Katy McDermott

# MEETING MURDER

*Katy McDermott*

Copyright © 2008 by Katy McDermott

ISBN  0-7414-4952-8

Cover art by Kenneth Carozza
Author photograph by Caroline Morris
Copyediting by Margaret Zelsnack

**Published by:**

PUBLISHING.COM

*1094 New DeHaven Street, Suite 100*
*West Conshohocken, PA 19428-2713*
*Info@buybooksontheweb.com*
*www.buybooksontheweb.com*
*Toll-free  (877) BUY BOOK*
*Local Phone (610) 941-9999*
*Fax  (610) 941-9959*

*Printed in the United States of America*

*Printed on Recycled Paper*

*Published  September 2008*

*For Peter*
*Much loved, much missed*

# Acknowledgments

They say writing is a solitary endeavor, and in many ways it is, but I've had lots of help along the way.

As a meeting planner for a large pharmaceutical company, I had the good fortune to meet and work with senior executives, hotel personnel, top-notch vendors, and of course, an enormously talented (and tireless) brigade of meeting freelancers. Although this is a work of fiction, those people inspired me to write this book, and for that I thank them.

In Miami Beach, I received invaluable information from Graham Winick, Film and Event Production Manager from the Office of Tourism and Cultural Development. His insight enabled me to add real-life details to this product of my imagination, and helped me tell a better, more credible story. Closer to home, Margaret Zelsnack gave me the benefit of her expert copyediting skills and her wonderful suggestions. I thank her for both. I'm also grateful to Kenneth Carozza, who turned a 5-minute conversation and my kindergarten-level "drawing" into a gorgeous piece of cover art.

On a personal level, I'm indebted to my brothers, sister, mother, nieces, and nephews, and my extended family of cousins, in-laws, spouses, friends, and children. I'm lucky to have them all in my life. I also give profound thanks to Dr. Erol Veznedaroglu and the staff at Thomas Jefferson Hospital.

I'm especially grateful to Hilaire Veith-Beran, my oldest and dearest friend. I wouldn't be the person I am today without her. And to my husband Jack, I give the deepest thanks of all. His love, support, encouragement, and patience throughout this lengthy process have meant more to me than I can ever tell him.

# Chapter One

Thirty-three thousand feet above North Carolina, shivering under an airline-issue blanket and praying for a smooth flight, Laurie Kilcannon was making a list. She liked lists. They reassured her that she had at least some control over the complicated logistics of events like the sales meeting she had planned. Besides, lists distracted her from thoughts of wind shear, failed landing gear, and cockpit voice recorders.

Six years of crisscrossing the country meant she had racked up enough miles to upgrade to first class on almost every flight. Having to fly in the first place was still the biggest sacrifice she made for her job.

Almost as if her nervousness had willed it, the pilot's voice sounded over the public address system:

*"Ladies and gentlemen, we've been advised by Air Traffic Control that we may encounter some mild to moderate turbulence for the next 25 minutes or so. We're going to try to find some clearer air for you folks, but in the meantime we ask that you remain in your seats with your seatbelts fastened. Thank you."*

Here it comes, Laurie thought. Still, he'd said "mild to moderate." That's not as bad as "moderate to severe." That red-eye home from L.A. last October… but she didn't want to think about that. List, work on the list, she scolded herself, picking up her pen, occasionally chewing on its cap. A little while later, her legal pad looked like this:

1

### On-site To Do:

1.  Set up mtg. ofc.

2.  Book staff dinner thru CSM.

3.  Meet w/ ground operator to cross-check A/D manifest against xfer schedule.

4.  Meet w/ staff for wkng. agda. review.

5.  Distribute staff skeds & assignments.

6.  Meet w/ F & B team & Catering Mgr., review BEOs, confirm final GTEs.

7.  Have B/O staff set up Box Rm., inventory all pkgs. ag. shpg. list.

8.  Stuff welcome packets.

9.  Cross-check rmg. list w/ E/A list.

10. Attend precon.

11. Do walk-thru.

The jumble of acronyms and abbreviations made perfect sense to Laurie, but nonetheless she worried that she had forgotten something.

That's all I need, she thought – a screw-up on a product launch as important as this one. She knew Zephyrex was already being hailed in the media as the next "blockbuster" drug, a breakthrough medication that relieved not only seasonal allergies but tough-to-treat food allergies as well, with virtually no side effects. The company needed this drug to be a success. After a string of lawsuits and regulatory problems on older products, and with a sparse pipeline of new drugs, Connor Pharmaceuticals was mentioned in the media almost daily as a prime takeover target for industry giants like Pfizer and Glaxo.

Laurie had weathered one merger already, when Connor bought the sputtering European pharma company Offenbach, and she had no desire to go through another – not on the buyee side, anyway. Mergers meant consolidation, and that could mean the end of Laurie's job. Next to fiery wreckage, losing her job was Laurie's worst fear.

Well, I'm not doing myself any good by obsessing over it, she thought. I'll talk to Wendell when he gets in on Saturday. He'll give me the scoop.

She relaxed as she thought of genial old-timer Wendell McCarthy, Senior Vice President of Sales for Connor Pharma, and a frequent beneficiary of Laurie's "spare time." She arranged limousine transportation, lavish suites and special amenities for the higher-ups, and had planned more than one executive vacation in addition to her official duties.

She'd even set up a few trips for Eugene Stockton, her company's president. Although only a manager, Laurie not only knew him, she called him "Gene" at his invitation.

Laurie sat up suddenly and smacked her fist on the tray table. *"That's* what I forgot," she muttered furiously, reaching for her pen and pad to write:

12.      Have Becky check VIP suites before arrival.

Laurie Kilcannon was a good meeting planner, one of the best around, if her staff and colleagues were to be believed. But she wasn't clairvoyant. If she had been, she would have added one more item to her list:

13.      Find murderer.

A stiff but relieved Laurie shifted her laptop case from one shoulder to the other as she sweated her way through Miami International toward the baggage claim area. Once there, she knew, a smartly dressed hotel chauffer would take the heavy carry-on, and her "meeting planner" status would kick in – not that she had any illusions about that. To hotels, meeting planners were just dollar signs with feet. *Sore* feet at the moment, she mused as she negotiated the endless, identical hallways of the airport.

She trudged along behind a family chattering to each other in Spanish. Their small daughter, wide-eyed, wore a sundress with frilly ankle socks... she supposed she'd been almost the same at that age, although she couldn't remember much. The dreamlike outlines of her lovely, laughing parents had given way long ago to the unchangeable fact that they were gone.

They'd been embarking on the trip of a lifetime, she'd been told, a trip they'd put off once they'd realized Laurie was coming. She tried to imagine them as they must have been that day. Happy, excited, thrilled to be making the long-dreamed-of journey to Italy at last. They'd said goodbye to Laurie at her aunt and uncle's house, reassuring the little girl that they'd be back in ten short days with pictures, stories, and (most important of all to an 8-year-old girl) presents. She'd only cried a little then.

The real crying still waited for her, when her aunt and uncle, hiding their own tears, gently explained to Laurie that her parents weren't coming back. Their plane had crashed. Aunt Charlotte and Uncle Matt, childless, had taken little Laurie in and loved her as if she were their own, and Laurie came to love them too. Later, she loved them for protecting her, welcoming her, never missing an "event" in her young life. Uncle Matt had even attended a ballet recital on crutches from a broken leg once, but it wasn't the same. Her parents – her real parents – were gone...

She forced herself not to look at the little girl with the frilly socks anymore. The past is just that, she told herself – past. Resolutely forcing herself into the present, Laurie noticed several other experienced travelers, the ones who wore comfortable clothes and weary expressions like hers. The ones who carried the sweatshirts they'd worn in flight, knowing planes got cold no matter where they were flying.

Strangely, Laurie had never been to Miami before. Connor had held dozens of meetings in Orlando, but this time around those properties didn't have the space she needed over the right dates. At least they were headed for a Hanover property, she thought as she glanced out the limo's closed windows at a scene that looked like urban blight with palm trees. Like Marriott and Westin, Hanover valued its corporate clients, and attracted the best people in the industry to serve them. She hoped.

Whereas her trips to Orlando's top hotels featured long miles of farmland (Laurie had been so surprised the first time she saw cows in Florida) the journey to the Miami Beach Hanover Hotel and Conference Center took her instead through an area that reminded her of Philadelphia. In August. She'd expected Miami to be hot, but this was *really* hot. It must be the position of the sun or something, she thought.

The view finally began to improve once they'd crossed the bridge into Miami Beach itself. The Fontainebleau Hotel shone dazzling white against the postcard pastels of smaller buildings. Getting a glimpse of a tropically turquoise, serene ocean, she could hardly believe that this area had been devastated by Hurricane Andrew just a few years before. Whether the residents decided to thumb their noses at fate or figured that type of storm wouldn't hit again for a hundred years, they'd built back. And then some, Laurie realized as she saw construction sites everywhere against a gorgeous backdrop of sun and ocean.

A calm blue sea.

Even if she wouldn't get to enjoy it, Laurie was glad to know it was there.


"Okay, everyone, let's save some animals today!"

Jake started every AAPT meeting this way, and it always worked.

Over twenty volunteers, linked only by their professed concern for animal welfare, sat on folding chairs or found spots on the floor in the shabby upstairs space. Jake Pratt III looked fondly at the wildly diverse crew in front of him. The middle-aged hippies, the social misfits, the grandmothers, the disillusioned Ivy Leaguers...

He'd been one of the last group himself. Attended Princeton on a tennis scholarship, double-majored in English and History. Everyone expected him to walk the same path as his father had done: assistant professorship at a small college, suitable marriage to a socially acceptable classmate, transfer to a larger college, tenure eventually leading to Deanship.

Jake had other ideas, though, ideas fueled by his relationship with Lydia Emerson, the coed who combined an impeccable pedigree with radical ideas about animal rights. She'd joined AAPT, he knew, as a way of thumbing her nose at her mink-wearing mother, but the cause had become real to her, and through her, to Jake as well. Surprising himself, he'd found another career path, and if it involved a move to Miami Beach, so be it. The celebrity endorsements might happen at the national level of AAPT (where Jake knew he and Lydia would wind up eventually) but for now, this small regional field office more than sufficed. They did *real* work here.

Moving to Miami Beach had been a bit of a shock, he had to admit. He and Lydia both hailed from Connecticut and attended college in New Jersey. They were more accustomed to scraping ice off their BMWs' windshields than remembering to apply sunscreen at all times. But the move had been a good one. AAPT needed a solid team at their Southeast Regional office, and after their Premarin protest made the news, the stock of AAPT's Miami Beach office continued to rise.

At today's meeting, as always, groups continued to chat, women and men with various hair lengths flirted and fidgeted. After what seemed like an hour, Jake began.

"You guys know why we're here. AAPT gives a voice to the voiceless, power to the powerless, and reminds us all that protecting animals is the most human thing we can do…"

Sitting cross-legged almost at the back of the room, Vivian Linsky fell in love all over again. Jake was so *handsome*. That thick sandy hair, the Kennedy-ish bone structure, those too-blue eyes… she could stare at Jake for hours and never tire of the sheer pleasure of it.

Not that she knew much about pleasure, of course, unless the cheeseburgers she'd eagerly consumed before the Great Conversion could be considered "pleasure."

She'd wanted to be a veterinarian until the animal rights movement (in the form of a fervent AAPT staffer at her local college's Career Day) had changed her life forever. Vivian loved animals – after all, her chief circle of friends consisted of stray cats and dogs growing up – but she didn't love science. Pre-vet students had to take a *lot* of science courses. Vivian had cleaned out cages at a shelter for two summers during college, when the boss at her other job would let her, and she saw herself as a champion for these smaller, more helpless beings. Unfortunately, the academic demands of her chosen profession – the idea of *having* a profession – proved too much for her.

AAPT represented the best of both worlds. As an AAPT volunteer, and hopefully as an AAPT staffer someday, she could say, "Yes, I'm taking pre-veterinary classes in college, and I'm active in the animal rights movement too."

And that was before she saw Jake.

"…elephants being held in chains," he was saying, "And the circus is coming to town. Chris and Gigi, I'd like you to organize the protests. Make signs, gather recruits, cause a commotion. Remember what Lydia's told us: people only know what they see on TV, so court the media whenever you can."

Someday I'll be tapped to lead a protest too, thought Vivian.

"Now on to other matters... we all know that most pharmaceutical companies test their drugs on animals, and sometimes *make* their drugs out of them too. We spear-headed a good campaign against Wyeth-Ayerst not long ago. More people than ever know that 'Premarin' stands for Pregnant Mare Urine. The question is, how do we follow it up?"

Vivian raised her hand a few inches.

"Yes, Vera, what information do you have?"

"It's Vivian," she replied tentatively. "A friend of mine at the catering company where I work? Well, he takes jobs doing food and beverage stuff at big conferences for extra money when he can. He's signed up for a spot on a Connor Pharmaceuticals meeting. Sometime next week, I think. Didn't I read in the AAPT newsletter that Connor's about to release a new drug that was tested on rabbits? Do you think that's what this meeting's about?"

Jake looked at her with new respect.

"Ve – I mean, Vivian, you may be right, and if you are, that may be just the opportunity we're looking for. Who's this friend of yours anyway?"

"His name's Jeremy," she answered, "And I know how to reach him."

"Terrific. Contact him tonight if you can and find out everything he knows about this Connor meeting. It could be important for us."

"I will. You can count on me."

"That's great. I knew I could. Now, on to the next order of business. Marcy, you're in charge of mailings. How's that going?"

Vivian was ecstatic. Jake needed her! Once she'd gotten the information from Jeremy, she'd celebrate. Maybe even with a cheeseburger. Not that she'd tell anyone from AAPT.

"Laurie, can I see you for a moment?"

Three hectic days later, Laurie blew her hair out of her eyes and glanced up from the pile of binders, manifests, and sticky notes spread out on the 6' skirted table that would be her headquarters for the week. The office was nearly set up – copiers, fax machines, walkie-talkies, coffee break station, and at least five dozen people crowding what used to be an average-sized conference room. She'd been lucky to get almost everyone she wanted for her lead staff. The top freelance meeting workers were in high demand from companies like hers. Good freelancers made a well-planned meeting run seamlessly on site, but less experienced ones could unravel even the most thorough arrangements. Laurie treated her freelance "leads" like the pros they were. She had, in fact, learned much of her job from watching and listening to them on earlier programs. As a result, she usually got her crack department heads with no trouble.

Equally important to the success of a meeting was the hotel staff, Laurie thought as she looked up at Juan Herrara, one of the hotel's Convention Service Managers and Laurie's counterpart for this meeting. The two had been in close contact during the months of planning, but she met her CSM for the first time several nights ago while touring the facility. No pre-meeting site inspection with a well-respected chain like Hanover, unfortunately. Now Juan wanted to speak with her. A problem, Laurie wondered?

"Sure," she answered, "You want to talk here or go somewhere else?"

"I thought we could head over to the café for a few minutes, if you can spare the time."

Uh-oh. *That* sounded like a problem.

"Okay, let me grab a walkie and we'll go."

On site, she and all her staff wore walkie-talkies except when they slept. On busy programs (and there were no other kind), they often slept so little that the walkies barely had time to recharge overnight. Clipping the low-tech device to the waistband of her jeans, Laurie followed Juan out of the conference room that had been converted to Mission Control for the Zephyrex launch.

As soon as they sat down in the café, Juan with a cappuccino, Laurie with one of many Cokes she would drink that day, she cut to the chase.

"Okay, Juan, what's the problem?"

He didn't try to deny it.

"We're overbooked tomorrow night, Laurie. I'm really sorry. You know how hotels operate. We book more rooms than we have, because the no-shows almost always balance it out. But we've got another meeting coming in tomorrow, and Reservations has been overrun with calls. It's Association business, not Corporate, so the attendees have to pay their own way. We thought they'd barely make their contracted room block, but – well, we were wrong."

"Who's the group?" Laurie asked wearily.

"The American Association of Funeral Directors," he answered with a straight face.

"You can't be serious."

"Dead serious – oh God, I didn't mean to say that!" Juan struggled not to laugh.

Laurie glared at him.

"What's our shortfall going to be?"

"At least 20 singles," Juan replied, back in control. "Your double-doubles and suites are safe."

"Thank God for that, anyway. I hate to do it, but I'm going to have to double up the staff."

Laurie made sure her staff always got single rooms on site, a luxury that would have incensed the paired-up sales reps in attendance, had they known it. Sales reps, however, didn't have shin splints and wrecked nerves by the end of a meeting, she reasoned.

"We've got around 50 staff on this program, mostly worker bee types, a lot of whom I don't even know, so hopefully they won't mind being doubled up too much. Or at least, they won't tell me about it. I want to keep my leads in singles if it's humanly possible, though. What if the shortfall goes beyond 20?"

"I'll walk tourist traffic if I have to. You won't have to double up your leads."

"Walking," Laurie knew, was when an overbooked hotel sent guests with confirmed reservations to a competing property. It hurt a hotel's reputation and was an altogether unsatisfying option. She appreciated Juan's willingness to do it.

"Thanks. Any other catastrophes looming?"

"Just possible bad weather and some protesters from AAPT. You know, 'Animals Are People Too.' They got their license to demonstrate from the county yesterday. Was Zephyrex tested on animals?"

"Rabbits, actually. Well cared-for rabbits. AAPT – Christ, that's just what we need. You can keep them off the property, can't you?"

"They won't be able to go past the front gate, and that's a quarter mile from the main entrance."

"Alright, I'll have the ground operator reroute arrivals to the side entrance. I do *not* want Gene Stockton's limo accosted by a bunch of tofu-eating extremists in bunny costumes waving homemade signs at the tinted windows."

"I'll alert Security, don't you worry," Juan assured her, chuckling.

"What about the weather?"

"Well, Miami Beach is usually what I call a 'self-cleaning city,' with quick showers that pass through in an hour or so, but we might be getting some real rain later in the week. I'll keep an eye on it."

"Okay. Now let's get back. We've got the preconvention meeting this afternoon, and I've got to have a staff briefing first."

"Well, you need to be sharp for the precon, that's for sure," Juan joked. "You don't want to be caught napping when all the hotel department heads thank you for your business."

Grudgingly, Laurie chuckled. Precons *were* pretty boring, even if it was important to learn all the hotel people's names.

They headed down the corridor, Laurie petite and unassuming in her polo shirt and thick auburn ponytail, Juan a more imposing figure at 6'4" in a well-cut navy suit. He'd boxed in college, and looked like Jimmy Smits' more athletic brother.

"You know, I'm almost glad this overbooking thing happened," Laurie said. "Every meeting has at least one disaster, and I like to get it out of the way early."

"Let's hope this is ours, then," Juan smiled back at her.

Suddenly, Laurie shivered.

For pity's sake, why did these hotels keep the air conditioning so high you could store furs in the lobby?

Vivian showered and dressed more carefully than usual, applying lip gloss and mascara in the small mirror above the sink. She wondered why those thirty extra pounds hadn't fallen right off when she'd (almost) become a vegetarian. Must be all that pizza.

Even so, she hummed as she strained to button the waistband on her khaki shorts and added a pretty floral blouse on top. Last night Jeremy had told her plenty, and she couldn't wait to share the information with Jake.

"You got class today?" her mother Earlene called from the grimy kitchenette.

"Class, then work," Vivian shouted back, neglecting as always to mention her planned detour to AAPT headquarters.

It was one of her mother's few days off from the hair-dresser's, and she planned to spend most of it waiting for a new dining set to be delivered. Sloppy, warm-hearted Earlene worried a bit about her only child.

Earlene used to dream of becoming a model (she'd been pretty enough, in her teens) or a famous actress, but then life had gotten in her way. She'd fallen for a guy, and her dreams changed from "famous actress" to "wonderful wife." Neither dream had come true. The guy had gone, leaving twenty-year-old Earlene with a few shiny memories and an infant to feed. Over the years, she'd become so focused on the escalating needs of her little daughter that she'd all but forgotten her own dreams.

Modeling, of course, was out of the question once she had the baby. The schedule was impossible and the income unstable, plus Earlene never quite lost her "baby weight." But more than that, pursuing her ambitions of modeling and acting seemed frivolous once she had Vivian. So Earlene cleaned houses, then waitressed at a local diner, then worked the checkout register at a nearby discount superstore. When the layoffs came, she'd felt lucky to get a job answering phones and scheduling cut-and-color appointments at the salon. At least she got to sit down all day. After all, Earlene was 42, and her back wasn't as strong as it had been. How

Vivian juggled college courses (college!) with the hours she put in at the catering company, Earlene didn't know.

"You work too hard," she told Vivian, pulling a stray plastic curler from her head as she entered the miniscule living room.

"Don't start with me, Mom," she said almost angrily. "After all, it's 1995, not 1895, and I've got to earn a living. You're a fine one to talk, anyway. What did you work last week, 60 hours? Why are you home today, anyway? Are you sick?" she asked in a less belligerent tone.

"We've got some new furniture coming. And you know me. I like to work. Keeps me young. Speaking of which, how are your classes going?" she finished, settling into a well-defined hollow in the plaid couch.

Vivian rolled her eyes. Mom wanted to bond.

"I'm gonna be late if I don't get going. Classes are fine, work is fine, everything's fine."

Well, if that wasn't an opening, Earlene didn't know what was.

"I'm sorry I've been so busy lately, honey. Maybe what we need is a vacation. You've always said you wanted to go to Disney World. How 'bout something like that?"

"What, did you finally win the lottery? That place costs a fortune," Vivian answered skeptically.

"We could manage, and nicely, too. I've got some savings, you know. You'll be graduating soon. What if I made the trip your graduation present?"

Vivian was intrigued in spite of herself. Over the years, she'd spent many hours with her mother poring over vacation brochures from the travel agency in the local strip mall, planning imaginary trips. One of Earlene's best friends worked at the agency, and was always trying to book them for something. Still…

"You mean like a package deal, where we'd stay in a motel and eat at Denny's every night except for the one time we'd go to that medieval place?"

Seeing Earlene's face fall, she added, "Not that I mind! But, you know, a *trip*."

"No motels," said her mother. "We could stay at the Grand Floridian, even. Take the Monorail, go on all the rides, eat at a different fancy restaurant every night!"

"You *did* win the lottery."

"Not exactly," answered Earlene, so happy to see the eagerness on Vivian's face.

"But even if we could stay in a place like that, where would we get the clothes?"

"Maybe we could buy some. Aventura Mall's got a sale coming up. Why don't we check it out?"

"Mom, are you *sure* you're not sick?"

Earlene just smiled.

The shopping, the trip, the nice hotel and gourmet dinners... they'd make a welcome change to the workaday routine she and Vivian had fallen into.

All she really wanted, though, was to spend time with her daughter.


Thoughts of a trip sidelined, Vivian indulged in the favorite of her many fantasies as her 10-year-old Toyota rattled down Northwest 41$^{st}$ Street...

> *"Vivian, you look so gorgeous today, I can hardly keep my mind on my work," Jake said as he eyed her appreciatively.*

*"Well, the animals aren't going anywhere, are they? And you've got a lock on your office door," she replied with a slow, sultry smile.*

*In her fantasy, the thirty extra pounds <u>had</u> fallen right off, and the hair she usually thought of as "bushy" framed her face in a cloud of curls.*

*Even better, there was no Lydia.*

*Slim, blonde, exquisite Lydia, Public Relations Director for AAPT and Jake's live-in lover, simply didn't exist. The perfect, patrician voice, which Vivian had once overheard saying "Thank God martinis aren't made from animals" after a particularly contentious press conference, didn't whisper into Jake's ear. Instead she, Vivian, claimed the place by his side. Working together to save the animals, preparing delicious meals in their meat-free kitchen, making sweet, earnest love in their enormous bed...*

"So, Vera, what have you heard?" Jake asked.

Vivian started, blushing. How had she made it to the AAPT offices so fast – and in that car, too? Then she sighed to herself. Jake still didn't even know her name.

"My friend Jeremy told me that all the top brass from Connor Pharma are coming to this meeting to 'launch' their new drug to the sales reps. It's Zephyrex. The one that was tested on rabbits."

"That's great!" Jake enthused, "For us, I mean. Not for the rabbits. Anyway, did Jeremy happen to mention when and where the big meeting is?"

"I asked him that. I figured you might want to stage a protest. It's at the Hanover, and the big session happens the day after they arrive. May 8th, 8:00 a.m."

"Terrific! We'll apply for a demonstration permit, and if there are any questions from the press, Lydia can handle them. Thanks, Vera."

"You're welcome. And it's Vivian."

"Alright, everyone, let's get started."

Laurie had to raise her voice a little to be heard over the multiple conversations going on all around her. Most of the staff had arrived on schedule, and drifted into the office throughout the morning. The veterans were catching up on each other's meeting horror stories, while the new ones just looked bewildered.

"We're going through the Working Agenda in a few minutes," Laurie began, "Even though I'm *sure* you all read through it on your flights."

This was met with a lot of guilty snickering, and some panicked looks from the youngsters.

"And I hope you can all join me at the staff dinner the hotel has arranged for us tonight. But first," she continued, "Staff assignments and schedules. Could you pass these around, please?"

"Sure thing, Laurie," replied one of the returning freelancers.

"I know a lot of you are new to Connor Pharma programs, and some of you may even be new to meeting planning. Well, let me start by welcoming you and introducing myself. I'm Laurie Kilcannon, the planner for the Zephyrex launch. Thank you all for taking this booking. You're the ones who will make this meeting shine, and it literally couldn't happen without you."

"Oh, God, I'm gonna cry. Who's got a tissue?" came a voice from the back of the room.

"Hello again, Dash," Laurie said with a wry smile. Tadashi "Dash" Tamaseko, one of her favorite freelancers, had given her a hug that almost collapsed a lung half an hour ago.

"No disrespect, Lauriebell. You know how I love your welcome speeches!"

"Thanks so much. And I know how *you* love checking meeting rooms and hauling boxes, so that's why I made you lead on Breakouts!"

Dash buried his head in Marc Masterson's shoulder and cried "Noooooo!" in mock horror. Running Breakouts was a dirty, exhausting job, but Dash had headed the department before, and Laurie knew how good he was.

"Everyone on the Breakouts team – it's listed as B/O on the staff assignment sheet for you new ones – report to Dash once we're through and he'll fill you in on your exact duties. As many of you already know, 'Breakouts' are the small district-level meetings that happen on Wednesday and Thursday. But don't let the name fool you. You guys will handle the setup for every meeting in the program. Now, on to Food & Beverage. Is Dagmar –?"

Loud voices interrupted from just outside the office.

"Let's raid Laurie's coffee break. The meeting planners always get the best food."

A pair of VIPs barged into the room, then stopped when they saw the staff gathered in a circle.

"Oh! Sorry, everyone," Wendell McCarthy said without a trace of embarrassment, "Fisher and I were just looking for a place to go over our slides. You mind, Laurie?"

"No problem, Wendell. Jim, glad to see you got in okay. Are your suites alright?"

"Amazing!" Jim Fisher replied in his familiar twang.

"You guys mind if we keep going? There's a light box on that far table for your slides. And Wendell, the croissants look especially fresh today," she added with a grin.

"Laurie, you always know the way to this old man's heart. Go on with your meeting. We'll stay out of your way."

She turned back to her staff.

"Okay, Dagmar, you know you're lead on F & B. We don't have any tight turnarounds, thank God, but keep an eye on the final night banquet setup. It's got full décor, floral, the works."

"Ja, I noticed that on the Working Agenda. Many vendors involved. Do you think they're up to it?" the "Danish Duchess" asked with a frown.

"They'd better be," Laurie responded, "They know how important it is, though, and we've used all of them before. I'm pretty sure they can handle it."

"Good."

"Now, Recreation. Marc, that's you. We've got lots of golfers as always, so start praying the weather doesn't turn nasty on us before Tuesday. The reports look iffy at the moment. You might want to check out local tour options just in case."

"God forbid," Marc replied crisply, "The only thing more annoying than a bunch of rabid golfers is a bunch of rained-out rabid golfers. Don't worry. I'll keep them in line, whatever the weather."

"Marc Masterson: Recreation Tyrant," Dash interjected. Marc shot him a "shut up" look while the others laughed.

What a strange couple those two are, Laurie thought to herself, not for the first time. Dash resembled a rumpled puppy dog, irreverent and cheeky, while Marc paired the reserve of a banker with a seemingly endless supply of perfectly pressed khakis. The two had been together for eight years, owned a show-stopping brownstone in Baltimore, and refused to work separate meetings. I wish *I* could find that kind of love, Laurie mused wistfully.

"Okay, let's get through this, folks. Becky's lead on Special Services Desk. She's not here right now because she's doing our remaining VIP meet & greets – "

"That woman is the sweetest thing on two feet," interrupted Wendell, who had clearly been listening.

"Thank you, Wendell. I'll tell her you said so. You guys on SSD, *make sure* you get Becky to brief you before major arrivals tomorrow. It'll be a zoo, so try not to drink too much tonight, and get to bed early after the welcome packets are done. We open the Desk at 7:00 a.m. Our final department is Transfers. Becky's handling the last few VIPs' transportation, so you guys get to handle everyone else's airport shuttle arrangements, lost luggage, and late limos. Our lead is Sue Palmer. Sue, I only hope this won't affect our friendship."

"What friendship?" Sue Palmer cracked. She'd run Transfers on dozens of Laurie's meetings, and somewhere along the way she sort of adopted the younger woman. Lots of people knew Laurie had been an orphan since the age of eight. Sue was one of the few who knew why.

Staff assignments finished, Laurie reminded her leads about the precon later that afternoon and was about to review the massive, detail-laden "meeting Bible," or Working Agenda, when another VIP arrived. Edward Tradd, Senior Vice President of Marketing, glowered at the Connor meeting planner.

"Goddammit, Laurie," he shouted, oblivious to the staff meeting she was leading, "Did you check the view from my suite? It's a goddamn parking lot! And the soap in the bathrooms – crap! You tell your hotel person I want some decent French-milled soap in those bathrooms by this afternoon. And a different suite, too!"

"I'm sorry, Ed," Laurie said quietly, wanting to disappear – just as soon as she slapped his smooth blond face. "The hotel's completely booked, so I'm afraid I can't switch your suite, but I'll have someone take care of the soap problem within the hour."

"Fine," he snapped, turning to leave. Seeing the other two VIPs running slides in the corner, however, he joined them at once.

"Wendell, good to see you, you crazy bastard! I see Jim's giving you a preview of my presentation."

Fisher almost choked on his croissant. *Tradd's* presentation! Jim had been working around the clock on the strategic marketing analysis for Zephyrex, and his boss was taking full credit for it. Unbelievable.

"Very impressive, Ed," Wendell said blandly. "What do you say we go rehearse it in the ballroom?"

"Sure. Give me a few minutes and I'll join you."

As Tradd sauntered out of the office, Laurie glanced over at his two colleagues. Jim Fisher was staring at Tradd's retreating back, an expression of pure hatred twisting his otherwise pleasant features. She looked away quickly. His face had scared her.

# Chapter Two

Behind the stage at 7:25 on Monday morning, the Bougainvillea Ballroom, now converted to hold the Zephyrex launch opening session, was almost pitch dark. Laurie stepped carefully over the maze of taped-down electrical cables that snaked across the floor, looking for Lew Paulson, Connor Pharma's Director of Multimedia Production.

"Lew, hold up," she called, spying his lumpy, semi-bald silhouette with its graying ponytail across the equipment-laden area. Someone needs to tell that man the 80s are over, she thought.

"Hey, Laurie," he looked up as she approached. "You ready to get this show on the road?"

"So far, so good. Everyone's plane got in last night – eventually – and no one got food poisoning from the sushi at the welcome reception, so I guess it's your show now."

"You got that right, kid."

Laurie hated being called "kid."

"We've got a video montage on this new drug that's going to blow them away, and the teleprompter hasn't broken down once," he added, looking around for a piece of wood, then knocking on his skull.

"All the VIPs here?"

"Every one. Wendell's up first, thank God. I still can't believe they didn't give him a slot for a full speech. He's the best speaker we've got, and they're pushing him aside for that a-hole Tradd."

"Wendell's being eased into retirement. Everyone knows that. I guess they thought it was time to showcase the new talent. How is Tradd this morning, anyway? He ripped me a new one yesterday. In front of my staff."

"What a jerk. He's done that to me too, it drives me nuts. He's been fine this morning though. A little quiet, which is odd. Usually, he never shuts up. Probably tired. He must have gotten some 'quality time' with that rep he's been seeing. You know, Brandi, the blonde?" he leered.

"You gotta keep up, Lew," Laurie responded, snapping her fingers. "Brandi's last year's model. The current flame's a brunette, Karen. She's got a territory close to the home office, hair down to her waist, and legs up to her ears."

She didn't talk about the VIPs as a rule. In her position, Laurie heard so much confidential information that a reputation for gossip would be a career-killer. Tradd's behavior was so flagrant, however, that she figured he was fair game. Besides, he *was* a jerk.

Lew was miffed. "How come you always have the best dirt?" he sulked.

"Elementary, Watson. The hotel rooming list showed that Karen didn't check into her room last night, but I knew from my transfers manifest that she'd made her flight and caught the airport shuttle. I mentioned it to Wendell, and he told me she was probably shacked up with Tradd in his suite. Apparently they've been an item for months now."

"Hey, Laurie, have you heard anything new about those merger talks?" Lew asked suddenly in an unnaturally loud voice. Laurie caught sight of Tradd walking toward them just in time and played along.

"No, I've been wondering about them too," she bluffed, hoping she could slip away before Tradd reached them. No such luck.

"Paulson, you limp dick, where the hell are my slides?" Tradd boomed, not seeming quiet in the least. Oh Lord, Laurie thought.

"I need to find Gene," she muttered, threading her way through sound equipment, lighting "trees," and slide projectors as she made her escape.

Gray-haired and patrician, Gene Stockton, President and CEO of Connor Pharmaceuticals, nibbled on a cruller by the skirted table that held the backstage coffee break. With him were Wendell McCarthy and Mike DellaGuardia, Vice President of Marketing Communications. Part of Mike's job was to make sure the reps had an ongoing supply of the "detail aids" and other selling tools they needed. Huge and shaggy, Mike always looked a little out of place in business attire. But his gentle nature concealed a ferocious work ethic, and the sales force wouldn't hear a word against him.

"Hi Laurie," Mike greeted her, "I wondered if I'd see you this morning. I wanted to thank you for the welcome basket in my suite. It was great."

"Oh, good, I'm glad you got it. Pretzels, dried apple chips, and O'Doul's, right?"

"Yup. What does Wendell get – pudding cups and warm milk?" Mike teased. Wendell lobbed a punch at his arm.

"I can answer that one," Gene interjected with a smile, "Tortilla chips with salsa and a bottle of Cabernet. Tell us, Laurie, how do you manage to send us all welcome baskets with our favorite food and drinks with everything else you have to do at the meeting?"

"Well, I probably shouldn't share this – it's kind of a meeting planning trade secret – but I call your assistants and ask them what you like. There goes my mystique, huh?"

"Never," Gene assured her. "I wouldn't trade jobs with you in a million years. But efficient as you are, even *you* can't control the weather. I've been meaning to ask what you plan to do about tomorrow's outdoor dinner if this storm I've been hearing about happens."

It was just like Gene, Laurie thought, to concern himself with an event that had more to do with showing the reps a good time than with sales forecasts and market share. Fresh out of pharmacy school 25 years before, Gene Stockton had started at Connor as a sales rep, studied for his MBA at night, and worked his way up to run the company with a sure hand and a talent for managing by example. No matter how high he rose, Laurie had heard, he never forgot what it felt like to be in the field – "carrying a bag," as pharma people say – and his employees repaid him, by and large, with loyalty and hard work. And now, despite the demands of his job and a hectic family life with his anxiety-riddled wife and 18-month-old son, he still found time to care about details like a theme party for his sales force.

"It's still too early to decide about the dinner," Laurie replied, "I've got the Weather Channel on in the meeting office, and my hotel contact is monitoring the marine forecasts as well. Who knows? The sun may shine all week. I don't have to make the call until noon tomorrow, and I have the hotel stocking up on weather-related props in case we have to turn 'Safari Night' into an indoor party. We may still get lucky, though. Cross your fingers."

The murmur of voices in the hall outside the ballroom was growing, and Laurie realized they were nearing the start time for opening session. She excused herself to the VIPs, and checked in once more with Lew.

"You'll walkie me when you want us to let the reps in?" she asked. "I'm on channel 4."

"Yeah, don't open those doors until I give you the signal."

Lew suffered agonies of nerves on site. He'd never quite recovered from a meeting several years ago where the reps saw the first five slides in Gene's presentation projected upside down.

Laurie left him to his nail-biting and exited the backstage area through a side door, almost bumping into Marc Masterson on her way out. Several hundred reps were gathered in little knots around the coffee break tables in the foyer, but Laurie knew that most would arrive, en masse, at five minutes to eight. As the time to the meeting's start approached, Dash's entire Breakouts team deployed outside the enormous ballroom to direct traffic.

Out of the corner of her eye, she noticed several scruffy-looking youngsters entering a nearby Men's Room, each carrying a bulky plastic bag. Probably on Spring Break or vacation, she thought idly. The South Beach area drew a year-round influx of partiers and families, in addition to business meeting groups.

A short time later, as she reviewed the seating strategy with Dash, a burst of nervous laughter arose from the attendees. Looking up, Laurie saw five figures emerging from the Men's Room, now joined by about twenty other "guests" who'd appeared out of nowhere. The men wore rumpled khaki shorts and dirty canvas sneakers, but covering them from chest level up were huge papier-mâché rabbit heads. Each one carried a sign reading "Connor Pharma Murdered My Family. AAPT Supporters Unite Against Corporate Tyranny!"

Laurie closed her eyes and allowed herself a moment of panic. Dear God in heaven, what if the media found out? What if the protesters caught sight of Gene Stockton?

*Jesus.*

Thinking fast, she told Dash to walkie Lew: fill him in, have him delay opening session, and at all costs keep the VIPs backstage. Grabbing her own walkie, she switched to the hotel channel and practically shouted, "Laurie to Juan! Come in, Juan!"

"Juan here. Over," the CSM responded calmly.

"Juan, meet me in the general session foyer *immediately* – and bring Security! We've got bunnies!"

A hectic twenty minutes later, the protesters had been escorted from the property, the attendees surged through the eight doors to the ballroom, and the "walk-in" music pounded in Laurie's ears. In time-honored pharmaceutical launch tradition, Lew had chosen Huey Lewis' "I Want a New Drug." Laurie smiled to herself as she urged the reps into the long rows of seats. Lew was so predictable. Still, it could have been worse. If she'd had to endure one more blaring rendition of "New Attitude," she'd have torn her hair out by the roots.

Even louder than the walk-in music was the amplified "Voice of God" (actually a Multimedia staffer with a commanding baritone hidden behind the control panel) futilely intoning "Ladies and gentlemen, please take your seats. The meeting is about to begin." Laurie raced from row to row, trying to get the keyed-up, chattering reps to stop greeting each other and move toward the middle, instead of taking seats at the end and blocking the whole row as they usually did.

Along with the annoyance, though, she felt a familiar rush of excitement. Moments like this were why she loved her job. After two months of nonstop preparation, and despite a sleeping room shortage, executive feuds, an impending storm, and even bunny-headed protesters, the Zephyrex launch was finally underway. And she, Laurie Kilcannon, had helped make it happen.

Remembering that less than a decade ago she'd answered phones and typed memos for a living, she couldn't help feeling grateful to Connor Pharma. True, she'd started her career at the company the same way as she had at other jobs, but organizing one simple board meeting had led to all this. Laurie had a staff now, an office at headquarters with a door she could close, and more responsibility than she'd ever hoped for. She'd never be an executive – didn't want to be – but her position was perfect for her.

She worked hard. As big meetings approached, she often found herself grabbing milk and cereal at her local convenience store because there was no time for grocery shopping. But she didn't mind the late nights, the weekend work, the endless flights (okay, those she did mind a little). Being busy at a job she did well kept her from thinking too much, and besides, Connor Pharma gave her a place to belong. At work, she never lacked confidence or felt hesitant about anything. She was as contented with her career as she was discontented with her personal life...

At last, the lights dimmed and the crowded room grew quiet as Wendell McCarthy strode onto the stage. Craggy-featured and confident, he'd opened more Connor Pharma meetings than he cared to remember. Laurie turned the volume on her walkie to "low" and stood in the shadows at the back of the room to listen for a minute. Watching Wendell in action was always a treat.

"Good morning," he began in a hearty voice, both hands on the podium.

A pause. A few hesitant "good mornings" from the audience.

He tapped on the microphone.

"Is this thing on? Let's try that again. Good morning!" he bellowed.

This time, the reps roared their response.

"That's more like it. I'm glad to see everyone arrived safely, and I'm sure you're all as excited as I am to be here in sunny Miami Beach."

A few whoops from the crowd.

"Alright, settle down. Recreation's not till tomorrow," he said to scattered laughter.

"And I'm sure you're as excited as I am to be here to launch a drug that's going to turn the Rx allergy market on its head…"

Polite applause.

"…a drug that's going to be such a blockbuster that we've had to allocate a special bonus fund just to accommodate the early projections!"

*Now* he had their attention. The crowd erupted with clapping, foot-stomping, and approving yells.

"We're expecting great things from each and every one of you, because we can all expect great things from… Zephyrex!"

Another riot of applause. Dash joined Laurie at the back of the room, leaning in to whisper, "This guy could've been a great televangelist if he hadn't gone into pharmaceuticals."

"And although, in light of this morning's events, you might be expecting the next speaker to be Elmer Fudd…"

He had to pause for a full twenty seconds as the reps howled with appreciative laughter.

"…I am actually here to introduce to you the man whose dedication and marketing savvy are going to help every one of you ride the Zephyrex Express right into a new tax bracket…"

He was forced to wait again.

"Ladies and gentlemen, it is my great pleasure to introduce Connor Pharmaceuticals' Senior Vice President of Marketing, Mr. Edward Tradd!"

The sales force clapped madly. At this point, Laurie muttered to Dash, the reps were so thoroughly under Wendell's spell that they would've applauded Hitler. Wendell's hand was outstretched toward the wing from which the marketing Vice President was supposed to make his entrance...but Tradd didn't appear.

"Ed, the protesters are gone, so whenever you're ready," Wendell joked to cover the awkward pause.

At the back of the room, Laurie's heart raced as she and Dash looked at each other. Where was he? What had gone wrong? Incongruously, she flashed on the Strasbourg Music Festival awards scene from "The Sound of Music." The emcee announcing the vanished Von Trapp Family Singers, a spotlight trained on the empty alcove...

As Dash and Laurie watched, a Multimedia staffer in jeans and a black t-shirt hurried onstage and whispered something to Wendell. He blanched, hesitated, then turned back to the microphone.

"Ladies and gentlemen, I've just been informed that Ed has been taken ill suddenly, so we're going to start our meeting with a video presentation on Zephyrex that we're sure will inspire you as much..."

Laurie didn't hear the rest. She and Dash had vaulted from the back of the room at the words "taken ill" and pelted down the hall to the backstage door. They raced into the darkened area – and straight into Marc Masterson.

"Marc, what is it?   What's happened?" Laurie asked urgently.

"Laurie, thank God you're here. Tradd is... he's..."

"Marc," she responded evenly, quelling her own fear in the face of his, "Where is he?"

Marc steadied himself with an effort, as Dash led him to a chair.

"He's over there, by the coffee break table, but – "

"Dash, stay with Marc," Laurie ordered, then walked quickly toward the cluster of men gathered by the break table. Fisher, Stockton, DellaGuardia, McCarthy, and Paulson hovered over a figure lying on the floor.

Edward Tradd was still blond, still immaculately groomed, and still wearing his custom-tailored Brooks Brothers suit.

He was not, unfortunately, still alive.

# Chapter Three

The media ignored the protesters. They already had a boating accident (with dramatic rescue footage), the wedding of a prominent local politician's daughter (with professional stills the family had released, as well as a guest's account), and an expanded weather forecast to fill up their evening news broadcasts. Besides, AAPT was always demonstrating against something. Hotel security men quickly ejected the imposters, gripping the dirty, tattooed arms as they all but threw them off the property. For Lydia, it was a dark day. For Vivian, it was an opportunity.

"I heard from my friend Jeremy last night," she told the dejected AAPT staff. "He said that three Food and Beverage staffers came down with the flu and had to go home. The Connor meeting people are desperate for new bodies, preferably ones that know about catering for big groups. Jeremy will recommend me, if you like. Maybe we could find out something else about them."

As quickly as they'd become discouraged, the AAPT staff grew excited, and the comments started flying.

"That's a great idea."

"They probably serve two *different* kinds of flesh at their banquets. A crime, but not newsworthy. Yet."

"Who knows what she could uncover?"

"*We* know Connor's evil, but maybe someone on the inside could find proof."

"Don't we have a video camera she could hide?"

Vivian trembled, and waited. The Southeast Regional field office of AAPT had few resources. Those bunny heads had finished off almost all of the "miscellaneous" budget for May, and it was only the 8$^{th}$ of the month. Were there extra tapes that Jake could allocate? Maybe, or maybe not. She could buy tapes herself, of course, but would Jake let her use the expensive video camera? Between postage for mailings and the professionally printed leaflets they distributed, funds were tight. Even their ramshackle "headquarters" (in a 90-year-old walk-up in the question-able part of downtown Miami) cost money every month. The copiers were broken more often than they worked. There weren't even coffee makers. Members brought their own coffee. In fact, if it hadn't been for the volunteers willing to picket outside SeaWorld, stuff envelopes, and canvas door-to-door in a town about as welcoming to them as it was to Jehovah's Witnesses, AAPT couldn't survive at the local level. Vivian had good reason to be anxious.

Finally, Jake spoke.

"Well, Ve – I mean, Vivian, I don't see what it could hurt, although I think the big show is over. Zephyrex was tested on rabbits, but the press doesn't seem to care. If we'd been able to grab their attention with those costumes... oh well, no use crying over spilt soy milk," he shrugged with a sigh. "But go ahead if you want. I don't think you need the camera, though. If you uncover something important, just tell us about it."

Laurie stared at the man on the floor. This couldn't be real. He *couldn't* be dead.

But he was.

Edward Tradd lay on the spill-concealing hotel carpet, gray eyes wide but sightless, body utterly relaxed, mouth open and wet with saliva, lips and skin a grayish blue. Laurie had never seen a dead person before, and she knew this image would haunt her. It was so…wrong. She hadn't loved this man or even liked him, but he was young, and he had children, and now he was dead. She felt like crying as she stood there transfixed, part of the wordless group that lingered over the body.

"Where is he?" a loud voice called as the backstage doors flew open. The stricken tableau disintegrated as Juan Herrara and two hotel security officers bustled into the darkened area. One of the security men dropped to his knees and began working on Tradd, in the obviously vain hope that he might be revived. Juan went straight to Laurie.

"Lew walkied me and told me what happened. Are you okay?"

"I'm fine. I'm fine. I just… Ed's dead, Juan. Why are they doing CPR on him? It's too late."

"Protocol, and liability. We have to be able to say we did everything we could. I called 911 as soon as I heard. They've got an ambulance coming from Fire Rescue, and they're sending a police officer too."

"The police?" Laurie said, horrified, "Why do we need the police? He had a heart attack, for God's sake!"

"Laurie, a man in his early 40s has died suddenly and without explanation on our property. We need to protect ourselves. It probably was a heart attack, but in a situation like this, calling in the police is standard procedure. Hotel security cameras don't work in dark areas. We need to know what happened here."

The security men had given up.

"It's useless, Juan," one of them said.

"What do we do now?" Laurie asked, feeling shell-shocked.

"Wait for the ambulance and the police," Juan answered, "But for the moment, why don't we cover this poor man up?" He plucked a spare cloth from the coffee break table and spread the rough cotton folds over the lifeless body.

His action seemed to release the others from their collective stupor. Mike DellaGuardia made the sign of the cross and murmured a Hail Mary, while everyone else began talking at once, trying to figure out what to do next.

"Gene, the video montage is almost over," Lew said urgently. "Do you want to cancel the rest of opening session?"

Laurie couldn't believe it. She had almost forgotten that the meeting was still happening! Apparently, she wasn't the only one. Gene Stockton stared blankly at the Multimedia Director for a long moment before collecting himself enough to say, "Yes, we must cancel the session. It – it would be indecent to continue. I should be the one to announce it. I should..."

Wendell interrupted quietly.

"Let me do it, Gene. You can address the reps later. There are probably things you need to do. I'll tell them to break until lunch and then go to their workshops this afternoon. Let me handle it."

"Alright," the CEO replied. "I don't know if I could speak to them right now, truthfully. Thank you."

Laurie had regained some of her composure during their exchange. She turned to Juan and asked him to have the three lunch-and-dinner restaurants opened early. The 2,000 reps would need someplace to gather and process what had happened, and the café couldn't handle the numbers.

"I'll take care of it."

"Laurie?" someone asked, touching her shoulder, "Could you ask him to have the bars opened too?"

She turned to see who had spoken. It was Jim Fisher, white-faced and trembling.

The ballroom area was quiet at last. The VIPs and Lew Paulson had gathered in Wendell's suite to decide if the meeting should continue. Juan waited in the lobby to escort the ambulance crew and police through the back corridors. Laurie had sent Dash and Marc to brief the meeting staff and instruct them not to discuss the death with the attendees. Alone except for a security guard and the late Edward Tradd, she waited backstage.

She was glad to have some time to think. Now that the initial shock had worn off, her mind spun with all the practical implications. Feeling ghoulish, but knowing it had to be done, she sat in a corner and began making a list, frowning over her yellow legal pad.

## To Do:

1. Ask police – when will body be released?

2. Ask Juan – how do we ship Tradd's body home? Paperwork?

3. Ask Wendell – what to tell reps re: meeting continuing?

4. Have Sue call airlines re: possibility of changing everyone's flights if meeting cancelled.

5. Call ground operator re: possible early airport xfers.

6. Cancel Safari Night? (Note: check weather soon!)

7. Ask Juan re: financial penalty if meeting ends early – how much?

8. Pack Tradd's luggage, ask Juan re: shipping home.

9. Ask Gene – who will notify Tradd family?

Laurie stopped writing and read the last two items again.

Packing up the effects.

Telling the family.

The irrevocable cruelties of death.

Briefly, she let herself remember the moment her aunt and uncle had told her about her parents… the bewilderment, the total rejection of it. Three hundred miles away, two little girls were watching Nickelodeon or chasing a soccer ball, with no idea that their lives were about to be shattered. Laurie folded her arms around herself, thinking about her past and those little girls' future.

The sound of voices brought her back to the present. Juan. Ambulance. Police. She sniffed once, hard, and wiped her eyes with her shirt.

A detective bent down and drew the tablecloth back from Tradd's body, disgusted.

"Who covered this body?" he asked accusatorily.

"That was me, Officer," said Juan. "It seemed like the decent thing to do," he added with just a hint of indignation.

"An admirable instinct, but you've contaminated the scene," sighed the detective.

"And what about our security people who tried to revive the man?"

"They contaminated the scene too. I'll need to speak with them, of course. You should have told them not to touch anything until the police arrived," he said testily.

Hidden in the corner, Laurie wanted to turn away, but she couldn't. As she watched, the officer examined the body without touching it, shining a penlight at the eyes and mouth, observing the gelled blond hair, peering closely at the exposed skin of the neck. Finally, he straightened and spoke to the ambulance crew.

"He's dead, alright. Take him over to Jackson Memorial and have a doc declare him, then take him to the M.E.'s office. I'll brief her later." Turning to Juan, he added, "Who's in charge of this conference, anyway? I'll need to get statements and interview everyone who was here when it happened."

"You want to talk to Laurie. I'll call her," Juan said, reaching for his walkie.

Laurie stepped forward from the shadows to join the men.

"I'm here, Juan. I was waiting for you, but you guys came in so fast you went right past me."

"Laurie. Good. This is Detective Tim Riordan of the Miami Beach Police Department. Detective, this is Laurie Kilcannon, Connor Pharmaceuticals' meeting planner."

"What the hell's a meeting planner?" he asked gruffly.

"I handle all the logistics for the meeting, Detective," she answered with a touch of irritation, "Sleeping rooms, meals, meeting space, VIP arrangements, travel. Everything but the actual content."

"Oh," he said, bemused, "I thought secretaries did all that."

If he'd wanted to annoy Laurie, he'd picked the right nerve to touch.

"I have a degree from Cornell, Detective Riordan, and advanced certification from the Convention Liaison Council in Washington, D.C. Two-thousand-person meetings don't plan themselves. Now tell me, what are we going to do about Mr. Tradd?"

The detective blinked and shook his head slightly. Jesus, she was a prickly one! Gorgeous – if you liked classy, slim, not-quite-redheads, which he did – but prickly.

"You didn't overhear?" he answered, trying to regain the offensive. "I'm having his body taken to the hospital and then to the Medical Examiner's office for an autopsy, and I'll need to collect some statements while we wait for the results. I might as well start with you. Is there somewhere we can go to talk?"

Laurie was flustered. What could she possibly tell this obnoxious man about Edward Tradd's heart attack? Knowing she couldn't get out of it, she suggested the café. At least it was close to the meeting office. It was too bad he was obnoxious, she found herself thinking as she stole a glance at him in the brightly lit hallway, automatically checking his ring finger and finding it bare. He had wavy salt-and-pepper hair, crinkly green eyes, and a face that could have graced an Irish Tourist Board poster. Under other circumstances, she would have found him extremely attractive. Those eyes... Now just cut that out, she scolded herself, casting around for something to contribute so he wouldn't guess what she'd been thinking.

"Detective Riordan," she said crisply, "You mentioned an autopsy. Maybe I've watched too many episodes of '*ER*,' but don't you need to get the family's permission before doing a postmortem?"

"Ordinarily yes, Ms. Kilcannon," he replied as they slid into a booth at the café, "But not in this case."

"Why not?"

"We don't need permission to autopsy a suspected homicide."


"What can I get you?" the waitress asked Laurie. She'd seen the planner with Juan earlier and knew she was an important client.

"A Coke, please. And an ashtray." Turning to Riordan, she added, "I won't smoke if it bothers you, Detective, but I'm a little stressed-out at the moment."

He ordered a coffee, then pulled a pack of Marlboro Ultra Lights from the inside pocket of his jacket and showed it to her with a resigned half-grin.

"I keep trying to quit between meetings, but when I'm on site it's hopeless."

"It must be pretty hectic," he sympathized, trying to gain her trust so she'd give him the information he needed. "I didn't mean to put down your job before, Ms. Kilcannon. I'd just never heard of it."

"Most people haven't," she acknowledged, "But it's more complicated than you might think. And you can call me Laurie if you like."

Good, he thought. She's starting to relax.

"Call me Tim. So tell me more about what you do, Laurie."

"Well, basically, I have to be the 'master brain' of the meeting. Know every setup, make sure the VIPs are happy, put out fires on site... and it's always a challenge getting 2,000 people to do anything on a tight schedule. But I have a lot of help, of course. It's a great job. Usually."

"Yeah, I imagine having someone turn up murdered puts a wrench in the works, alright."

"Detective – I mean, Tim – about that. Why do you think Ed Tradd was murdered? That was his name, incidentally. Edward Tradd," she emphasized, wanting this policeman to see Tradd as a person, not just a "victim." "I didn't see any blood or anything. Why couldn't it just have been a heart attack? They do happen, you know. Ed was a top executive, very Type A. He was probably a total stress case and just hid it well. Aren't you sort of – well, professionally predisposed – to think of murder every time you see a body?"

"So Tradd was a bigwig. Did he have any enemies at the company that you know of?" Tim asked, ignoring her comments. "What was he like?"

"Oh for God's sake, you can't be serious! What do think I am, a spy? For one thing, I'm convinced the man had a heart attack. For another, I already told you I like my job."

Tim mentally kicked himself for handling her clumsily.

"Laurie, listen to me," he said more gently, "I need your help with this. I have good reason to believe Tradd was killed. Things I noticed about the body, things the Medical Examiner may confirm. Herrara already told me that access to that backstage area was restricted, so I don't think an outsider did it. You guys are going home in a few days, right? I can't find out what I need to know before then without your help."

"Why me? I'm no detective," Laurie asked, but she was stalling.

She knew why.

"C'mon, Laurie, you're not stupid. You *know* the people who go to your meetings. You know the top hotel people too, and I'm guessing you can go wherever you want in this place. You understand the politics of your company. I can shut down this meeting if I have to and order every single person to stay here until I can interrogate them. You could avoid all that by helping me."

Shut down the meeting? Keep the attendees in Miami Beach indefinitely? Laurie's head was aching now, but still she hesitated.

"There's something else you may not be considering," Tim added, playing his last card.

"What else could there possibly be?" she asked dully.

"I think Edward Tradd was murdered. And once a person has crossed the line to murder, it's easier the second time. If you can help me find out who killed Tradd, you might be helping to prevent another tragedy."

Tragedy. Not crime. Riordan wasn't stupid either. He'd used the word deliberately. As Laurie sat stunned, trying to sort through everything he'd thrown at her, he smoked quietly and said nothing.

Finally, she sighed.

"I still can't believe it was murder. But I'll make you a deal. If the Medical Examiner says it was – and you'll have to tell me why – then I'll help you as best I can. No promises, though."

"Fair enough."

"Dagmar to Laurie, come in, Laurie," her walkie crackled suddenly.

"Laurie here. Over."

"The Catering Manager wants to know if we're still planning to do the Safari Night dinner tomorrow. Can you meet me in the office? Over."

"On my way, Dagmar. Over and out." She turned to the detective. "I have to get back. You'll let me know when you hear from the Medical Examiner?"

"I'll let you know," he nodded.

Tim watched her as she hurried from the café.


The meeting office had felt crowded the day before with all 60 freelancers and a few VIPs. Now it was crammed with wall-to-wall bodies – meeting staff, hotel employees, and attendees – all hoping for some inside scoop about Tradd. Laurie pushed her way to her desk and wondered about fire code violations.

At least a dozen people approached, each needing to speak with her immediately. Glancing at her watch, Laurie started with Dagmar and the Catering Manager.

"Okay. Safari Night. What's the latest weather report?"

"I've been checking it every hour," Dagmar answered in her lilting Scandinavian cadence, "It looks like the storm is heading back out to sea. The latest report said it would miss us."

"Well, then, I say we chance it if the weather holds. I have another 24 hours to cancel it anyway. These reps are going to need some diversion by tomorrow, and God knows we could use *one* positive event at this meeting."

"So the meeting is going to continue?"

"Oh, Jeez. Good point, Dagmar. I don't know. Let me call up to Wendell and see what they've decided."

A few minutes later, she put down the phone and turned back to her F & B lead. Other staffers gathered nearby, waiting to hear the decision. If the meeting were cancelled now, they'd lose three day's pay.

"We're staying," Laurie said. "They all seem to feel it's what Ed Tradd would have wanted. Wendell's going to announce it at the end of lunch. Dagmar, you'll need to get a microphone and podium into the banquet room pronto."

Dagmar and the Catering Manager immediately left to see that the equipment was added. Laurie scanned the office quickly, looking for her friend and most reliable lead, Sue Palmer. Spotting her juggling alphabetical and chronological departure manifests with the ground operator across the room, Laurie called her over.

"You poor kid. How're you holding up?" the fiftyish freelancer asked kindly, easing her solid frame into the chair next to Laurie's.

"Oh, you know, just dealing with the usual on-site glitches," Laurie responded with a straight face.

Sue shook her head, laughing.

"I've been working meetings for twenty-three years, but this is a new one on me, I gotta admit. I've had an attendee die once – stung by a bee during one of those corporate team-building wilderness deals, turns out he was allergic, can you *imagine* the lawsuits? But a VIP keeling over right before a speech? That takes the prize. The attendees are pretty flipped out, I don't mind telling you. They're pumping the staff like you wouldn't believe."

"I believe," Laurie answered, "But you can't really blame them. Anyway, that's what I wanted to talk to you about. Wendell McCarthy wants me to go up to his suite to talk to the VIPs about the arrangements for Tradd. Could you talk to the staff for me? I know Dash and Marc already did, but I just want you to reinforce to them that they *cannot* talk to the attendees about this whole thing. There's enough gossip flying around as it is, I'm sure."

"No problem, hon. You go do what you need to do."

"Thanks, Sue." She turned to leave.

"Hey, Laurie?"

"Yeah?"

"Who was that handsome guy you were chatting with in the café?"

Happily married herself, Sue was determined to see Laurie settled down someday.

"Just a detective, and a royal pain in the butt, if you must know. What do you have, anyway – eyes in the back of your head?"

Jim Fisher was leaving Wendell's suite just as Laurie walked up.

"Jim," she called to him, "How's everyone doing? Wendell asked me to come up."

"They're trying to decide who's going to tell Tradd's family. Gene wants to fly home and do it himself, but Mike and Wendell don't think it should be left that long. They want to send the Finance VP, Evans. He's home in Philadelphia, and he knows the family socially."

Laurie was glad to see that Jim was in better shape than he'd been earlier. She guessed he'd braced himself at the bar before joining the others.

"You heard we're going on with the meeting? Our first instinct was to cancel it – we all want to show respect to Marcia, of course – but we also need to get these reps trained on Zephyrex." he was saying.

"Well, then, I guess it's a good thing we're staying. Plus, the police need time to get statements from people," she said casually, watching for his reaction.

Aside from a slight widening of the eyes, there was none. She left him and walked into the foyer of the suite.

"Wendell, it's Laurie," she said loudly. VIPs didn't appreciate people interrupting them unannounced, she knew.

"Come in, Laurie, come in," Wendell replied, crossing the hall to meet her. "We wanted to ask you what, ah, arrangements are being made for Ed. Charlie Evans is going to talk to the family this afternoon, and they'll want to know when they can hold the service, when the funeral home can pick up the – body, that sort of thing."

"And he was a Catholic," Mike DellaGuardia put in. "I'd like to see about getting a local priest to perform the Last Rites for him. I know he's past helping, but I think it would comfort Marcia to have him, you know, blessed."

"I'll check into that this afternoon, Mike. Anything we can do to make it easier for her. The thing is, I'm not sure when his body will be released to send home. The police had him taken to the Medical Examiner's office for an autopsy."

"An autopsy? Why?" Gene asked.

Poor Gene, Laurie thought, this must be so hard for him. He'd always been a "company man." Despite his devotion to his wife and baby son, he really did care about Connor Pharma.

"They're not – they don't seem to be – 100% sure about how Ed died," she stammered. She certainly wasn't going to repeat Riordan's suspicions to the top executives of her company, not without more proof than she had at the moment.

"Laurie, do you mean the police think Ed was *murdered*?" Wendell asked, incredulous.

"I don't know, Wendell. And they don't know either. It's probably just a liability thing, ruling stuff out, you know? Let's not make it worse than it is."

Mike was shaking his head. Gene looked sad but calm.

"You're right," the CEO said, "This has just been so unimaginable. I guess we're all a little on edge."

"I know. The meeting staff and the reps feel the same way. For what it's worth, the good weather seems to be holding."

"That's a break, anyhow," Wendell said. "It's funny. We were wondering if it was appropriate to go on with the dinner tomorrow and the big banquet the night after, but then we all remembered how much Ed enjoyed that kind of thing on other meetings."

"He always loved to get a chance to interact with the reps one-on-one," added Mike.

I'll bet, Laurie said to herself automatically, remembering the gossip about Karen Shearing. She was instantly ashamed of the thought.

"What would you think of doing some sort of tribute to Ed at the final night banquet?" she said hastily to Gene to soothe her guilty conscience.

"That's a fine idea, Laurie. I'll start working on a speech this afternoon," Gene replied. He seemed glad to have something positive to do.

"And now, if you gentlemen will excuse me, I've got to get back to the meeting office. The reps are on their own for dinner tonight, so I've got to alert the Bell Captain to have extra taxis on hand."

"Sure thing," Wendell answered. "And Laurie?"

"Yes, Wendell?"

"Let us know if you hear anything from that policeman."

"He's a detective, I think. I'll keep you posted."


Later that afternoon, after she had dealt with two slide projector breakdowns, three sick freelancers, six complaints about the food at lunch, and eleven requests for roommate switches, Laurie got the call she'd been dreading.

"Laurie, it's Tim Riordan."

"Yes. Hello."

She waited.

"It was murder, Laurie. No question whatever. Edward Tradd was poisoned with a massive injection of a curare-based drug. Anectine or Pavulon, probably. A test in the lab found a measurable amount of curare in his system. We need to talk."

Listening to all this, Laurie felt perfectly fine. After all, it wasn't happening.

"Laurie?"

Silence.

"Laurie? Are you okay? Are you there?"

"I'm here."

"I've got to be in court this afternoon to testify in another murder case... "

Another.

"...so how about if I swing by the hotel around seven and we can talk then?"

"Yes. Sure. Fine. See you then."

She hung up.

Suddenly, she felt a wave of nostalgia for the impending rainstorm and the bunny-headed protesters.

# Chapter Four

Nobody should have to work in this heat, thought Tim as he pulled into the garage at police headquarters. After fifteen years, he still wasn't used to it. He dwelled gloomily for a moment on the air conditioning at the station. It would barely make a dent in the astronomical late-afternoon temperature. Back home, it'd barely break 60° this time of year.

Sighing, he forced himself to focus on his latest case. A murder (and he was sure it *was* murder) at the Hanover, during a big meeting, may offer variety, but the challenges of solving it made him rub his temples for a minute. Once in his cubicle, jacket off, tie loosened, and sleeves rolled up, Tim spared a thought for the other cases he was working at the moment. They dealt with drugs too... but illegal ones, not media-touted pharmaceutical darlings like the medication Connor was launching.

Hoping in vain that his iced coffee would cool him off, Tim contemplated the pile of files that confronted him. Miguel Gonzalez, murdered in a drug war. Maybe the girlfriend would talk if he promised her entrance into the Witness Protection Program. Miguel was a major figure in the Miami Beach drug trade. Jaime Trujillo, on the other hand, was just a minnow among sharks. A small-time dealer killed on the street for a few ounces of heroin. Tim made a note to recheck the witness's stories in his case.

What could he do with this most recent file, though? Edward Tradd had been an executive at a nationally known pharmaceutical company. Who'd want to murder him... and why? Tim had a feeling that that meeting planner – Laurie, was it? – held the key. Trouble was, she was suspicious. Pretty, true... but suspicious. How could he win her over?

He needed to.

For professional reasons, he assured himself.

It was 6:45 p.m. The afternoon workshops were over, and for the last two hours, Laurie had been pitching in at the Special Services Desk. Most attendees, sales reps accustomed to spending every day, unscheduled, on the road, were hungry and antsy after four hours in darkened meeting rooms. There was no planned dinner function that night, so the desk was mobbed; Laurie felt like a concierge as she booked restaurant reservations and ordered cabs. She was glad she'd guaranteed a lower number for the group breakfast tomorrow. It was an unwritten law of meeting planning that fewer and fewer attendees showed up for the morning meal as late nights (and hangovers) added up over the course of a program.

Finally, the onslaught slowed. Most of the reps were on their way to a night of drinking and revelry, and only a few stragglers still approached the desk. At a quiet "Excuse me," Laurie glanced up from her binder full of menus and saw Tim Riordan. For a while, she'd been able to lose herself in the comforting familiarity of meeting logistics, but now reality was back, staring her in the face.

Reality was looking mighty good, she noticed grudgingly. Tim had changed clothes, and now wore faded jeans and a moss-green polo shirt that seemed to make his eyes change color. For a split second, she wondered if he'd worn it on purpose. To weaken her.

"Detec – Tim, you're here already," she said with a discernable lack of enthusiasm.

"Well, let's not have a parade or anything," he responded, acknowledging her mood. "You said we could talk at seven."

"Yes, I remember. I'm trying to think of where. How about the hotel restaurant?"

"Too public for what we need to talk about. How about your meeting office?"

"You mean Grand Central Station? Don't think so. I'd say the backstage area – we have it booked until Friday, and I'm sure it's deserted. I have to admit the idea creeps me out, though."

"Well, then, how about your room? Would you mind?" he asked carefully.

"I have a junior suite this trip, as it happens. Don't give me that look, hotels always spoil meeting planners. Anyway, there's a sitting room, so I guess we could go there."

"Done."

This is a murder investigation, he reminded himself, and you need her cooperation. You are *not* looking forward to it.


Drinks and dinner ordered from Room Service, Laurie and Tim faced each other uncomfortably. She coiled herself onto the sofa; he sat in a wing-backed chair.

"So how was your day?" he asked with exaggerated casualness.

His inflection caught her off guard and she laughed, looking down at her feet and shaking her head. After a moment, she looked back up at him and smiled – a smile Tim could have done without.

"Let me put it this way: I've had worse days, but they've usually involved root canal or intestinal parasites. I still can't believe this whole thing has happened."

"I know. That's one thing I think all the TV cop shows get wrong. They seem to gloss over how completely shocking murder is."

"You know, you're right. I never thought of it like that. But I guess I have to deal with it, shocked or not. Where do you want to begin?"

"The timeline," Tim said promptly. "We need to figure out the time of Tradd's death as closely as possible. Let's start with when you last saw him alive."

"That's easy. I was doing a final check backstage before the opening session. Call it about 7:30 this morning. Ed seemed fine. Quite his usual self. Then I didn't see him again until Wendell announced from the stage that Tradd was sick. I ran backstage, and he was lying on the floor."

Tim took notes as she spoke. Without looking up, he asked, "Who else was backstage when you got there?"

Laurie closed her eyes for a moment to visualize the scene in her mind.

"All the guys who were scheduled to speak. Gene Stockton, our CEO, planned to do the medical stuff since our Vice President of Medical Affairs couldn't make it. Gene graduated from pharmacy school years ago, so I guess he figured he'd be able to handle the science. Wendell McCarthy must have run from the stage and only just gotten there before me. Mike DellaGuardia and Jim Fisher were there too. They're both Vice Presidents. And Lew Paulson, of course – he runs our Multimedia department – plus his freelancers. He can give you their names."

"What about hotel staff or your own people?"

"I don't remember seeing any hotel people back there until Juan came in with the security guys, but the double doors along the far wall lead to the back of the house, so someone might have slipped out that way."

"Back of the house?"

"Sorry. That's what hotels call the behind-the-scenes area of a hotel. Kitchens, back corridors, storerooms, that kind of thing. There would have been a banquet server backstage very early this morning to set up the speakers' coffee break, but after around 7:00 they'd been told to steer clear. It gets too chaotic right before opening session."

"Okay, I'll have Herrara track down the coffee break person. Maybe they can tell us something. So who else?"

"That's all, I think. No, wait… when Dash and I were running to the backstage area, we almost bumped into Marc. He was on his way out."

"Dash and Marc. Who are they?"

"Two of my leads. Freelance meeting planners who oversee different aspects of the program. Dash is lead on Breakouts – that's meeting room setups – and Marc's heading up Recreation. He's been going nuts today setting up golf foursomes and shopping tours for tomorrow."

Tim looked thoughtful.

"How well do you know those two?"

"As well as I do any of my leads," she answered, frowning. "We've worked programs together for years, and exchange Christmas cards and such. Why?"

"At this stage, we can't rule anyone out. I'm just wondering what Marc was doing backstage right before the big meeting when his job was Recreation."

"You think Marc…? That's crazy! What possible reason could he have to want to hurt Tradd?"

"I'm not thinking about reasons yet, Laurie," Tim answered. "I'm thinking about times. The Medical Examiner believes that Tradd was only dead for 10 minutes or so before he was found, so he must have been killed right before the meeting started. That's why I need to know exactly who was backstage. Let's not rule out Marc just yet. Let's prove he didn't do it."

"But it doesn't make any sense! I was talking to Ed not half an hour before the session was supposed to start, and there were 5 or 6 people there then. The same people who were there after he was found. How could he have been murdered without any of the others noticing any– " She stopped suddenly. "Oh, my God. I just remembered something. The protesters."

"What are you talking about?" Tim asked, leaning forward, "What protesters?"

"Just after I left the backstage area, these protesters from AAPT – you know, the animal rights group? – started prancing around the meeting room foyer wearing papier-mâché bunny heads and chanting slogans. It took us about 10 minutes to have Security clear them out."

Tim couldn't resist asking.

"Bunny heads?"

Laurie rolled her eyes.

"The drug we're launching, Zephyrex, was tested on rabbits. Anyway, I reached Lew Paulson on my walkie-talkie and told him to keep the VIPs backstage, out of sight. He must have told them about the protesters, and they were probably all trying to get a look through the hallway door – it's got a round window – to see what was going on while Lew's freelancers were busy setting up for the session. The door to the foyer is on the other side of the room from the coffee break table. *That* must be how the killer could poison Tradd and not be noticed by the others. All the VIPs were distracted by the bunnies!"

Tim sat back in his chair and grinned at her enthusiasm.

"You see?" he said, half-mockingly, "I'll make a detective of you yet."

Laurie reddened.

"I didn't mean to go on like that. When you're just trying to figure out the logical parts – who was where and when – it seems almost like a game or a puzzle. But he really is dead, and it's not a game at all, is it?"

"No, it's not," he agreed as a knock came at the door. "I'll bet that's Room Service. Why don't we take a break? I have a lot more questions for you."

"Terrific," Laurie sighed, turning her attention to the cart being rolled into the suite. A chilled bottle of J. Lohr Chardonnay for her, a 4-pack of Guinness Draught for him, plus the crusty bread, soft Camembert, enormous cocktail shrimp, and miniature crab cakes they'd agreed to share.

Tim eyed the spread appreciatively.

"Beats the hell out of cold pizza at headquarters. I should work hotel cases more often."

"What kind of cases do you usually get?" she asked, biting into a savory crab cake, her first food in nine hours.

"Drug murders, mostly," he answered through a mouthful of shrimp. "I see things you wouldn't believe in this town. Revenge murders, murders to scare people, sometimes just murder for the fun of it. I'm thinking of getting out soon, before I lose what's left of my faith in human nature. I'm from up north originally, but I've been staying down here to see my kid through high school."

"You're married?" she asked.

"Was married. Way too young, it was a disaster. Tim Jr.'s the only good thing that came of it."

Dolores was a perfectly nice woman, Tim mused. Attractive, loving, funny, and supportive. Supportive until she realized the daily dangers a beat cop faced, he corrected himself. Tim still remembered The Talk, the one that had led to their divorce. He'd grown up on Cape Cod, but they lived in New York City then...

"I've been doing a lot of thinking, Tim, and I've decided I just can't stay with you anymore unless you leave the Force. Every time the phone rings, I jump three feet, thinking it's someone at the station calling to tell me you've been killed. You don't know what it's like. The worrying, the waiting, the constant fear... and now that we have a baby, it's a hundred times worse. Do you want your son to grow up with a flag-draped coffin and the sound of bagpipes as his only memories of you?"

He'd pointed out that he could die any day. So could she, so could anyone. A drunk driver. A freak accident. A sudden illness. He'd also pointed out that she knew what he did for a living before she married him. It was no use. He'd tried, for the sake of his marriage, for Tim Jr., to do something different with his life. Became an insurance agent, sold real estate on the side. But the marriage crumbled anyway, perhaps because of his own misery. Once a cop, always a cop, he guessed. When she left, he went back to the Force. At least being a cop made sense...

"His mother and I are on good terms, but as soon as he heads off to college, that's it for me and the Sunshine State. He's chosen a school in Boston, thank God, so I can move back to the Cape and still see him. How about you, Laurie? Married? Divorced?"

"Door Number Two, Detective. I can't claim to have been too young. Just colossally stupid and completely blind. No kids, though. If there were, I wouldn't be doing this job. Where on the Cape, by the way?"

She'd caught him in the middle of a hunk of baguette. Swallowing, he answered, "A little town called Barcliff, right next door to Chatham. Don't tell me you've heard of it?"

Laurie couldn't believe it.

"Heard of it? I love it! My grandparents used to have a house in Eastham, right down the road. I've been renting a place on the Cape for a week every summer for ten years!"

"Son of a bitch! Small world, isn't it?" He had a sudden mental image of a sunburned, wind-tousled Laurie walking along Barcliff's rocky beach in a fisherman's sweater.

"Let's get back to work," he said abruptly.



Tim had been grilling Laurie for over an hour. He'd sorted out the VIPs' names, titles, and relative power levels, learned all about the threatened takeover, and gained a fresh appreciation for the intricate logistics of a large-scale product launch. Now he needed to know about the people.

"So, let's start with Edward Tradd. What was he like?"

Laurie had cooperated fully up to this point, but at that question she began to grow nervous.

"I'm not sure what I can tell you, Tim. I didn't know him that well. I don't know any of these guys that well. I'm afraid of saying something that might implicate someone."

"Laurie, the only thing that's going to implicate anybody is hard evidence or a signed confession. All I'm asking for are your impressions of the people you know from work. It will give me a place to start, and help me with my interviews tomorrow. Now please – tell me about Edward Tradd."

Laurie paused for a long moment, then began.

"I don't know any way to sugarcoat this, so I'll just say it straight: he was pretty much an asshole, and I can't think of anyone who genuinely liked him... except his family, presumably. Maybe he was different with them. But at Connor, he was known for using people, taking credit for his colleagues' work, and treating his subordinates like dirt. He's been sued for sexual harassment at least three times that I know of, although nothing ever came of it. The women

57

always dropped their cases after a meaningful discussion with Connor's lawyers. Basically, Tradd was a bastard."

Tim whistled.

"Jesus, he sounds like a real hard case. So who do you think hated him enough to kill him?"

Laurie felt as annoyed as she had in the café earlier that day.

"How on earth should I know? Are you asking me to just speculate about one of our employees being a murderer? How can I do that?"

Tim lit a cigarette and opened his second beer.

"Listen, I realize this is hard. You know all these people. Just try to think of it the way you were before. As a puzzle. Forget your own feelings for now. Just use logic, and tell me who you'd categorize as 'possibles' versus 'impossibles.'"

She sipped her wine and thought for a minute.

"Alright. That I can do. But put your notebook away, would you? It'll be easier if it seems like we're just talking."

He stowed the wire-bound memo pad in the back pocket of his jeans and waited.

"Okay. First off, I think you can forget about the sales reps. One of them could have slipped into the backstage area through the back-of-the-house door, but it doesn't seem very likely. Besides, Tradd was as well liked by the reps as he was disliked by the folks in the home office. His attention could get a rep promoted. No, I think the best bet is one of the VIPs. They worked most closely with him, and the ones at this meeting were all backstage when he was killed."

"That makes sense," Tim said. "You're doing fine. Now, let's take them one by one. Remember, this is just a puzzle to be solved. Start with Wendell McCarthy."

"Oh Jeez, this part's hard. I can't imagine Wendell killing anyone in a million years."

"I know. I'm just trying to find out if he had anything against Tradd."

"Well, Wendell's retiring next year. The rumor I've heard is that he doesn't want to go. There was a time when everyone thought Wendell was a lock to take over for Gene Stockton one day, but Tradd kind of edged him out. Maybe Wendell will get the promotion now that Tradd's dead. I guess you could call that a motive."

"I'd say," Tim put in dryly. "Now how about Tradd's #2, Fisher?"

"Jim's not quite as hard to figure, hypothetically, anyway. He hated Tradd and made no secret of it. Tradd didn't stop abusing him once he'd promoted Jim to Vice President. It was like watching a cat bat around a mouse. Torture for the fun of it. Tradd was always poaching Jim's ideas and passing them off as his own. I think I heard somewhere that Tradd once made a pass at Jim's wife, too. In any case, there was no love lost there."

Tim nodded.

"Excellent. That leaves us with – who? Stockton and DellaGuardia among the VIPs, right?"

"Yes," Laurie answered, "But I'm drawing a blank on both of them. Gene is just a saint. A dear, good man, and a damn fine CEO. Everyone loves him. He was even featured in *BusinessWeek* a few months ago. The article went on and on about how great he is to work for, all the charities he and his wife support. As for Mike, he's a devout Catholic. I can't see him committing a mortal sin like that and then saying a Hail Mary over the body ten minutes later."

"Hmm. He did that?"

"Yeah. I saw him making the sign of the cross as well. You Catholic?"

"Recovering," he answered, and got a rueful laugh in return.

"Same here. But the point is, Catholics – real ones – believe in the sanctity of human life. I just can't see Mike DellaGuardia as a killer."

"Yes, but remember, Catholics believe in absolution, too. Maybe Mike thought he could be forgiven if he saw the sin as somehow justified, and did a heavy enough penance for it afterward."

Laurie shook her head.

"I don't think so. By the way, you were going to tell me more about *how* Tradd was killed. Won't that have some bearing on who you suspect? I didn't recognize either of the drugs you mentioned on the phone as possible poisons."

"No, they're not marketed at all. I checked. Pavulon and Anectine are your basic workhorse drugs, designed to work with anesthetics. They're used in operating rooms and ERs to make all the muscles completely relax, for surgery or when a patient has to get a tube down the throat."

"So how was the drug given to Tradd?"

"Injected straight into the big artery in the neck. Both of these medicines cause total paralysis, and patients who get them are always put on a ventilator. Otherwise, they couldn't breathe. That's what happened to Tradd. Paralysis leading to asphyxiation. Looks a lot like a heart attack."

"So what tipped you off?"

"Well, for one thing, I saw a small puncture wound in Tradd's neck. For another, his chin was wet, like he'd been drooling. Both these drugs can cause excessive salivation."

"Jesus, how did you know all that?"

"I didn't. The puncture mark was enough for me to order the autopsy, and when the M.E. gave me the probable poisons, I went on the computer and did some research. Disappointed?"

"Hardly. Impressed is more like it. But it does make things more confusing in a way. How could anyone but a doctor get hold of that stuff? And how would any of our guys even know about it?"

"Anyone can do research, Laurie."

"I suppose. So what's next? You're going to interview all the VIPs tomorrow, right?"

"Yes. Do you think you could do your meeting planner thing and find me a conference room?"

"I think I might be able to swing that. Play your cards right, and I'll throw in some breakfast."

He smiled. He could really get to like this girl.

"You know, there's one more thing I wanted to ask you about Tradd. Did he have a mistress?"

Laurie hesitated again. She barely knew Karen, but it seemed disloyal somehow to tell Tim about her affair with Tradd.

"I'll find out anyway, Laurie. You might as well tell me," he said.

Laurie exhaled noisily.

"Alright, but don't jump to conclusions, okay? Her name is Karen Shearing. She's one of the reps, and I understand she and Tradd were lovers."

"Was the relationship still going on?"

"Yes."

"How can you be so sure?"

Laurie told him about the hotel arrival manifest with Karen's name missing, and Wendell's theory that she had checked into Tradd's suite.

Tim swore.

"We'll have to find out for sure. But if it's true, it's a real setback."

Laurie couldn't figure that one out. She asked Tim why it mattered, and he explained that he'd wanted to get into Tradd's suite and search it himself before anything was disturbed. He couldn't do that if Karen were there.

Laurie gave him a patronizing smile.

"Just give me a moment," she said, turning to her overflowing binder. Scanning her rooming list and the hotel's Expected Arrivals manifest, she picked up the phone and dialed the front desk.

"Yes, hello, this is Laurie Kilcannon, the meeting planner for the Connor Pharmaceuticals launch. I'm updating my rooming list. Could you tell me if an attendee named Karen Shearing checked into a double-double with Ellen Markowitz today?" A pause. "She did? Thanks, I'll make a note of it."

Hanging up, she turned to Tim.

"I guess she didn't want to stay in Tradd's suite after he was killed," she said.

"I guess not. Now can you call them back and ask for an extra key to the suite? I'd like to get in there as soon as possible."

"Don't need to. I have duplicates of all the VIPs' keys, so I can check their bar setups and stuff."

"Great! You sure are handy to have around. Let's go!"

"Both of us?" she asked, suddenly afraid.

"Both of us," he replied firmly. "I want your insights. Don't worry. Nothing bad is going to happen. I'm armed, remember?"

Well, *there's* a comfort, Laurie said to herself.

# Chapter Five

Nine o'clock at night was an oddly silent and deserted hour. Later, the hotel corridors would be filled with rowdy reps eager to continue their evening of freedom. But for the moment, the hall outside Tradd's suite was quiet. Almost sinister, Laurie thought.

Pausing outside the double doors, she knocked lightly. Tim's puzzled look made her drop her hand.

"Force of habit," she explained. "I was taught never to enter an attendee's room unannounced, even if you know the person's not there. I've only forgotten once," she added with a slight shudder.

"And I'm sure you could tell me a pretty wild story about *that* little lapse," he grinned.

"Some other time. After you," she gestured, opening the door with her duplicate "key" (actually a coded passcard with Tradd's name taped to the front).

He entered, flipped on the lights, and stopped short.

"Mother of God."

Laurie rushed forward, expecting to see another dead body based on the shock in his voice, but he was just staring at the suite.

The sitting room was enormous, with sleekly designed modern furnishings and a carpet that looked like a Braque canvas. Subtle recessed lighting highlighted distinctive artwork on walls and tabletops, but the real star of the room was its view. Through a wall-length bank of sliding glass, which led out to a magnificent balcony, yachts off Miami Beach glittered on the horizon.

"Unbelievable," Tim marveled.

"You bet it is. Tradd had a temper fit with me yesterday about his view being substandard!"

"He must not have seen it by night, then. Honest to Christ, Laurie, this suite is amazing."

The veteran planner was long past being impressed by hotel suites. She spotted the slight disorder and figured that Juan must have told Housekeeping to leave the suite alone after Tradd's death, but she had to admit that it still looked pretty nice.

"You should see Gene's," she laughed. "Two floors, spiral staircase, a grand piano, and *his* balcony overlooks the ocean directly – at high tide you could practically sail a boat right up to it. But even that's pretty modest compared to some. At the Dolphin in Orlando, the Presidential Suites each come with, I swear to God, their own butler."

"Jesus. What do these rooms run a night?"

"Normally around $2,500, but all our VIP suites are comped. We're not paying a cent for them."

He whistled.

"How'd you get them to do that?"

"I asked," Laurie said simply. "This meeting is bringing over two million dollars to the Hanover in five days. They generally offer a few freebies as a courtesy, so I just asked them to comp the suites before I signed the contract. They're not losing money, believe me."

He looked at her with new respect. A multimillion-dollar contract, and she was negotiating the terms.

"So what are we going to look for in here, anyway?" she asked.

"Anything that will tell us more about Tradd and why someone wanted to kill him. I need to get a better feel for this guy."

"Then let's start in the bedroom. Clothes make the man, right?" she suggested gamely, her jitters forgotten.

Unfortunately, Tradd's wardrobe revealed more about the skill of his tailor than about his own personality. His business suits were flawlessly cut on classic lines in muted grays and blues. Dress shirts of heavy cotton/silk blends, golf shirts from Cutter & Buck, silk boxers and pressed Orvis khakis… they told of nothing but an appreciation for quality and the means to indulge it.

His ties gave the only glimpse into the character of Edward Tradd. Several bore "Save the Children" tags – gifts from his wife, Laurie guessed – but there were two, rich with sensuous jewel tones, that she imagined he'd picked out himself. Tucked at the bottom of a drawer that held socks lay one more, patterned with pill capsules in green and blue. She put that down as a gift from Karen.

"Hey, Tim," she said, as something odd occurred to her, "Did you notice there are no pajamas?"

"He probably slept in the nude."

Laurie grimaced.

"Okay, don't need to be visualizing that right now. Let's check the bathroom."

The first thing she noticed in the master bath was the French-milled soap, remembering Tradd's fury yesterday. The bathroom yielded a few more insights into his habits – expensive hair gel, ginseng tablets, and a large bottle of Cinnamon Scope – but there were no telltale heart medications to cast doubt on the murder theory.

Drawer by drawer, closet by closet, they searched the suite and found nothing of interest. Laurie was about to give up when Tim asked, "Did he have a briefcase?"

"Of course he did. A Hartmann, naturally. The best you can buy."

"Where is it, then?"

"Probably by the desk," he replied, "Or maybe we missed it between the sofa and chair."

They pulled the chair away and bent down to peer under the sofa. Just to be sure, they checked the bedroom again. No briefcase.

"Would he have brought it down to the backstage area?" Tim asked.

"No," Laurie said definitively. "His speech was already loaded into the teleprompter, and he wouldn't have wanted to lug the briefcase around anyway. None of the VIPs carry them at meetings."

"Then it looks like someone took it."

"Who would do that? Who could get in?"

"Laurie, think for a minute, would you? Who else had a key? I know who my first interview subject is going to be tomorrow, anyway. I need to have a chat with Karen Shearing."

Back in Laurie's suite, they went over plans for the following day. Tim wanted to interview Karen, Wendell, Jim, Gene, Mike and Lew, and he wanted Laurie there when he did.

"You can tell me if they seem unusually nervous. The problem is, I'd rather they didn't know you were there. If they did, they might be less open."

"I agree. I don't want them thinking I'm helping you either." After checking her enormous binder, she said, "I think I know what might work. The Hibiscus Boardroom. It's a small executive meeting room with a built-in projection booth. They wouldn't be able to see me, but I could hear them. How's that?"

"Perfect."

"I'll call Juan and set it up," she said.

"Now? It's after 10:00!"

Laurie laughed. "He's used to it. Oh, and I have two other suggestions as well. Go to Gene's suite instead of asking him to come to the Boardroom, and don't let Lew know you're interviewing him. People always notice what Gene does, and Lew tells his freelancers too much. I won't be able to watch your interviews with them, but you can tell me what happens later if you want."

The meeting room was available, and Laurie put a hand over the phone to ask Tim what he wanted for breakfast. Doughnuts?

"Brioche, if they have it," he answered. Doughnuts! Who did she think he was, Baretta?

Hanging up, she turned back to him.

"I've been thinking… how about if I talk to my staff in between interviews? They might have some useful information."

"I can have my people do that," he replied. "I know how busy you're going to be tomorrow."

"I can make time," Laurie persisted. "Why not let me? I know who was doing what and I'm pretty sure I know what questions to ask. My folks have lists and records of when everybody arrived, whose plane was late, all that stuff. And the F & B people – "

"F & B?" Tim interrupted.

"Food & Beverage. They can tell me things like who drank too much at the welcome reception and how the VIPs were acting. Gossiping about the attendees is practically a contractual obligation for these people. If there's dirt, they'll have it. And they're more likely to share it with me than with a Miami Beach cop."

Tim whistled softly.

"When you decide to do something, Ms. Kilcannon, you really do it. Quite a change from the coffee shop this morning."

Laurie wasn't sure how to respond to that. In fact, she wasn't sure herself why she wanted so much to help.

"It must seem a little odd, I know," she struggled to explain, "But finding out it was definitely murder shook me. I mean, for one thing, it's *really* screwing up my meeting, which I do not like…"

Tim chuckled at that.

"Murder as inconvenience. Well, it's a fresh spin, I'll admit."

"I'm serious," she glared at him. "Helping find whoever did it just seems like the most productive thing to do, under the circumstances."

She hesitated. "But it's not just that. I can't – " she stopped.

"What?" Tim prompted, curious at the sudden change in her face, "Can't what?"

"I can't stop thinking about Tradd's children. He has two daughters. I've seen their pictures in his office. Listen, I know the guy was a bastard, but to those girls he was just 'Daddy.' Now they're going to grow up with this – this *hole* in their lives because of whoever did this to their father. I'm sure the murderer was only thinking of hurting Tradd, but those kids are damaged for life, and I want the person who did it to pay!"

She stopped suddenly, embarrassed by her outburst.

"Laurie," Tim said, taking her hands without thinking, "Something's really gotten to you about this case. What is it?"

He paused.

"*Tell* me, Laurie. Please."

She sighed, deciding to trust him for reasons she didn't quite understand.

"I lost my own father. Both parents, actually. Plane crash when I was 8. It's not usually that near the surface."

"My God, I'm sorry."

"Thanks. The past can't be changed, though, and I've done plenty of time in therapy to get over it."

"It's funny," Laurie went on. "I always used to get upset by stories of senseless accidental death. Raging at God or something. But I've gotten more fatalistic about that sort of thing as I've gotten older. This thing with Ed Tradd, though... well, with this, there's someone to blame, someone *real*. I'm kind of surprised by how vengeful I feel."

"That's natural," Tim said, "But you have to keep those emotions in check if you can. Finding the killer, especially during a three-ring circus like this meeting, is going to take focus and logic. That's the only way we'll get at the facts."

She leaned back into the sofa cushions, releasing his hands.

"Alright. I promise I'll stay focused. Listen, I should probably draw up a schedule for your interviews tomorrow. I'll need to leave messages for everyone tonight so they know when and where."

"Messages? On their hotel phones? How can you be sure they'll get them at this hour?"

"I can't. I'm going to leave them on the Connor voicemail system. Voicemail's an addiction with these people. They check it every chance they get. And don't worry. I'll make a note of it if anyone tries to weasel out of their interview."

His eyebrows went up.

"You catch on fast."

"Too many mystery novels," she confessed.

"Dick Francis or Sue Grafton?"

"Lots of Dick Francis, but I read those mostly for the horsy stuff. My secret obsession is an English writer from the 1930s, Dorothy L. Sayers. Her detective's an aristocrat named – "

"Lord Peter Wimsey," Tim finished, to Laurie's complete astonishment.

"First the brioche and now Lord Peter," she laughed. "How many more surprises do you have in store for me?"

"Buckets of 'em. You know, I think you need to take your handbook of hard-boiled cop stereotypes and throw it out the window."

"You're right. I've been prejudging you, and I *hate* people who do that! Forgive me?"

"No need," he answered, "I was only teasing. Besides, now I've been repaid for that secretary comment."

Laurie laughed.

"So you have. Well, it's getting late, and I still have to draw up that schedule and leave the messages, so we should probably say goodnight."

He looked down at his watch.

"Of course. Jesus, I didn't realize what time it was! Sorry I kept you up this late."

"Oh, don't worry about that. My body's pretty used to sleep deprivation. I only average around 5 hours' sleep a night on site."

He got up and walked to the door, then stood there looking awkward for a moment.

"Um, Laurie?"

"Yes?"

"Make sure you put the deadbolt and the chain on after I leave, okay?"

"I promise, Detective," she said solemnly.

"Alright, then. Oh, and Laurie?"

"Yes?"

"If we get this case solved, there'll probably be a trial or some, um, follow-up investigation. Do you – get down to Florida much?"

Follow-up investigation. Right. She grinned as she eased him out the door.

"From time to time. Goodnight, Tim."

She clicked the deadbolt and fastened the chain, then listened to his footsteps as he walked away.

Laurie rested her forearms on the railing of her tiny balcony, tired and comfortable in baggy plaid pajama bottoms and a white tank top. She'd drawn up the interview schedule and left her voicemails, and was enjoying a final glass of J. Lohr and a solitary cigarette before tackling the last task of her 18-hour day.

She exhaled slowly as she watched the moon dancing on the water several hundred yards away. Now that darkness hid the raucous colors of the city, the sound of waves and sea birds made her think of Cape Cod. How many more summer vacations would she be able to afford there? The talk of a buy-out had been worrying enough, but with the murder of Edward Tradd her future looked even more uncertain.

Would the VIPs blame her for not providing better security? Would meeting planning be outsourced by the new management if the merger went through?

Laurie was no stranger to questioning things, not after her experience with Etienne...

Movie-star handsome, quick-witted, and with an accent to boot, Etienne had captured her heart in no time. He caddied at a local golf club, and his permanent tan only accentuated his hazel eyes. They'd met at a friend's party, and within two weeks were talking on the phone every night. They began to date, and Laurie gave herself unabashedly to the charming Frenchman she'd fallen for so quickly. When he proposed, she thought all her little-girl dreams were coming true.

She visualized their future – the two adorable children (Jacqueline and Jean-Paul), their first house (small but homey, filled as it would be with mementos of his homeland – Chagall and Monet prints on the walls, perhaps a few cloisonné vases), his comforting embrace as the two of them watched the children graduate from high school...

"Etienne," she'd asked one night, after a blazing and glorious session in bed, "Do you think you'd like to get a regular job? I could get you an interview at Connor probably. I mean, I'm just a secretary, but it *is* a huge company, and I'm sure they'd jump at the chance to have you." (I certainly did, she'd thought.)

Etienne's mood soured then. "Caddying suits me fine, Laurie. And I don't want anything that comes from you." He withdrew his arm from around her shoulders, his eyes cold.

It was the first of many cracks in their seemingly perfect marriage. Things came to a head one night when she arrived home, exhausted, from a meeting her boss had taken her to ("so she could learn"). She'd worked over 70 hours in five days, but to her aggressive, demanding husband, his needs clearly outweighed her tiredness. She'd gone along, although her fists were clenched the entire time (a fact he'd either not noticed or not deemed important). The next morning, they'd gotten into a huge fight about something. It culminated in Etienne revealing that he'd only married Laurie in the first place so he could get his green card. Soon after that, she'd asked him for a divorce...

Sighing heavily, she stubbed out her cigarette and decided she had enough real problems to worry about without borrowing hypothetical ones – or dwelling on the past. She concentrated on Tradd's murder for a while, trying to decide what motive could have been strong enough to drive someone to actually kill him. When she remembered how many people had hated him, though, she gave up. She couldn't figure this thing out. That's what the police were for. At the moment, tomorrow's "to do" list was still unwritten. She went back inside and curled up with a fresh legal pad.

### To Do (Wednesday):

1. Confirm interviews.
2. Check meeting rooms.
3. Check in with Recreation staff.
4. Check weather.
5. Meet with hotel, vendor re: Safari Night dinner (?)
6. Watch interviews. Take notes.
7. Check with Sue re: departure notices for Thursday.
8. Check Safari Night setup again before start time.

She thought some more, added a few more items to her list, called the hotel operator for a 5:00 a.m. wake-up call and finally fell into bed.

Fortunately, she didn't remember her dreams in the morning.

# Chapter Six

"So what do you have today?" asked Earlene. "Work, class, or a hot date? I know it's early, but…"

Vivian laughed as she brushed her curly brown hair.

"Just work, Mom. I'm taking a few days off from classes. Don't worry, though, I won't flunk out this close to graduation. I've talked to my professors, and I'm in good shape for finals."

Earlene looked relieved. Vivian had gone through so much to get her degree these past four years. Working at Elegant Eats, studying late into the night, having no father to help out…

"Remember that extra job I told you about? The one I got through Jeremy at the catering company? It's for a big company that's meeting at the Hanover, Connor Pharmaceuticals. They're having an event tonight."

"Connor Pharmaceuticals?" the older woman asked.

"Yeah. Why? Do they get *Drug Bigwig Monthly* at the salon or something?"

"No… no reason," Earlene said. "I'm just interested in what you're up to, that's all."

"Well, I don't know all the details yet. Jeremy just told me when and where to show up, and I guess I'll find out then. The money's good, anyway." As always, Vivian let her mother believe that was her main motivation, saying nothing about her involvement with AAPT. Or her infatuation with Jake.

"Jeremy?" her mother was asking. "Is that Jeremy Smalls, the guy you've worked with for a few years?"

"That's him."

Earlene did her best to sound offhand.

"Well, that was nice of him. Getting you extra work and all. I'd love to hear how it goes."

"Oh, I'll let you know. If there's anything interesting to tell, anyway."



Wake-up calls should be illegal, Laurie thought dimly. Her arms were flippers, stone numb from the shoulders down. She'd barely moved since burrowing into the pillows and flinging the blankets over her head five hours before.

"H'lo?" she mumbled in the direction of the telephone mouthpiece, once she'd nudged it off the receiver with her chin.

"Good morning! It's another beautiful day at the Miami Beach Hanover Hotel," a computer-generated voice chirped.

I hate automated wake-up calls, Laurie thought. Big hotels were great for high-profile launch meetings, but in some ways she preferred the smaller properties, where real live operators commiserated with anyone who had a wake-up call earlier than 6:00 a.m.

"Well, at least I know where I am," she consoled herself on the way to the bathroom. During one cross-country string of two-day meetings, she'd had to call a hotel operator back after her wake-up call to find out what city she was in.

By this point in her career, Laurie's on-site morning routine was automatic: one bottle of Evian, one Coke, fifteen minutes of CNN to make sure the world hadn't blown up overnight, local weather, borderline scalding shower, semidry ponytail, minimal makeup, and down to the meeting office.

Dagmar had beaten her, though, and the room was already open. Laurie clipped on her walkie and got her second Coke of the day from the staff coffee break.

"How can you stand that at 6:00 in the morning?" Dagmar asked with a disapproving frown. She was drinking strong black coffee, her hair fully dry and swept gracefully back from her tanned face.

"Nectar of the gods," Laurie replied, "You don't know what you're missing." She was used to Dagmar by now. When they'd first met on a Connor management meeting three years before, the elegant Danish woman had obviously resented Laurie because of her inexperience. Since then, they'd worked on close to a dozen programs together, and Dagmar had gradually admitted to herself that the younger woman was coming along. Laurie often asked for – and took – Dagmar's advice on Food & Beverage issues, which helped their relationship as well.

"I'll stay with coffee, thank you," Dagmar said as she gathered her Banquet Event Orders and found her walkie on the rack of chargers.

"Going to check the breakfast?" Laurie asked.

"Ja."

"They'll be late this morning."

"Hungover, too."

"Probably. Listen, Dagmar, will you kind of keep a special eye on the VIPs this morning? I know they're all upset about Edward Tradd, and I just want to make sure they're okay." God, that sounded lame, she thought, but I can't come right out and admit that I'm investigating my own bosses.

Dagmar gave Laurie a long look, then smiled briefly.

"Ja, it makes sense," she said cryptically. "What do you want me to keep a special eye for, exactly?"

So much for subtle inquiries. Well, at least Laurie knew Dagmar would be discreet.

"Just let me know who shows up and who doesn't, if any of them are acting strangely or seem especially nervous. Anything that strikes you as odd."

"Alright. And I'll keep a special eye on that beautiful rep from Philadelphia too, you think?"

Laurie laughed.

"Jesus, Dagmar, you don't miss a trick."

"All that fish makes them smart," Dash said as he bounced into the office in time to hear Laurie's last sentence. "You Norwegians pretty much live on herring, dontcha?"

Dagmar ignored him. "I'll talk to you later in the morning, Laurie," she said on her way out.

Dash swiped coffee and a muffin from the break table.

"How ya doin', Lauriebell?"

"Hanging in, Dash. How about you and Marc? I know he was pretty upset about Tradd."

"Yeah, the whole thing spooked him for a while, but you know Marc. He got it together in an hour or so."

"Did he sleep okay?"

"Yeah. I made him take some melatonin and we crashed early. I'll probably help him out with Recreation once the morning workshops are through, if that's okay with you, Mistress Kilcannon."

Laurie smiled. She knew Marc would be pitching in on Breakout setups tomorrow once his own toughest day was over.

"Yes, my lowly minion, you may help your sweetie with Recreation. Just make sure your team sweeps through every workshop room and collects the leftover paper for shredding."

"Yes, ma'am. Thankee, ma'am," Dash said, touching an imaginary cap.

"And listen," Laurie added, no jokes in her voice now.

"What is it?" the younger man asked, taking his cue from Laurie and becoming suddenly, incongruously, serious.

"Dash, the police are going to question everybody who was in the backstage area when Tradd died, just as a formality. They'll need to talk to Marc about why he was there."

"Oh," Dash said. "Well, that's no problem. Marc told me all about it. None of the VIPs had filled in their recreation forms – they never do – so he'd gone backstage to ask them what they wanted to do today. He said it was the only place he could be sure to find them all together."

"Good. That's cleared up, then."

"But I'm sure Marc won't mind being questioned if it's necessary… especially if the questioner is that cop we saw you hanging out with yesterday. Yum, yum, gimme some!"

"Don't you have about 30 workshop rooms to check on, Dash?"

"On my way," he said cheerily, then added, "If you ask me, I say go for it. You two look adorable together."

"Dash, you're hallucinating again, and after you *promised* to stop dropping acid on site. Now get to work!"


The meeting office came to life as staffers and leads arrived to collect their walkies and wolf something from the coffee break before heading to their assigned duties. Sue showed up on the late side, since today would be a light one for her with no major arrivals or departures. Laurie waited until the office had emptied out before confiding in her friend.

"Sue, I need you to pinch-hit for me a little today. Tim – the detective, I mean – has asked me to listen in and take notes while he interviews some people about Tradd's death."

"My God, Laurie. Do you mean Tradd was murdered?"

"Yes, he was. Poisoned. I didn't believe it either, but they did an autopsy and some tests that confirmed it yesterday afternoon. And the detective wants me to help him with the investigation, because I know all the people involved."

"Dear Lord, a murder. That's just awful. But of course you have to do whatever you can to help the police. I'll be glad to cover for you during the interviews."

"Thanks, Sue. Just keep it to yourself, okay?"

"Not a word. Now tell me, before I die of curiosity, *what* is going on with you and that gorgeous man?"

"Me and Detective Riordan? Are you crazy?"

"Well, he seems like your type. You know, tall, hand-some…"

Laurie looked pained.

"Thanks, but I've had enough 'tall' and 'handsome' to last me a lifetime, as you well know. Okay, Tim's nice-looking, I'll grant you that. But he's also bossy and intrusive, and we have nothing in common. *Nothing*," she emphasized, deliberately ignoring thoughts of Cape Cod.

"Well, it sounds like that's a non-starter," Sue replied. She wasn't entirely sure she believed Laurie, but she could sense this wasn't the time to push it.

"I've got to get going. The first interview's in 10 minutes. I'll have my walkie on, but turned down low. I'll be in the Hibiscus Boardroom if you need me, in the projection booth. I'm supposed to stay out of sight."

"Such intrigue! So who's first?"

"Karen Shearing."

"Ah. The gorgeous girlfriend. Off you go, then. You might want to put on a little lipstick, by the way."


Tim was already reviewing his notes when Laurie got to the boardroom. "Good morning," she said, feeling a little uncomfortable with him now that he was on duty. "Is the room okay?"

"Perfect, thanks. And the brioche are great," he replied smoothly. "Did you get through to Ms. Shearing?"

"Left her a voicemail, and she responded right away. She'll be here at 9:00. After that, you've got Wendell McCarthy at 10:30, Mike DellaGuardia at 12:30, Gene Stockton in his suite at 1:30, and Jim Fisher at 5:00. Paulson you can talk to whenever."

"Why the big delay between Stockton and Fisher?" Tim wanted to know.

"Because Jim's got a 1:30 tee time and he wanted to get in a full 18 holes," Laurie answered. Seeing Tim's expression, she added, "Hey, I know they're suspects to you, but they're still VIPs to me, and I have to keep them happy."

"Whatever. I guess I can update some case files in the meantime. I'm always a month behind on my reports."

"Fine. You've got this room all day."

She started to say something, then stopped.

"I'd better get back in the projection booth before Karen gets here," she said. "Do you still want me to take notes?"

"If you could, that would be great. Pay attention to her expressions and gestures. We can compare notes afterward."

"Okay, see you later then," Laurie responded, leaving the Boardroom and accessing the projection booth through its side door. Once inside, she turned on only a small lamp next to the control panel, so that none of the interviewees would be able to see her.

They waited just a few minutes for Karen to arrive. Laurie felt a sudden surge of envy as she watched the stunning rep greet a clearly impressed Tim. God, I'd love to look like that, she thought, taking in the perfect tan, crisp white linen shorts, sleeveless pink silk oxford, and elegant strappy sandals Karen wore. Her toenails actually matched her shirt. For a moment, Laurie dwelled gloomily on her own sun-repelling complexion and bitten, unpolished nails before reminding herself that she had a job to do. Tim had already started his questions.

"Ms. Shearing, do you know why I wanted to interview you today?"

The rep hesitated, then said, "I suppose it's because Ed's death wasn't natural. After all, how could it have been a heart attack when he was so healthy? And I had reason to know because of my – relationship with him. I tried to be discreet about it, but Ed liked to take risks, and I think the other VIPs knew. I suppose you know about it too, and that's why you called me here today."

"What can you tell me about him?" Tim asked, not denying his knowledge of the affair.

Karen looked away for a long moment, then turned to look straight at Riordan, her lovely blue eyes filled with tears.

"He was good to me. Oh, I know how he seemed to other people. Too ambitious, not compassionate enough. But he could be so sweet. He was kind to me, and I loved him for it. I even thought…"

She stopped, unsure of how honest she should be.

"What did you think, Karen?" Tim asked gently, leaning forward.

No longer "Ms. Shearing," Laurie noticed.

"I let myself believe that he was going to leave his wife and marry me. It's embarrassing to admit in this day and age, but I'm so tired of being a sales rep. I just wanted to marry Ed and have a couple of kids. Everyone probably thought I was sleeping with him to try to get a promotion, but it wasn't like that at all."

Laurie was surprised. She had thought that herself.

Tim continued to ask probing, sensitive questions. It seemed more like a therapy session than a police interrogation, Laurie mused, and then wondered if that was intentional. After all, he'd used much the same technique on her.

"What don't you like about being a rep?" Tim was asking.

"The never knowing," Karen responded promptly, as if it were the obvious answer.

"You lost me," Tim said. "Never knowing what?"

"Never knowing why I do so well. I studied hard in sales training, Detective, and I work hard in the field. But in this business it's all about access, whether or not a doctor or surgeon will see you when you make a call. Most of my doctors are men. They see me. Even in hospitals, where it's always tougher for a rep to get in, they see me. How do I know they're not just prescribing my products because they find me attractive?"

"I see," Tim said.

"Listen, I don't mean to sound vain, but I'm not blind. I know how I look. But that's just an accident of genes. It's not an *achievement*. You know, sometimes I wonder what I could have done with my life if I'd been born, well, average-looking. I know it isn't fair, but all my life I've gotten special treatment because of my face. Not my brain, not my personality. My face."

She sounded so tortured that Laurie began to feel sorry for her. Laurie knew she was pretty in a low-maintenance sort of way, but she also knew she was no bombshell. Maybe that wasn't such a bad thing. Being as beautiful as Karen must be like being extremely rich. You could never really trust people's motives.

"Maybe you should find a job where your looks wouldn't matter," Tim was saying. "Why don't you become a computer programmer or something?"

"Because it would bore me silly," Karen said immediately. Tim laughed, and in the hidden booth, so did Laurie. Damned if she wasn't starting to like this woman in spite of herself.

"Well, I don't want to keep you much longer, Karen, but I do have just a few more questions for you. First of all, where were you between 7:30 and 8:30 yesterday morning?"

"I was wondering when you were going to get to that," Karen said. "Sorry to throw cold water on your theory, but I was at the big group breakfast with a bunch of reps from my district. We got to the general session a few minutes late, and one of those meeting people had to help us find seats. I would never have hurt Ed, Detective. I loved him. But I can give you the names of the reps I was with if you need them."

"I'll let you know," Tim said easily, "But for now I have one more question: where is Edward Tradd's briefcase?"

Karen looked like she had been slapped.

"Why are you asking me?" she asked in a low voice.

"I searched his suite last night, and naturally that was one of the things I wanted to look at," Tim answered. "I figured you had been in the suite with Tradd, and maybe even had a key," he said blandly. Laurie was grateful that he didn't mention her or Wendell to Karen.

"What about the maids? Ed's briefcase was expensive. Maybe one of them stole it," Karen suggested.

"I don't think so. The hotel guy told me that most of the staff are immigrants supporting large families back home. Their jobs are too valuable to risk. Besides, the suite hadn't been cleaned when I searched it. Listen, Karen, I can get a warrant to search your room with one phone call. Why don't you save us both the trouble and tell me what happened?"

The rep was scared. From the booth Laurie could see her twisting her hands and shifting in her seat as she tried to make up her mind. Tim waited quietly. Laurie began to think Karen wasn't going to talk, and then:

"I thought there might be letters in the briefcase. Letters I wrote to him. When I heard he was dead, I panicked. I was so afraid someone would send the briefcase home to his wife and she'd find them. I know it must sound ridiculous, since I tried to steal her husband, but I didn't want her to be hurt that way once I knew he was gone."

Tim looked puzzled, but Laurie understood, and liked Karen all the more for it.

"I went up to the suite during the afternoon coffee break. I found the briefcase and was going through it, looking for the letters, when there was a knock on the door. It was the maid coming to clean. I was scared. I wasn't thinking straight. I grabbed the briefcase and walked out of the suite like I belonged there. She said something to me in Spanish, but I kept going. I just wanted to get the hell away."

"And you put the briefcase in the room you're sharing with Ms. Markowitz?"

Karen's eyes flickered toward him. "You do know a lot, don't you? Yes, I put it in the room."

"Can we go and get it now?"

"Yes, but... do you have to look at my letters?"

"I'm sorry, I do. But I promise you this: if they have nothing to do with the investigation, I'll give them back to you privately and I won't include them as evidence."

"Thank you," she whispered.

Laurie waited until they had left before stepping out of the projection booth into the hotel corridor. After half an hour in semi-darkness, the light hurt her eyes. Squinting at her watch, she saw she had close to an hour before the next interview. Plenty of time to check on Marc at the Recreation Desk. The attendees were still in their workshops, but she wanted to make sure he was prepared for the crush when the meetings ended.

"Ready for the golf hordes?" she asked as she walked up.

"As we'll ever be," Marc replied. He looked as pressed and polished as ever, Laurie was glad to see. Apparently Dash's care had helped him recover from yesterday's shocks.

"The weather's holding, anyway," she said.

"Thank God. They're saying overcast but no rain for this afternoon. All our foursomes are arranged, finally, and the carts have been stocked with ice, beer, and waters since 8:00 this morning."

"That's great, Marc. I knew you'd have it under control. How about the non-golfers. Any problems I should know about?"

"No... well, yes, there is one group of attendees who might complain. They'd signed up for the deep sea fishing trip and were pretty upset when we cancelled it because of the weather."

"Okay. Just send them to me if they cause any trouble. That storm's still out there somewhere, and the water's pretty rough. We couldn't take the chance. Besides, they'd be a lot more upset if they spent their one free afternoon at this meeting projectile vomiting into the ocean."

85

"Amen to that," came a new voice.

Laurie turned to see Mike DellaGuardia and Gene Stockton standing nearby, casually dressed in polo shirts and khakis.

"Gene, Mike, I didn't see you there. Is everything okay?" she asked.

"Fine," Gene said. "We just wanted to find out if those – appointments – you left us messages about were still happening."

Laurie nodded goodbye to Marc and walked down the hall with the two executives.

"I'm afraid so. Detective Riordan needs to talk with everyone who was backstage yesterday. I'm sorry about the times, though. Were you planning recreation? Maybe I could reschedule your interviews. I did it for Jim – he's got a tee time – but I hadn't heard from either of you, so…"

"Laurie, relax!" Mike urged. "The times are fine. We both have work to do this afternoon."

"Yes," Gene added, "And I hate golf anyway. What did Mark Twain call it? 'A good walk spoiled?'"

"I couldn't agree more," Laurie smiled.

"Well, we need to pop our heads into some of the workshops and see if anyone's still awake," Mike said. "See you later, Laurie."

"Have fun," she said, then headed back to the Hibiscus Boardroom. Tim was already there, and he looked worried.

"What is it?" she asked as soon as she saw his face.

"The briefcase," he said. "It wasn't in Karen's room where she swears she left it. It's gone."

# Chapter Seven

Laurie whistled. "Well, that tears it," she said. "There has to be something in the briefcase that points directly to the killer." Before she could explore the possibilities, however, a new thought occurred to her.

"Tim, listen. Are you 100% sure the briefcase is really missing? Couldn't Karen have been lying to you so you wouldn't see her letters?"

"She could have been, but she wasn't. She'd taken the letters from the briefcase yesterday and put them in her own luggage. She showed them to me, and I read a few. Healthy girl, Ms. Shearing."

Laurie made a face.

"I'm sure. But now the big question is: what else was in there?"

Tim looked at his watch, then settled back into one of the leather captain's chairs at the boardroom table.

"We've still got time before McCarthy's interview. Why don't we brainstorm?"

Laurie sat down and turned to a fresh page on her legal pad.

"Okay, but you start. My job's pretty straightforward. I don't get a lot of practice with free association."

"Just let your imagination go," Tim said. "Think of anything you can that could fit into a briefcase and suggest a motive for murder. We know it's probably papers or a computer disk. How about evidence of a shady stock deal?"

"Like insider trading?" Laurie asked, writing "shady stock deal" on her latest list.

"Exactly. Now you try."

"Oh Jeez, I don't know. I've got one idea, but it's so bad I can't picture any of our people doing it. Not even Tradd."

"Tell me anyway."

"Well, you know how new drugs get approved, right?"

"Not in detail, no."

"Basically, it comes down to the drug company conducting tests called 'trials.' They do animal trials first, then human, to prove that a certain drug does what it's supposed to do – its 'indication.' If they have two separate human trials that prove the drug's indication, and there aren't any horrific side effects like kidney failure or spontaneous baldness or whatever, the drug has a good chance of being approved."

"So?" Tim said, running a hand through his hair absentmindedly.

"Well, I once read about a company that falsified its clinical trial data so the FDA would approve their drug. You have to understand, the research and development phase of pharmaceuticals costs millions of dollars. If a drug collapses in late-stage trials, it can mean a huge loss to the company. Anyway, the executives who were behind it had to pay enormous fines and a few of them went to jail. Country club jail in Connecticut, mind you, but still."

"So you're saying maybe Tradd was conspiring with another VIP to tamper with the results on this new drug of yours, and his partner was afraid Tradd would get cold feet and talk to the FDA, so he killed Tradd and then stole the briefcase in case there was evidence of the data falsification inside it."

"Well, it's possible, but I'm telling you, these guys would not do that. It's totally unethical, not to mention illegal."

"Your faith in your bosses is touching, but write it down anyway as a possibility. Now what about those animal tests you were telling me about? You mentioned that you guys had protesters here on the day of the murder, didn't you?"

"Yeah," Laurie laughed. "Those crackpots from AAPT."

"What's their beef, exactly?"

"Nice choice of words, Detective. They think we tortured bunny rabbits during the testing of Zephyrex, if you really want to know."

"And did you?"

"Of course not! We've got monitoring in place like you wouldn't believe. SPCA, Humane Society, you name it. The Zephyrex rabbits had clean hutches, all the carrots they could eat, and clear sinuses in the bargain."

"Alright, alright!" Tim chuckled, "You know, if you ever get sick of planning meetings, I'm sure the PR department would be happy to have you. But just to humor me, put 'compromising bunny pictures' on your list. I don't see how it could be a motive for murder, but I'll look at anything at this point."

"Okay, so what else?"

"What else is we have to find that briefcase. The answers we need are in there, I know it. I want to search the VIPs' suites."

She didn't like the idea.

"But that's crazy! If you ask them to do searches, they'll know they're under suspicion, and if one of them's the murderer, he'll just cover his tracks."

"They don't have to know, Laurie. Didn't you say you had duplicate keys to all the VIP suites?"

"Forget it," she said flatly. "I won't let you have them. For one thing, it could cost me my job if anyone found out, and for another, you couldn't use any of the evidence in court if you did find something."

"Damn cop shows," he said in exasperation, "They make everyone think they're an expert."

"Too bad," she retorted. "You're not getting the keys."

"Fine," he shot back, "But we still have to think of a way to find out if any of the executives have that briefcase."

"Why don't you just offer a reward?"

"A reward to whom – the VIPs?" he asked, confused.

"Nope. The maids. Only the top echelon of housekeepers is assigned to clean suites. The tips are bigger, it's a seniority thing. So we get them together and show them a picture of the briefcase and offer a cash reward to any of them who sees it. They're not to touch it, of course."

"What's to prevent every one of them from saying they've seen it just to get the reward money, Einstein?"

Laurie was stumped.

"Ha!" she cried after a moment, snapping her fingers. "We'll give each of them a disposable camera with her name written on it and tell her to photograph the briefcase if she sees it. What's wrong with *that*?"

Tim threw up his hands.

"Uncle, already! That's a really great idea, Laurie. Forget PR. Your future's in police work."

"Not for a million bucks. I'm too chicken."

"You get used to – " Tim stopped suddenly, and Laurie turned to see Karen Shearing standing in the doorway holding a piece of paper and looking scared.

"Detective, I've found – " she noticed Laurie.

"It's okay. Laurie's helping me. I'd appreciate it if you'd keep that quiet, by the way. Now, what have you found?"

She looked at the meeting planner uncertainly for a minute, then seemed to accept Laurie's role as she realized the details the planner must know. "I found this. It was in between two of my letters to Ed. He must have dropped it in with them without realizing it, or maybe he was hiding it. I don't know. You'd better have it." She seemed upset.

Karen held out a piece of paper to Tim. He motioned her to place it on the conference table, then used the tip of a pen to carefully move the paper toward him so he could read the writing without disturbing any fingerprints. It was a draft of a letter, but there was neither salutation nor signature, just the words:

> *You've covered your tracks well, but not well enough. You can delude yourself all you want, but soon the time will come when everyone will know what you've done. When that day arrives — and it will, I assure you — you can say goodbye to every-thing you value most. Unless, of course, you give me what I want.*

"Well, there's our motive," Tim said quietly. "Tradd was blackmailing someone, or being blackmailed himself."

Karen was sobbing now.

"He wasn't being blackmailed. He was doing it to someone else. That's his handwriting. I'd know it anywhere. The *bastard*!" she cried, her tone betraying the utter shock and revulsion she felt.

Laurie was sickened, but not surprised.

Tim handed Karen a tissue and sighed.

"In some ways this makes the job easier. Ten to one that blackmail note was Tradd's death warrant. But in some ways it's harder now too. We need to go hunting for secrets."

Wendell arrived a few minutes early for his 10:30 appointment. Laurie had to wave to him and walk away from the room so he wouldn't know she was observing the interviews. She was just about to step into the projection booth when she spotted Dagmar. The older woman reported that the banquet kitchen had unexpectedly run out of the snow crab legs that were supposed to highlight the Safari Night seafood station. What did Laurie want to do?

"How are they doing on shrimp?" Laurie asked.

A pause while Dagmar walkied the chef to check.

"They have very many shrimp, and lobsters too," she reported.

"Then tell them to load the buffet with shrimp, and add lobster claws for variety."

"Lobster claws. I will tell them."

"So how was the breakfast?" the planner asked, motioning Dagmar to follow her into the soundproof area.

"Much as usual. Lots of people wanted the bacon and eggs you ordered," the austere F & B lead responded with faint distaste. "But I'm supposing you are not interested in the menu?"

"Not really, Dagmar."

"Well, then, here is what I saw: Mr. Stockton arrived almost at the very end, drank a quick cup of coffee, and spoke only to Mr. McCarthy."

"Probably tied up with phone calls, or else he knew he'd get a million questions from the reps. What else?"

"Your guess is accurate. Mr. McCarthy did answer many questions this morning. He arrived at breakfast just as we opened the doors."

"Sounds like Wendell. How about Jim Fisher?"

"He also came down early. He talked to many people as well, and seemed almost happy."

"Happy?"

"That is how he looked. Cheerful, even. Quite different from Ms. Shearing. She arrived at the last moment, and looked very despairing."

"Hmm. I guess that's understandable."

"The biggest surprise was Mr. DellaGuardia. On past meetings he has always been one of the first to arrive for breakfast, and has made his plate full of everything you Americans like to eat in the morning."

"But today?"

"Today he arrived early, like always. But he barely ate."

Glancing swiftly at her watch, Laurie said, "Thanks so much, Dagmar. You've really been thorough. Oh, and about tonight's buffet – tell the chef I'd like to get the lobster claws at half price. The hotel shouldn't have run out of crab legs."

"Ja, Laurie," Dagmar replied with a hint of amusement, reaching for her walkie as she left the projection booth and headed back to the banquet kitchen.

Laurie listened for a moment, trying to figure out how much of Wendell's interview she'd missed.

"...and then Lew came over to tell us about the protesters and their signs and costumes, so we all crowded over to the side door to have a look. It was like a car wreck. You know it's horrible, but you just have to watch. Plus, we wanted to see if there were any media around."

"I can understand that," Tim said. "Now I need you to think back very carefully. Who was watching at the door with you? Was Mr. Tradd there?"

"I guess he couldn't have been, if he'd already had a heart attack. But if that were the case, why ask me who else was there? Do you think Tradd was murdered?"

"It's one possibility," Tim said calmly. "We're looking at everything. You were backstage before the meeting started.

Your insight would be extremely valuable. Was Mr. Tradd watching the protesters at any point?"

The VIP thought for a moment, squinting as he tried to recapture the scene in his mind.

"As a matter of fact, I don't remember seeing Ed at the side door. Jim was there, that I know. He made some comment about his younger sister being a protester for some crazy group or other, and how all those kids needed to set them straight was a job and a mortgage."

"Did he say which group?"

"Can't remember. 'Save the Spotted Emu' or some such nonsense. I asked him why there wasn't a group out there demonstrating to Save the White-Shirted Executive."

Tim chuckled. "So who else do you recall being there when you were watching the protesters?"

"Let's see. Oh, yeah, I told Mike DellaGuardia to get the hell out of the way. He's big as a house, nobody could see over him. And then – that's right – Gene came up and told me I should make a joke about the protesters in my intro. You know, acknowledge it and get it out of the way so we could go on with Zephyrex."

"But you never saw Mr. Tradd?"

"No, I didn't. I guess I figured he was going over his speech again before the session started."

"Okay. Tell me, what did you think of Mr. Tradd?"

Wendell busied himself pouring a fresh cup of coffee.

"Ed was a rising star at Connor, Detective. He had uncanny instincts about successful product marketing, and made many valuable contributions to the company. He'll be difficult to replace. And of course, he has a loving wife and two young daughters, which is the real tragedy in all this."

"Mr. McCarthy, with all due respect, I can get his corporate bio from your PR department. I'm asking what you thought of him personally."

"Why? Are you expecting me to say that I hated him and incriminate myself? If you want to know whether I killed him, the answer's no. I may not have liked him much, but I don't like my accountant either and he's still breathing."

"Point taken, sir," Tim said, smothering a smile. "But listen, I need to know everything I can about Mr. Tradd so I can figure out who did kill him – if he was in fact murdered. He's the only person in all this that I can't interview, and he's the one I need to understand."

He paused for a moment.

"If it helps, you're not the only one who didn't like him."

Watching from the darkened booth, Laurie leaned forward. Tim wasn't going to tell Wendell what she'd said about Tradd, was he?

"Alright," Wendell said, "Where do you want me to start?"

Tim relaxed into his captain's chair and took a sip of coffee.

"How about with Mr. Tradd's business dealings? I've heard he was ambitious to the point of being ruthless, and he had a habit of using anyone he could to increase his chances of getting ahead. Would you agree with that assessment?"

Wendell laughed.

"Well, well, well, you have been busy, haven't you, son? To answer your question, yes, I suppose I would agree. I never had to work under him, thank God, but I've heard stories, of course. Some of the stunts he pulled..." Wendell shook his head. "I remember one time... I'm not boring you too much, am I?"

"Not at all," Tim assured the older man.

"Well, there was a job opening in the marketing department, for an Associate Director of Something or Other. The position reported to Tradd, but it was Tradd's then-boss who was going to make the final hiring decision. It came down to two candidates for a third interview, one inside Connor and one outside. Tradd liked them both well enough, but he preferred the Connor candidate. Being seen to promote from within would help Tradd's reputation, you see, and Tradd figured the guy would be so grateful he'd let Tradd 'borrow' his work on occasion. So do you know what he did?"

"I can't imagine."

"Sent a fax to the outside guy telling him the time of the interview had changed, making sure the outside guy would be an hour late, and making sure the inside guy would look better by comparison."

"He sent a fax with a fake interview time? Seriously?"

"Absolutely. And here's the kicker. The inside guy? Who got the job, of course... was Jim Fisher. Tradd's been 'borrowing' his work ever since."

"Unbelievable."

"You know it. And the real irony is, Tradd didn't need to do any of it. As hard as it is for me to admit, he was talented enough on his own. But he always tried to look as good as possible to the senior execs. He was angling for the top job himself eventually, of course. He wanted it, and he didn't care who he had to step on to get it."

"Did that include you?"

"To a degree, yes. For a time, I was gunning for Gene's slot myself, I'll admit it. You see, Gene's been CEO for eight years now, and he's still only in his mid-40s. Chances are, he'll be moving up soon to the executive board of our parent company. Anyway, a few years ago, I was in a pretty good position to take over from him, and then they promoted Ed. He had a huge success launching Gromax, our baldness drug that came out in '92. He never looked back. And he was a good twenty years younger than me. Don't think that doesn't count these days."

"And what about you? What made you think he was pulling ahead of you for the CEO job?"

"Oh, you know. Subtle things and not so subtle things. Cafeteria gossip. What kind of projects we were assigned. I headed up the new Organizational Efficiency Campaign... a bullshit job, hiring a bunch of 25-year-old consultant MBAs to tell us our secretaries were wasting copy paper. Ed was put in charge of new product development."

Laurie hadn't realized OEC was a make-work assignment. At the time, company memos touted it as the most important initiative since installing computers.

"So you stepped aside?" Tim asked.

"Not consciously. I've been with the company for over 30 years, so I'd be lying if I said I wasn't a little ticked off. More than a little, to tell the truth."

Wendell stirred his coffee.

"But that's how it goes sometimes. A lot of factors you can't control, you know? Believe me, smoke-filled, big-city election headquarters have nothing on pharma companies when it comes to politics." Wendell smiled. "But over the course of a couple of months I got a few wake-up calls and realized the quest for the CEO spot was taking me over. I sprouted an ulcer you could drive a truck through and my wife almost left me. One day I just realized it wasn't worth it. I'm 62 years old. Time to empty the In-box and get to know my grandkids."

"Sounds like you dealt with the situation pretty well, Mr. McCarthy. Where are you planning to retire?"

"Jenny and I are looking at condos on a golf course in Hilton Head. Do you play, Detective?"

Tim shook his head. "Tried it a few times and didn't like it. I prefer basketball. Better odds of getting the ball where it's supposed to go, and you don't have to dress up. Would it surprise you to know that Edward Tradd was blackmailing someone?"

If he'd been trying to catch Wendell off guard, he didn't succeed. The older man narrowed his eyes and looked at Tim for a long minute.

"No, it wouldn't."

"May I ask why not? A fake fax is a long way from blackmail."

"Because of three sexual harassment complaints, Detective. Coercion and blackmail are first cousins, don't you think?"

"I'd heard about the complaints, sir, but how can you be so sure that he coerced those women?"

"Because one of them was my daughter."

"Holy shit!" Laurie thought. Wendell's daughter worked for the company and Tradd had put the moves on her? She had never heard a whisper about it.

Tim was almost as flummoxed as Laurie. "Do you mean to tell me that Mr. Tradd knew your daughter was a Connor employee and he targeted her? What purpose would that serve?"

"He didn't know. Julie was divorced at the time, and still using her married name. She was adamant that no one know I was her father. She didn't want to be accused of trading on our relationship. She got her job fair and square. She was a rep, mainly selling pain meds to hospitals, and she was damn good at it. Tradd targeted her for the simple reason that she's beautiful. He never bothered with the plain ones."

For the first time, Wendell's voice betrayed his real loathing of Tradd.

"He told her that if she didn't sleep with him, he'd see to it that she was reassigned to the lowest-performing territory in her district, with no hope of advancement. She complained, but the lawyers got to her and she decided to leave rather than fight. It turned out to be a good decision, oddly enough. She went to SmithKline a few months back and just got a promotion."

"I'm glad to hear it, sir," Tim said, looking at his watch. "And I thank you for being so forthright with me. Your information has helped a great deal."

"Has it? Well, I'm glad. I may have despised the man, but I don't condone murder – if that's what it was," he added perfunctorily. "I hope you find whoever did it."

"We'll do our best, Mr. McCarthy."

"That's all any of us can do, Detective," Wendell said as he rose to leave.

In her dim hideout, Laurie tried to sort out everything she'd just heard. One thing was clear: if he was anything like most fathers, Wendell McCarthy had a reason for wanting Edward Tradd dead.

# Chapter Eight

"Elegant Eats," a gracious voice announced. "How may I help you?"

As soon as the receptionist learned the caller was an employee, however, she dropped her overly polite phone manner.

"Hey, Vivian," she said. "You want Tammy?"

"That'd be great, Jill."

"You got lucky this time. She's actually in her office. You looking for more work or less?"

"Less, at least for the next few days. Think she'll mind?"

"Nah. She'll probably give you some grief, but the schedule's pretty light. No big weddings or anything. Let me put you through."

After a relatively short wait, the boss picked up.

"Hello, Vivian. What can I do for you?"

Which, Vivian knew, meant "how many days off do you want?"

"Hi, Tammy," she responded, "I was just wondering how the next few nights were looking. I've got finals coming up, and I really should put in some extra studying time."

There, Vivian told herself, that wasn't an actual lie. And she hadn't come right out and asked for time off.

Tammy pretended to sigh heavily.

"Well, I don't know, Vivian. I guess I have to allow you extra time to study, but you've always been such a reliable employee. Try to give me more notice next time, okay?"

"Sure thing, Tammy. But if these exams go well, I'll be graduating soon, and then I'll be available all the time. For the summer, anyway. Until I find a full-time job."

"That's great, Vivian," the older woman said. "Well, good luck on your exams, and call me when you're ready to work."

"So what did you think of Wendell?" Laurie asked once the VIP had left.

"I like him. He seems like a stand-up guy. I still suspect him, of course, but it sounds like being pushed aside for that CEO job wasn't that big a deal after all."

"You suspect everyone," Laurie replied ruefully, "But I don't know about Wendell. Before he said that about his daughter, I thought there was no way he could have been involved in Tradd's murder. But think about it... what Tradd did to Julie was pretty awful. I can't imagine Wendell taking it as well as he seemed to. Understand, I'm not saying he was the killer, just that I couldn't see a motive before."

"I know," Tim said. "It does put a different spin on him. You know what I'm having trouble with, though?"

"What?"

"The murder itself. Sometimes when I can't get a solid hold on a crime, I try to picture the actual moment of it. In this case, that means someone sneaking up behind Tradd and pushing a needle full of poison into his neck. I can see McCarthy trying to beat Tradd up when he found out about his daughter, and I can even see him shooting the guy, but I'm thinking that if McCarthy killed Tradd, he'd want Tradd to know why. It's the sneaking up on him that I can't get my head around."

Laurie thought about that for a moment.

"You're right. It's not dramatic enough. Wendell's a great guy, and I really like him, partly because of his, well, flair. A lot of these executive types seem to shed their personalities on their way up the ladder, but not Wendell. Maybe he could kill a man who had wronged his daughter, but not without making a speech about it beforehand."

"That's what I mean," Tim agreed. "Listen, are you hungry?"

"Starved! Why don't we steal a couple of box lunches from the Recreation area? I need to check on those guys anyway. Okay?"

"Sure," Tim said, although the idea of box lunches held little appeal. He remembered too well the tasteless baloney-on-white of his childhood. But what the hell, he figured, it was just fuel anyway.

As they approached the foyer where the reps were gathering to collect lunches and depart for their chosen activities, Tim wandered over to a gift shop display and pretended to examine it while Laurie checked on the meeting's progress. She appreciated his tact as several reps approached her with questions. Her job was tough enough without having to explain the presence of an armed detective, even if his gun was hidden and he wore khakis like everyone else.

"Hey, Laurie!" one of the District Managers from Nebraska called to her, "Man, that was a shocker about Mr. Tradd, wasn't it? You never know, I guess."

"I guess not."

"So what's the deal with dinner tonight? Our agendas just say 'Buffet Dinner, Casual Attire.' Are we doing something fun like that M*A*S*H party we had at the last launch?"

"Why don't you wait and see, Jeff? It's supposed to be a surprise."

"Oh, c'mon, Laurie, give me a hint."

"My lips are sealed. And anyway, if I told you guys what the theme was, there'd be no surprise left and you'd all blow off the dinner and go carousing in South Beach clubs half the night."

"You've got a point there," the DM admitted. "Can you at least tell me if we're going to have to listen to more speeches?"

"That I can do: no speeches. Tonight is relaxation only. It should be a *wild* time," she added, hoping he wouldn't read too much into her clue. "Are you golfing, Jeff?"

"Nah, I suck at golf. Always puts me in a bad mood. It's been in the 20s for two weeks back home, so I thought I'd just sit by the pool and soak up some sun."

"Sounds good. Have a great afternoon."

"You too. See you, Laurie."

Up at the Recreation Desk, she watched Marc and Dash efficiently steer the reps to their appropriate shuttle buses, answering the same questions over and over as the controlled chaos sorted itself out. Somehow, she knew, everyone would get to where they needed to be, and in half an hour the foyer would be practically empty. She picked up two white boxes and rejoined Tim.

"We've just got time to eat if we hurry. Here or in the Boardroom?"

"We're spending enough time in there. Let's grab a couple of chairs in the lobby."

"Good idea."

Tim watched as Laurie sat down and began to unpack her box. She reached in and removed two small sandwiches (smoked turkey and brie on a miniature baguette and fresh shrimp salad on a croissant), a container of carrot and celery sticks, a serving of pasta salad with sun dried tomatoes, an oversized brownie thick with walnuts, and one perfect navel orange.

"Is mine the same as yours?" he asked.

"Mostly. I got you one with roast beef and cheddar on crusty rye and honey mustard chicken breast on a seven-grain roll, but if you want to trade, I'm game. Why are you looking at me like that?"

"When you said 'box lunches,' I was expecting... well, I should've known better. You plan one hell of a meeting, Laurie."

She smiled broadly and felt herself beginning to blush.

"At home I subsist on Corn Flakes and Lean Cuisines. I guess I pour all my frustrated gourmet tendencies into menu selection on my meetings. Glad you like it," Laurie said, as Tim tore into the roast beef.

"Iffs deliccgwf!"

She laughed.

For the next ten minutes, they both concentrated on eating – suspecting, if for different reasons, that they might be too busy to have dinner. Laurie finished first.

"Polish off that sandwich and let's get back to the Boardroom. Mike should be arriving any minute. You can have your brownie after you've finished with him."

"Yes, Mom," he sighed as he turned his brownie over to her.

"Sorry. Didn't mean it to sound like that," Laurie said.

"Don't apologize, okay?"

"It's not like Mike to be late. He's very considerate as a rule," Laurie said after they had been waiting for ten minutes for DellaGuardia.

"I hope he's not trying to get out of it," Tim replied.

"I doubt that. He probably just got held up. I'm going back into the booth in case he shows up soon."

She had just gotten herself settled behind the control panel when the door to the Hibiscus Boardroom opened and Mike DellaGuardia rushed in. At 6'4", with thick black hair and a full beard, he made the solidly built Tim seem almost compact.

"Detective Riordan, please forgive me for being so late," he said as he grasped Tim's hand in both of his.

"It's not a problem, Mr. DellaGuardia. I figured you got held up with meeting business."

"Call me Mike, please. No, it wasn't work. I was on the phone with Marcia – Ed Tradd's wife – widow – helping her decide on the readings and hymns for the Mass. I've been talking with her almost nonstop since it happened. Do you know how soon they'll be able to – have his body sent home?"

"I believe the Coroner's gotten all the information she can from Mr. Tradd's body. I'll give you the number of the Medical Examiner's office so you or Mrs. Tradd can call to give them instructions."

"Thank you, Detective. I know it will help Marcia to see Ed buried decently. I mean, it will be horrible, but better than the Limbo she's in now."

"Limbo. I remember back in my CCD days when that's what the nuns called Purgatory," Tim said, figuring the earnest VIP would speak more easily with a fellow Catholic. Right on cue, he saw DellaGuardia's eyes flash in recognition.

"What order did you have?" the bigger man asked.

"IHMs. Immaculate Heart of Mary. You?"

"Sisters of Mercy up until high school, then my parents figured the only thing that would keep me in line was Jesuits."

Tim laughed at that. "Did it work?"

"Well, I've never been arrested, so I guess it did," DellaGuardia responded. Then he remembered what he was there to discuss, and became serious once more.

"Detective, I want you to know that I'll do anything I can to help with your investigation of Ed's death. Please, tell me what I can do."

"I appreciate that, Mike. First of all, I'd like you to tell me as much as you can remember about the morning Mr. Tradd died. Who was where backstage, what was said, what you saw. Just take me through the morning as you remember it, from when you first walked in to the backstage area."

For the next twenty minutes, DellaGuardia followed Tim's instructions to the letter, relating the events of the morning in painful detail. Tim let him talk, and found his account matched Wendell's almost exactly. When DellaGuardia reached the moment when Tradd's body was discovered, however, he stopped.

"Forgive me, Detective. It's a very difficult thing to talk about."

"I understand, Mike. Let's get off that topic for now, okay? What would really help me is your personal opinion of Mr. Tradd."

DellaGuardia hesitated, his desire to see only good in his fellow man clearly battling his respect for the truth.

"I think Ed was misunderstood," he said finally.

"Okay," Tim replied. "Can you tell me more about what you mean by that? Who misunderstood him, and about what?"

"Almost everyone misunderstood him, Detective. Oh, I know what they said about him, that he was overly aggressive in business and less than moral in his personal life. But I don't believe it. Sure, Ed was ambitious. He wanted the best of everything for Marcia and his girls, and he wasn't afraid to take whatever opportunities came his way professionally."

"Did that include stifling other people's careers to advance his own?"

"You mean Wendell, don't you?" Without waiting for an answer, he went on. "Yes, Ed's success with Gromax led him to – I guess you'd say 'outshine' – Wendell, but it wasn't Ed's fault that he was good at his job. If anything, Ed was a real champion for his colleagues. A true team player."

"How do you mean?"

"Well, just to give you an example, he recently supported Jim Fisher's promotion to Vice President, but Ed made sure Jim would still report to him, so Ed could always go to bat for him. In fact, I think Ed played a big role behind the scenes when Jim was first hired in the marketing department."

That's one way of looking at it, thought Laurie as she rolled her eyes in the control booth.

"Fisher must be very grateful," Tim was saying.

"You'd think so, wouldn't you? Lately, though, I've sensed that Jim's been a bit distant with Ed. I'll admit, I don't have any idea what that's all about. I'm probably imagining it anyway."

"What about the rumors of infidelity?"

"Don't believe 'em," DellaGuardia said promptly. "Ed loved Marcia and he was besotted with his two girls. He'd never have done anything to jeopardize his marriage. Besides, he was a devout Catholic. We attended the same church!"

Laurie couldn't help smiling at Mike's naïveté, even as she added "hypocrite" to her mental list of things she didn't like about Ed Tradd.

"You think the reps who accused Mr. Tradd of sexual harassment were lying?"

DellaGuardia shifted in his seat, obviously uncomfortable, and perhaps startled by the amount of background information Riordan already had.

"It's not for me to accuse anyone, Detective. But men in powerful positions, like Ed, are vulnerable to those sorts of allegations. Ed Tradd was a good man, and I have better reason to know it than most people. He pretty much saved my life a few years ago."

Tim maintained his composure, but Laurie could tell he was as surprised by this new development as she was.

"Saved your life?"

"That's right, Detective. A couple of years back, I found I was having trouble with alcohol. It started out just at parties, but then I started losing control, drinking on the job, and by the time I realized it was out of hand, I couldn't stop. Every night I swore to myself that I'd put an end to it tomorrow, but I never could. After a while, it started to affect my work."

"So where does Tradd come in?"

"Ed noticed what was going on, and one day he took me aside and talked to me privately. He told me how concerned he was, and helped me understand what I was doing to myself and my career. He reminded me how awful it would be if Gene found out about my problem from someone else."

Tim stared hard at the floor. Safe inside the projection booth, Laurie didn't have to hide her amusement. Tradd had tried to blackmail DellaGuardia, but DellaGuardia had been too naïve to realize it.

"Well, what he was saying finally got through to me. I walked right into Gene's office, told him myself, and checked into rehab that same day. I've been sober for over three years now, and I owe it to Ed Tradd."

"Mike, did it ever occur to you that Mr. Tradd was trying to blackmail you about your drinking problem?"

The usually mild-mannered DellaGuardia shot out of his chair like a mountainous archangel.

"That's the most despicable thing I've ever heard! How dare you!"

"I'm sorry to tell you this, but I have conclusive evidence that Mr. Tradd had been blackmailing someone recently, and his death may not have been natural. He might have been murdered because of it," Tim said quietly.

DellaGuardia sank back down into his seat. He sat there for several minutes shaking his head.

"Detective, are you absolutely sure about what you're saying? There can't be any mistake?"

"There's no mistake. The Coroner's report is pretty clear, and we have a draft of a letter, in Tradd's handwriting, threatening someone with exposure of what would obviously be a devastating secret."

"Who did he send the letter to?"

"We don't know, but we'd like to. If you can think of anyone who has something to hide, it could help us a lot. We'd keep the source of the information quiet, of course."

"Dear God, I just can't believe it. It's so *sordid*."

"Yes, it is. Will you try to think about who it could be? Even if you just have a theory, I'd like to know."

DellaGuardia shook his head again and sighed.

"My brain is just paralyzed right now, Detective. I'm wondering what to tell Marcia, for one thing. She thinks it was a heart attack."

"It sounds like Marcia has enough on her plate with the service and her daughters. Hopefully, we'll find the killer, if there is one, in the next day or two, so we can inform her of the circumstances after the fact."

"I need to go away and think for awhile. It's times like these when I wish I were still drinking."

"What do you do instead now?" Tim asked curiously.

"Lift weights and watch cooking shows."

"Interesting combination."

"I learned in A.A. Whatever works."

Tim stood up. "I'm sorry to have upset you with the information about Mr. Tradd, Mike, and I thank you for your help."

"You're welcome. I know I should wish you good luck with your investigation, but if Ed really was a blackmailer... I don't know what to wish you now."

"To be honest, I'm not sure what I'm wishing for myself."

Laurie waited until DellaGuardia had gone, then joined Tim in the Boardroom. She'd been planning to joke with him about Tradd's foiled blackmail attempt, but the last few moments of the interview had clouded her mood. She could tell Tim felt the same from the way he slumped, head down, into the leather chair.

"You okay?" she asked quietly.

"Yeah," he responded. "DellaGuardia's a genuinely decent guy – it's almost comical how good he is. I didn't enjoy disillusioning him." She felt oddly privileged that he would share that thought with her. She pulled a napkin-wrapped lump out of her pocket and placed it gently on the gleaming conference table.

"Your brownie."

He didn't look up.

Promising to meet up with Tim after he'd interviewed Gene Stockton, Laurie left the Boardroom and walked toward the meeting office. Even as she dwelled on thoughts of the case, she realized that it was no wonder reps got so tense. Sitting in a darkened room was pretty exhausting in its way. As a matter of fact, Laurie thought, she *didn't* want to go back to the office. She needed to move. A quick check with Sue on the walkie assured her that no crises loomed, so Laurie allowed herself the luxury of a stroll through the Hanover lobby.

It felt almost like playing hooky from school. Her attendees were either away from the hotel enjoying their activities or baking and drinking by one of the three pools. Some were probably up in their rooms having "meeting flings." Whatever. Laurie saw only a lobby full of people she didn't know, and that was enough.

First stop:. gift shop, where she found presents for a friend's kids back home. She lingered longingly over a display of bikinis and bright cover-ups before conceding that pool time was probably not in the cards. Finally, she added a $12 bottle of Advil (for 18 caplets!) and a few mindless magazines for the flight home to her load, and put the lot on plastic.

After storing her purchases in her suite, Laurie lingered there for awhile, enjoying the solitude and wondering about Tim. There had been a moment last night... but she knew from experience that all contacts seemed more meaningful on site, even without a murder. Better not to force things. Better to focus on her job.

Leaving the suite, she began the lengthy hike to the Special Services Desk, using two elevators, traveling what seemed like miles of hallway, and finally descending the hotel's "grand" staircase. Becky, smiling and calm as always, greeted her when she finally arrived.

"It's good to see you, Laurie! And it's a perfect time too. We're in a bit of a lull right now."

"Hi, Becky. Glad to hear everything's quiet at the moment. Any problems I should know about?"

"Nothing out of the ordinary. Mostly lost name tags, which we've been able to replace, thanks to my secret supply of hologram stickers. I don't think you'll have to turn away too many attendees tonight!"

Laurie always adhered to the corporate edict that Connor enforce a strict security policy at their meetings. All name tags featured special stickers, kept only at the SSD, and every attendee, even Gene Stockton, had to wear one to every official function.

"Mostly, the reps have been talking about Mr. Tradd's heart attack. That poor man. And his poor family!"

"I know what you mean, Becky," Laurie answered, glad the "heart attack" explanation had taken hold. "They're planning a tribute to him at the banquet tomorrow night. But first, I have to go check the setup for tonight's big event. You haven't told anyone what it is, I assume?"

"Not a soul, but don't think they haven't asked!"

"Well, that's good. Between the theme dinner tonight and the Breakouts tomorrow, they'll be too busy to think much about the other. And speaking of Breakouts, do you know where Dash is?"

"Probably with Marc, closing down the Recreation Desk. Would you like me to walkie him?"

"No thanks, Becky. The Recreation Desk's on the way to the beach pavilion, so I can talk with him on my way to check out how Safari Night's coming along."

"Sounds good."

"Oh, and Becky, I hope you get a chance to relax a little this evening. The SSD shouldn't be busy. Why not put some other staffers on it and get some sleep?"

"I'll do that, Laurie, and thanks. If I don't see you later, I hope your theme dinner goes smoothly."

# Chapter Nine

"Here are the Banquet Event Orders for the meals you'll be working on," Dagmar was saying, "And thank you for changing your plans on such short notice."

Vivian nodded along with the other two new freelancers, adding the papers to the bulging stack that already held her schedule, assignments, hotel map, and Working Agenda.

"Just follow the BEOs, and you'll all be very fine. Make sure the hotel setups match everything that's listed, keep the bars nearest the entrance closed at first to draw people in, the usual. Your first assignment will be the theme dinner tonight. You may have heard that an executive attending this meeting died from a heart attack yesterday, so the sales reps will probably want to drink many beers and gossip even more than normal. The hotel Catering staff has been alerted. Don't worry about the safari elements – other staffers will see to them. And of course, don't forget your name tags. Now you all have several hours until you need to begin. You may want to spend them reading."

"Safari elements?" Vivian could hardly believe it – would Connor actually bring in *live animals* to entertain their sales reps? She read, alright. Quickly flipping through her Working Agenda, she found information that made her mouth hang open.

Then she called AAPT headquarters to ask how soon a volunteer could arrive with that hidden video camera. There was no question that she needed it now. And the lens could fit right into one of the "Os" in "Connor" on her name badge...

"Dash, could you walk with me a little bit? I don't have a lot of time, but I want to know how Breakout setups are going."

Dash joined Laurie almost instantly. The Recreation Desk was as good as closed anyway.

"It's a good thing you booked all those sleeping rooms for last night as well as tonight. The hotel staff has already converted most of them into meeting space – God knows where they put all those beds – and my people are checking on the last few now."

"That's great, Dash. I'm sure we'll have the standard complaints about the rooms being too small, but with 189 Breakouts, they'll just have to make do with what they get. Of course, some malcontent will find out that certain districts get a 'real' meeting room," she sighed.

"It always happens," sympathized Dash. "At least they can't bitch about their materials. Every single box has been sorted. I know, because I counted them. They're in the right rooms as we speak."

"Dash, you're the best."

"So I'm always saying. Too bad no one believes me! Now let's not worry about Breakouts anymore. Let's talk about the important stuff... what's the deal with you and that policeman?"

Laurie stopped short. Typical Dash. Even with nothing to go on, he'd try to invent an attraction. She'd better set him straight...

"Nothing's going on. Sorry to disappoint, but there's honestly nothing to discuss."

She certainly wasn't going to tell Dash about the possible chemistry between her and Tim. Much as she liked the free-spirited Breakouts lead, she'd just as soon rent out a billboard as tell him anything personal. Besides, she wasn't sure how to interpret things herself yet, or even if there was anything to interpret in the first place.

"Well, Dash, this is where I leave you, unless you'd like to see how preparations for tonight's dinner are coming along."

Dash pursed his lips.

"Are you kidding? I've seen plenty of theme nights in my time, and so has Marc. I'm going to do a final check on the Breakout setups, then Marc and I plan on having a quiet dinner in our room before going to bed early," he said virtuously.

"Now why don't I believe that?" Laurie asked with a smile.

"Well, we *are* planning to go to bed early…"

"Spare me the details."

"Yeah, you'd just get jealous. See ya, Lauriebell!"

"So long, Dash."

For all his talk, she knew Dash would check every Breakout room himself. At least one part of this meeting would come off without a hitch.


Exiting the hotel building, Laurie made her way down to the Beach Pavilion, grateful that the hotel's three pools left one available exclusively for groups. Even now, hours before the dinner (and still no rain, thank God), sweating hotel staffers in shorts and t-shirts were setting up tiki bars and Safari-themed buffet stations. Laurie hoped it would cool down a bit before tonight. Most of the reps weren't used to this kind of heat, and even the experienced banquet servers would probably be too hot in their beige pants and white polos.

Later, the event company Laurie had hired would arrive, bringing with them the wild animals and (she fervently hoped) handlers who would bring Safari Night to terrifying life.

Laurie knew the rickety bridges and abandoned vehicles would only be props, but still she wished she'd chosen the Mardi Gras theme instead. Safari Night suddenly seemed a little creepy.

Too late now.

She spied Tim searching for her in a grove of palm trees and strolled over to join him.

"So how was the interview with Gene?"

"It went fine, but I'm glad you warned me about that suite. Holy God! He seemed – I'll tell you about it later."

Perplexed by his sudden change in mood, Laurie turned around and saw Lew Paulson.

"Hey, Lew, what's up? I thought there weren't any presentations tonight."

"There aren't, but I thought I'd see what props you had going, what kind of food you had planned, that sort of thing."

Typical Lew. Always wanting to be in the know.

"Well, you're a little early for props, but I know you got a copy of the Working Agenda. You won't tell any of the attendees what the theme is, will you?"

"Me? Of course not! Besides, you've obviously let the policeman in on your big secret. If he won't tell, I won't."

"Certainly not," Tim said. "I just wanted to confirm yesterday's timeline with Ms. Kilcannon, but you were even closer to the action. It must have been incredible to be right backstage when Mr. Tradd passed away, Mr. Paulson."

Laurie seized the opportunity to look at a bar setup. She was far away enough to feign interest in something other than the interview Tim clearly had planned, but close enough to eavesdrop.

"In twenty years of running multimedia presentations at meetings, I've never seen anything to beat it. I mean, a VIP dying! And just before his speech!"

"It's a good thing you were there," Riordan encouraged.

"Oh, absolutely," Lew said importantly. "I was shocked, like everyone else, but at least the environment was familiar. I do a lot of my work in darkened areas."

"As I said, it was fortunate. May I ask if you noticed anything unusual?"

"Before Tradd died, you mean? Can't say that I did. I got there early, of course. I wanted to make sure the equipment was working properly. Rear screen projectors, I-mags, prompters, monitors, you know..."

"Of course, Mr. Paulson," Tim replied smoothly, although he understood almost nothing about technology. "Please, go on."

"Well, let's see. My freelancers arrived a little bit later, taping down cords and scarfing coffee and a doughnut here and there..."

"I wanted to ask you about that. Was the break all ready when you got there?"

"I'm almost positive it was. Laurie takes care of all that. I think one of the hotel banquet people came in at around seven to refill the coffee and make sure there were plenty of bagels and stuff, but he'd been told to do his job and get out quick. Once the VIPs arrive, it gets pretty crowded."

"And when was that?"

"Oh, they started coming in just after seven, I guess. They like to go over their slides."

"Who got there first?"

"DellaGuardia, as usual. He doesn't drink, so he had no hangover from the night before. Some of my freelancers, let me tell you, I don't know how they do it..."

Tim cut him off.

"When did Tradd arrive?"

"Oh, he didn't get there 'til late. He was one of the last to show up, I remember. You'd think that with a big speech to give..."

"And the protesters started making trouble when?"

"Let's see... pretty close to eight, I think. That's when the session was supposed to start, but we had to delay it while Security got rid of them. I wish I could've seen Laurie's face when *she* got wind of the protesters!"

Laurie would have winced at the memory, but now it seemed almost quaint.

"And what was Tradd doing?"

"I wish I'd noticed, Detective. After Laurie walkied me, I stayed in my control booth trying to figure out how to cut a few minutes out of the general session. Those things are timed almost to the second, of course. Turns out I shouldn't have bothered."

"No, sir. What about before you got called on the walkie?"

"I was talking to Laurie for a bit. She gets a little nervous on site for some reason. Good thing she doesn't have to deal with all the equipment I do, that's for sure!"

Overhearing, Laurie smacked a bar top as Tim hid a grin. She didn't seem like the nervous type to him.

"Tradd came up to check on his slides... not that he needed to, of course. Laurie'd gone off somewhere. Tradd and I chatted for awhile about the Zephyrex video, and then I think he said something about getting another cup of coffee. That was – let me think – yup, that was the last time I saw him before the session started."

So Paulson knew nothing, Tim realized. Still, there was no sense in alienating him. He might come in handy eventually.

Paulson snapped his fingers.

"You know what? Now that I think about it, Tradd *did* look kind of tired that morning, although I admit I didn't feel too sorry for him. Not to speak ill of the dead, but Tradd was *such* a jerk. Still, maybe looking tired was a sign that he was really sick!"

"Could be."

"If I was a nurse like my wife, maybe I would have noticed more, but I guess we can't all be good at everything."

Over by a bar setup, Laurie rolled her eyes. She'd heard about the wife before. Sounded like the woman had settled big-time.

"So your wife works for a heart doctor, then?" Tim asked pleasantly.

"Nah. She's an ER nurse. They get a lot of heart attacks in the Emergency Room."

"I guess they do."

"But as I said, I just thought Tradd looked extra tired. I put it down to the night before. I don't imagine he got a lot of rest, and it wasn't his conscience keeping him awake. Had you heard that he was seeing one of our reps on the side?" Paulson leaned in and whispered, practically swelling up with his imagined inside information.

"Had he really?"

"You bet. And from what I hear, she's a real babe, too. I've got my sources, you know..."

"Well, it doesn't look like I have much of a case, Mr. Paulson, although you may see me asking questions for the next day or two."

"I guess hotel duty must be a real step up for you, considering what you must usually have to deal with," Lew responded, clearly wanting to hear more.

Behind her palm tree, Laurie almost gagged. Tim seemed to share her opinion, because he ended the conversation there.

"It has its moments, Mr. Paulson. Thank you for your time. You've been a big help."

"Anytime," Lew replied before he sauntered back up the path. Once he had gone, Laurie rejoined Tim.

"God, he's such an idiot!" she exploded, glaring at Paulson's lank ponytail in the distance.

"Agreed. But you never know. So, do you have a lot more to do here?"

"Not really. Dagmar could check a theme night setup blindfolded. I just like to show my face now and then so she knows I'm still interested."

"And of *course* you don't double-check everything."

Laurie grinned guiltily.

"If you really are done here for now, there's plenty of time for you to hide in that sound booth or whatever before I talk to Jim Fisher."

"Hide?"

"Okay. 'Make crucial observations,' if you prefer."

"I do. Definitely," she remarked as they reentered the hotel and headed to the Hibiscus Boardroom. "So how did things go with Gene, anyway?"

"Stockton? Nice guy. Shocked and saddened about Tradd, of course, but mostly he talked about his wife and kid. Did you know he even has a couple of framed pictures of the two of them *here*? I mean, his wife's pretty enough, and the boy is cute – hell, Tim Jr. was adorable when he was a baby too – but Stockton seemed practically obsessed with them."

"He does talk about Cassandra and Ben a lot," Laurie admitted. "I guess for someone like him, who never thought he'd be a father, seeing Cassie finally 'give him a son' made family that much more important."

"Stockton's wife had trouble getting pregnant?"

"No. Staying pregnant. From what I hear, she had something like four miscarriages before she gave birth to Ben. People would laugh at Gene for adoring them both so openly if they didn't like him so much. But I'm getting off the subject. What did Gene have to say about the murder?"

"Unfortunately, he wasn't too helpful on that topic. Maintains he was watching the protesters when it happened, and only realized Tradd was dead after the meeting started and Tradd didn't react to McCarthy's intro. Stockton did tell me who found the body, though."

"Okay, I'll bite. Who was it? The hotel coffee break person? A Multimedia freelancer? Lew Paulson?"

"Wrong, wrong, and wrong, Ms. Kilcannon. Try Jim Fisher."

Slipping into the darkened booth attached to the Hibiscus Boardroom, Laurie wondered if Tim really suspected Fisher. He'd found the body, and he'd hated Tradd. Could it be him?

She watched as Fisher hurried into the Boardroom sporting khaki shorts, a polo shirt patterned with crossed clubs, and a "golfer's tan" – sunburn on his forearms, neck, and face only. He checked the watch on his powerful wrist.

"How long will this take, Officer? I've got to shower before dinner. The course was great, but man am I sweaty!"

Every inch of Fisher's lanky frame registered eagerness to be back in his suite.

"Not long at all, Mr. Fisher. You'll have plenty of time for your shower," Tim answered calmly. "I just have a few questions for you, so if you'll take a seat…?"

"Sure thing, Officer," Fisher relied, taking a leather chair with alacrity. "Shoot."

"Thanks. Let's start with when Tradd got down to the ballroom. You were already there, I believe, looking over his speech?"

"Yup. He came down late as usual."

"Tradd sounds pretty trusting. Assumed all his slides would be in order, sure that his speech would be loaded on the prompter."

Tim learned fast, Laurie acknowledged.

"I guess so," Fisher's southern twang became more pronounced. "S'pose he knew everything would be taken care of for him like it always was. 'Course, I did most of the work," he added bitterly. .

"So you weren't one of Tradd's biggest fans?"

"Hell, no. Couldn't stand the guy, if truth be told. But I never wished him dead, Officer. Hoped he'd go to another company, maybe, but not *die*."

"You must have been pretty shocked when you found his body."

Fisher's eyes widened for a moment.

"Well, yeah, you could've knocked me over with a feather when I went over to get a bagel and saw him lyin' there. Couldn't believe he was really dead."

"It must have been a real surprise. And based on what you just said, maybe a bit of a relief as well?"

Jim fidgeted in his seat, clearly uncomfortable with the direction of the conversation.

"I wouldn't call it relief, Officer. No," he said more confidently, "Not relief at all. I don't think I even felt a minute's worth of 'thank God I won't have to work for him anymore.' You know I didn't like him at all. I've told you that. I'd put out feelers for a new job, even, but I wasn't glad to see what had happened to him. Nobody – not even Tradd – should die that young."

"What did you do when you discovered Mr. Tradd's body?"

"Nothing, really. I was just shocked. Paulson must've gotten on his walkie-talkie to Laurie or the hotel guy. They were both there in minutes. Hotel security people tried to revive Tradd, but it was no use. He was gone."

"And were you surprised? Did Tradd enjoy good health as a rule?"

"Always seemed to. I didn't go to the doctor with him, but... he was healthy enough to sleep around, anyway!" Fisher burst out.

"Hmm," said Tim. "With the sales reps, you mean?"

"I mean with any pretty women he could find. Sales reps, secretaries at the home office, women he met at parties. Hell, he even tried to go after my wife once."

"Your wife is attractive?"

"I think Leslie's beautiful, Officer. Smart, too. She's a doctor!" All Fisher's impatience faded away when he talked about his wife. The man was clearly in love. Or in awe.

"She sounds like a wonderful woman," Tim smiled. "What kind of doctor, by the way?"

"Craniofacial surgeon, specializes in fixing cleft palates. She even uses some of her vacation time to visit those poor countries and work for free. Can you imagine?"

"Amazing," Tim enthused, doing his best to match Fisher's tone. "I'll bet Tradd didn't get too far with her."

"No sir. For one thing, Leslie would never do that, and for another, she figured out Tradd's game right quick."

"May I ask how you met your wife, Mr. Fisher?"

"What does that have to do with Tradd's heart attack?"

"Nothing. I'm just curious."

"Well, I guess it won't take too long," Fisher answered, looking at his watch again. But obviously, he loved talking about Leslie.

"We met at school, Officer. I went to Duke on a basketball scholarship, then stayed on to get my MBA. Leslie hails from Connecticut, but Duke has a great medical school. I used to watch her studying at the library, and one day she looked at *me* instead of her textbook." Fisher still seemed amazed.

"She got an internship at Pennsylvania Hospital, and when she moved up there, I got the job at Connor and the two of us got married. No kids yet, but there's still plenty of time. If we do have them, I hope they take after Leslie."

"She must be incredible," Tim replied dutifully. "Well, Mr. Fisher, I won't take up any more of your time. Thanks for talking to me."

"Sure thing, Officer. Hope you get all this cleared up soon."

Once he'd gone, Laurie practically ran from the booth.

"Why didn't you ask him more questions?" she demanded of Tim. "Why didn't you find out more about him finding Tradd's body?"

"Because I didn't need to."

He knew that "finding the body" wasn't important in what must have been the whirlwind backstage. It was "who gave Tradd the injection" that really mattered.

As the two of them left the Boardroom, Laurie bewildered by Tim's attitude about Fisher, they almost ran straight into Karen Shearing.

"Karen," Laurie said, "I saw you chose a shopping trip at Aventura Mall for your activity this afternoon. Did you enjoy it?"

"I didn't go," the lithe brunette answered. She looked upset. "Once Ellen left, I stayed in our room and did a lot of thinking. Detective, I want to ask you something."

Tim barely looked at Laurie, but he must have caught the planner's sudden wave of panic. Whatever Karen had to say, the hotel hallway was clearly not the place for the conversation.

"Maybe we should go to the Boardroom, Ms. Shearing. It's more private there."

"Yes, of course," she stammered, following them into the darkened area.

"Have a seat," Tim motioned once he'd turned the lights back on. "So what's on your mind?

Karen sat nervously on the edge of the offered chair.

"I've been wondering…" she started. "What if the killer finds out I had a copy of that note? You said yourself that the blackmail note was probably Ed's death warrant. What if the same person who killed Ed – I don't know – looks for me?"

"I haven't told anyone about that note, Karen, and I'm sure Laurie hasn't either. You can't live in fear," Tim said gently. "I understand why you're frightened, but you have to try to get the better of it. After all, you could get hit by a car any day of the week, right?"

Or your plane could crash, Laurie thought.

His answer seemed to calm Karen down somewhat, but still she asked, "So you can't offer me any protection?"

"Has an actual threat been made?"

"No, but I still think – "

"Then I'm sorry," Tim replied. "I'm afraid I can't. Try not to worry, Ms. Shearing. We're doing everything we can to find out who killed Edward Tradd. And to stop them."

# Chapter Ten

Leaving her room on the 45$^{th}$ floor, Laurie wondered again who the murderer could be. Wendell, the outraged father? Jim, the seething and overlooked assistant? Mike, Gene, even Lew... they'd all been there when Tradd was killed. For what seemed like the hundredth time, she tried to put those thoughts aside and focus only on the meeting. But then the elevator doors opened, and suddenly all the men she suspected stood before her.

Don't be ridiculous, she told herself as she got in. You've known all these guys for years.

There's no way they can guess what you're thinking, she admonished herself again. Mike, Wendell, and Jim knew nothing about the darkened hideaway off the Hibiscus Boardroom. They thought they'd been speaking just to Tim. Lew hadn't noticed you listening from behind that palm tree. And you weren't even there when Tim interviewed Gene!

Laurie tried to maintain her unworried façade as fleeting phrases from the last few days came to mind... "Think of anything you can that could fit into a briefcase and suggest a motive for murder..." "Tradd targeted her for the simple reason that she's beautiful..." "I think Ed was misunderstood..." "Couldn't stand the guy, if truth be told..." "Not to speak ill of the dead, but Tradd was *such* a bastard..."

Any of them could have done it.

Suddenly dry-mouthed, she wished she'd brought a bottle of Evian from her room.

She inventoried the contents of her pockets: copy of the meeting agenda, folded and unfolded so often the stiff cardstock had become soft, the bundle of VIP keycards held together with a rubber band, her Visa card, a half-empty pack of cigarettes, a lighter. A lighter. Maybe she could use that to defend herself.

Now that *is* ridiculous, she thought, reminding herself again that as far as the men in the elevator know, she was just Laurie the meeting planner, efficient but unimportant.

Still, 45 floors...

"Hi!" she said brightly, concealing her uneasiness as best she could. "What's everyone up to? It's a little bit early to be going down to the dinner!"

"I'm heading to that service desk of yours. Need to get a new name badge," Wendell volunteered in a completely unabashed voice.

"Same place for me," added Jim. "I want to get a look at which districts are in which rooms for Breakouts tomorrow. Might look in on a few."

Mike said "I thought I might check out some meeting rooms to make sure there are plenty of detail aids for everyone."

"No work for me," put in Gene. "I'm going straight to the gift shop to get a few things for Ben. How about you, Lew?" the CEO added kindly. The usually voluble Multimedia manager, having just met with Gene in the Presidential Suite about the tribute video for Edward Tradd, seemed awed by the executives for once. His reply was brief.

"I'm looking up a few of my staffers before the dinner."

As the car began to descend, Laurie found herself thinking morbid thoughts again. Did one of these men kill Edward Tradd? Did they know she suspected them? Preposterously, she wondered if they were all in it together, providing alibis for each other. Her fears made the relatively short ride seem endless.

And then the lights went out.

Oh God, thought Laurie. What if the killer really *was* one of these passengers? What if he killed *her*? No one would know for sure who'd done it...

Questions and comments floated out of the blackness.

"What happened?" asked Gene, sounding concerned but not frightened.

"It's just the light, right? There's nothing wrong with the elevator?" That was Lew, sounding nervous.

"Well, this is a fine how-do-you-do!" added Jim in an exasperated tone.

"I'm sure it's okay. Let's just try to look on the bright side," Mike put in earnestly.

"There isn't one," observed Wendell.

Nervous laughter greeted that last statement, and Laurie joined in quickly. Already paranoid from her earlier suspicions, she'd unthinkingly reached for her walkie before remembering that she couldn't get any reception from it inside the elevator shafts.

Talking, she thought. Keep them talking. She asked question after question, knowing manners would dictate that they answer, no matter how stupid she sounded. Normally, her job depended on her keeping quiet about all she saw and heard, but now her life might depend on the opposite.

Here, silence was her enemy.

After less than a minute that felt like an hour, the descent finally ended and the doors slid open.

Blinking, she stepped into the reassuring light of the Hanover lobby and turned to her companions once more.

"I'll let the hotel know about the elevator light immediately."

She forced herself to walk away slowly, but stopped a moment later. What was it Tim had said to Karen?

"You can't live in fear."

He was right, Laurie realized.

Her suspicions in the elevator embarrassed her now. If I'm going to help with this investigation, she thought, then I need to *help*, and not just by talking. I need to *do* something. But what? What did investigators do? Dust for fingerprints? Well, I don't know how, she reasoned. Interrogate suspects? That sounded better, but Tim had already done it. Okay then, what else?

Follow people, maybe. That she could do.

There and then, Laurie decided to take a more active role in figuring out who killed Edward Tradd.

She thought she'd have to wait until after Safari Night was over, though.


"Becky, you're still here!" exclaimed Wendell as the cheerful strawberry-blonde gathered her things.

"I was just getting ready to leave. Laurie told me I could make it an early night, bless her heart. But I'm really glad I didn't miss you! What can I do for you on this gorgeous evening?" the Special Services Desk lead asked, setting aside her purse, happy to help as always.

"Well, I was hoping you could make me a new name badge. I can't find mine anywhere, and I know how strict you guys are."

"For you? Of course! It'll just take me a minute to get the printer ready to go. I hope you don't mind waiting?"

"Not at all! Gives me more time to admire the scenery," Wendell replied with a mock-wicked grin.

"Oh, you! Mr. McCarthy, you're impossible!"

Laurie watched this exchange from behind a potted palm tree in the hallway. Or was it a ficus? Either way, it was a cliché.

All she needed, Laurie admitted ruefully to herself, was a Sherlock Holmes hat and a magnifying glass...

"There you go!" announced Becky, proffering a new "Wendell McCarthy, Sr. Vice President, Sales" badge.

"Thanks, Becky," Wendell said, pinning the new tag to his lapel as jauntily as if it were a corsage. "This should keep you meeting people happy."

"Have a great time at the dinner, Mr. McCarthy!"

As Becky gave a few last-minute instructions to her replacement, Wendell wandered off, unaware that Laurie wandered after him, stealing from behind her potted palm to behind a high-backed armchair, and feeling slightly ludicrous. Why on earth am I following Wendell, she asked herself. He's one of the nicest guys I know. This was a really stupid idea. God knows, I'm not telling Tim.

On his way to the dinner, Wendell fished in his pocket and tossed a piece of paper into a hotel trashcan. Laurie, feeling more ridiculous than ever, waited until he was out of sight and retrieved the paper from the top, first discarding a cellophane cigar wrapper and an empty soda bottle. She expected it to be yesterday's meeting agenda, a phone number he'd long since called, or a simple reminder of what he wanted to do tomorrow.

She wasn't prepared for what she *did* find.

It was paper packaging from a medical supply house.

And it was for a syringe.


"The hotel banquet people do most of the work," Jeremy told a wide-eyed Vivian. "Our job is to make sure that the attendees know where the food and drinks are, prevent bottlenecks, that sort of thing. You'll catch on fast. You'll see."

Vivian knew all about food from the parties she'd worked with Jeremy, her fellow employee at Elegant Eats, but nothing had prepared her for the Safari Night dinner. As fast-moving hotel servers loaded buffet stations with ribs, shrimp, vegetables and "African" peanut soup, she thanked heaven for Jeremy. He might not have been Jake, but Jeremy's pockmarked face displayed only calm in the midst of what looked like chaos.

"You've got the agenda for tomorrow memorized, right? You'll probably get more questions about that than about the food. Either the reps really don't know, or they just like to mess with us. If you ask me, Connor spoils them. Half the meeting staffers will be 'human arrows' in a bit, leading the attendees here like they couldn't find the place on their own!" he laughed. "Oh well, it's all money, and these meetings do pay pretty well. Though when you think of what's involved in tonight's shindig…"

"Connor does seem like it's good to its people," Vivian answered, trying not to be disgusted by the mounds of filet being added to the buffets, to be covered and kept warm until the attendees arrived.

"They sure are. I should have stayed in school and become a pharmaceutical rep! I mean, look at this setup – specially imported trees, props out the wazoo, even live animals!"

Vivian hoped Jeremy wouldn't notice her feel her pocket for the secret video recorder an AAPTer had delivered less than an hour ago. She'd carved out a space for the camera lens in her name tag, and carefully taped the wire to her skin in the Ladies' Room. To distract him, she asked with as much astonishment as possible, "*Wild* animals?"

"You know it, but don't worry. The handlers will keep them under control."

Vivian closed her eyes. The suffering of animals upset her even more than the steaks.

"Scared?" Jeremy asked, mistaking her revulsion for fear. "Well, as I said, you'll be perfectly safe. And anyway, all you'd have to do is yell and I'd come running..." he added with a blush.

Was short, dumpy Jeremy actually suggesting he could protect her? From anything? To cover the awkward moment, she asked him what kind of animals Connor had trucked in for this travesty. Not that she phrased it exactly that way.

"I don't know all of them, but I do know they have alligators, tarantulas, parrots, a boa constrictor, even a bobcat and a leopard. Can't wait to see them!"

And I can't wait to film them, Vivian thought.


Without thinking, Laurie reached for her walkie, then remembered she couldn't contact Tim that way. She was on the verge of calling police headquarters when he approached her in the hallway.

"Glad I caught you before I left," he said, looking a little wilted from the heat. "Would it be okay if I came back later? After seeing it this afternoon, I have to admit I'm curious about how that pool area's going to look."

That sounded normal, he thought. And neutral. She'd never guess his real motive was wanting to see her again.

"Of course, Tim. Whatever you like," she answered distractedly. "But first I have to tell you what I just saw!"

Her eagerness amused him.

"Okay, I'll bite. What was it? A sunburned executive? A bunch of meeting-goers with no name tags?"

"No – and I'll thank you not to treat me like a 5-year-old," she snapped. "You're the one who got me into this investigating mess, if you recall."

She was right, he realized. And prickly again!

133

"That's true, and I apologize for sounding patronizing. Don't get your Irish up, okay? So, you saw something related to the murder?"

"Yes," she replied, too concerned about her discovery to indulge in temper anymore. Drawing the crumpled packaging from her pocket, she handed it over, telling Tim how she'd found it. Pride and anxiety dueled in her mind. Anxiety won.

"Wendell *can't* be the murderer, can he? I mean, I know him, sort of. And you said yourself that you couldn't see him actually committing the crime."

"No, and I still can't. But what you found is a clue, and I'll need to follow it up. Remember, though, you can't be sure it was McCarthy who threw it out."

"I got to that trash can right after him, Tim, and it was the only bit of paper I saw."

"You didn't take fingerprints from it, though."

"No, how could…"

"And this hallway's pretty busy, right?"

"Sure, but…"

"Listen, Laurie," Tim said, truly shaken by the possibility that she'd come so close to a potential murderer. "I know I was the one who suggested this 'investigating mess,' as you put it, but I didn't think you'd start tailing people and rooting around in trash cans!"

"But you told Karen Shearing not an hour ago that she couldn't live in fear. It was good advice, I thought."

"Karen Shearing has nothing to do with it!" he exploded. A few people in the hotel hallway turned to look, and with an effort he lowered his voice.

"You can't go around following people, Laurie. It could be dangerous. Really. You could get hurt! In fact, you've helped me plenty as it is. Just focus on your meeting."

"How can I, now?"

"It's what you're best at, Laurie. And investigating crimes is what *I'm* best at. I need you on this case, but to talk to, to get your take on things. Good God, I don't want you to run risks!"

His voice had risen again. Could it be that he was taking this personally, Laurie wondered?

"Okay, okay. I need to check on the dinner anyway, so I'll get going now."

"Alright, Laurie. Just promise me you'll stay away from anything dangerous."

"I will, don't worry," she lied, thinking of the approaching darkness, the fog machines, and the wild animals.

"And remember, I won't be far away," he reminded her before he walked off. "I need to catch up on some reports, but I'll be back soon."

On her way to the pool area, Laurie thought about what Tim had said – and how he'd said it.

He was handsome, to be sure. She'd admitted that to herself from the first. He had a nice body, too. Bulky but not fat, just big and solid and real. Strong, protective Tim. Who worried about her.

Wendell's syringe didn't even enter her mind.


Stepping carefully over one of two "rope bridges" the vendor had erected at the entrance, Laurie coughed a little. It was still early, but the fog machine was already churning away. As night fell, she knew the scene would get scarier, but at least the vendor seemed to be doing her job.

Juan caught up with her just as she started to do a last-minute check of the arrangements, consciously not thinking about her last discussion with Tim.

"I know my freelancers will have counted," Laurie said to the Convention Service Manager towering above her, "But you do have 200 rounds of 10, right?"

"Absolutely. And all the buffet stations are stocked. Sorry about that crab leg fiasco, by the way. We'll be happy to give you the lobster claws at half price."

Laurie smothered a grin, remembering her conversation with Dagmar that morning and wondering whose head had rolled in the banquet kitchen.

"And the bars are set up all over, 20, as you requested. No vendor trouble. The Wild Nights people have worked with us many times in the past."

"Terrific, Juan," Laurie replied as she watched a hotel staffer installing the last of the many tiki torches that would add to the Safari Night atmosphere, "But what I'm really concerned about is the weather. It seems fine for tonight, but what if the storm blows back inland tomorrow? I've been monitoring the weather reports, and it looks like it might."

"I've been watching them too. For one thing, the Banquet Manager's digging out miniature umbrellas to add to your centerpieces if necessary tomorrow night. For another, and more importantly, the hotel can switch to generator power if the electricity goes, but that's never happened in May before. We don't start getting our major storms until August as a rule. Let's hope for the best."

"I would, Juan, but I get paid to worry."

"Well then, you certainly earn your salary," the CSM said with a smile.

Relaxed from their afternoon of recreation, the reps began to arrive at the dinner in small groups. Laurie stopped worrying long enough to watch the early arrivals choose which of the two bridges to take. The left side led past a "Quicksand Pit" that housed several alligators, while the right brought astonished salespeople to the "Creature Tree," home to the snake, tarantula, and numerous parrots. Just when they thought their path was clear, the reps had to navigate past a bobcat and a giant leopard. Laurie knew the animals were tame, but even she had to admit that they looked ferocious in the waning light. Following a semi-dark pathway, she cut ahead to the edge of a torch-lit clearing to listen.

"Wow," murmured Jeff, the Nebraska-based District Manager who'd spent the afternoon by another hotel pool. Turning to one of the attendees who accompanied him, he whispered, "That's not an *actual* crashed airplane, is it?" as he stared at the half-submerged craft in eight feet of water. A few dozen bags of garden mulch had made the pool as murky as an African puddle.

"I don't think so, but it sure looks authentic."

"And that crocodile snapping at the windows seems pretty real to me," added another.

"Hey, look at that panther!"

"Where are those drums coming from?"

"Let's keep going," Jeff said, sounding shaken. "There's bound to be a bar up ahead. I don't know about you guys, but I could use a beer!"

Dagmar found Laurie standing in the shadows.

"Looks like those Wild Nights folks really outdid themselves," the meeting planner remarked. "This place is practically unrecognizable! And I'm guessing the bars are going to see a *lot* of traffic tonight."

"They're prepared," responded the polished F & B lead, "And yes, it does look good. Even the hotel people are enjoying your Safari Night. Many arrived early so they could pet the animals."

Laurie assumed Dagmar meant the bobcat and the leopard. Nobody could really want to pet a tarantula. She hoped.

"Well, they're allowed. I spent a little time with the animals myself. Checking out the vendor, of course," she added innocently. "You know, seeing the proposal on paper is nothing compared to the actual event. The prerecorded jungle drums, for example. I never thought they would come off, but they sound so real the reps are actually nervous!"

"I suppose it's like you Americans say: presentation is everything. The hotel may be serving spareribs and filet, but the 'Antelope Antlers' and 'Serengeti Steak' labels definitely make better the illusion," the freelancer answered with a rare laugh.

"You're so right, Dagmar. Oh, by the way, I saw a couple of newcomers staffing this function. Are they the replacements for the sick F & B folks?"

Dagmar was impressed that Laurie had noticed.

"Ja, one of my regulars is a local, and he works for a catering company in town. He was able to call in some friends at the last moment. They have no meeting experience, but at least they know food and beverage."

"I'm sure they'll do fine. Well, Dagmar, I won't keep you. I know you want to check in with those bartenders, and I should probably see how the VIPs are doing." Laurie had just spotted Mike looming over the growing crowd.

"I'll find you later, Laurie," said the Danish woman before she walked away.

"A helluva job as always, Laurie. Fantastic!" Wendell thundered. "I took a stroll along this beach earlier today, and you'd never believe it was the same place!" Looking at his relaxed, open face, Laurie struggled anew with thoughts of the suspicious syringe.

"Yes, very convincing, Laurie," Gene added. "The reps seem to be having a great time."

They watched as a group of attendees nearby laughed and chatted, pointing at the animals.

"I'll be honest," put in Mike, "I thought it would be disrespectful of Ed's memory to have an event like this, but he would have enjoyed every second of it."

"That's good to hear, Mike. Now if that storm will just hold off… "

"Any news?" Gene asked anxiously.

"We won't really know anything until tomorrow morning, but I've started talking with the hotel about contingency plans. Try not to worry about it this evening. I know there are lots of attendees who want to talk with you."

"Yeah, I'll bet they'll have lots of questions about yesterday's general session," added Wendell grimly. "And speaking of, have you heard anything more from that policeman?"

"Not a word," responded Laurie, just a shade too quickly. She wasn't about to mention her discovery to Wendell. Or the fact that she'd brought it to Tim's attention.


"Hey, Wendell, over here!"

The aging Vice President ambled good-naturedly toward a group of reps examining a vehicle of some sort. Closer inspection revealed it to be an antique Land Rover complete with old-time luggage, frayed ropes, canteens, and mosquito nets. It gave a Pith-helmeted photographer the perfect opportunity to start snapping away.

"Here, Sean, turn this canteen upside down like you're trying to find more water… and Susan, look bewildered while you're staring at the map... Matt and the rest of us can wave from the jeep's windows... "

"Great shot. Now just hold that pose." A flashbulb exploded as the photographer captured the tableau. "Got it! Thanks, guys."

The reps wanted to look at the props some more, but other groups began to line up, all with their own ideas about how to pose, how to use the Land Rover. No one asked Wendell any questions about Ed Tradd's death, but they all clamored for him to be in their pictures.


Karen's group had already gone through the buffet, but all she could stomach was the "Jungle Foliage with Iguana Meat" (chicken Caesar salad). She picked at her dinner and drank some wine, hoping it would calm her nerves. Her roommate Ellen tried to interest her in the array of animals and props that surrounded them, but even she drifted off after awhile, sensing Karen's disinterest.

Her outfit and flip-flops betrayed Karen's anxiety. She hadn't bothered to select one of the many dazzling pairs of high-heeled sandals she'd brought with her, and forgot to wear earrings with her simple khakis and plain white blouse.

Her fellow reps, even those who didn't know about her relationship with Edward Tradd, instinctively left her alone. The women were jealous of her beauty, the men had been rebuffed often enough to know she didn't want their company.

When Gene Stockton approached, however, asking with raised eyebrows if he could join her at the empty table, she nodded vigorously.

"Please, Gene, sit down."

He deposited his own untouched plate of "Forest Fritters" and "Lion's Teeth" (crab cakes and lobster claws) in front of her, declaring, "I couldn't eat either. This whole thing has been so awful – and I imagine you've been having a worse day than most."

"Oh Gene," she said gratefully, turning luminous blue eyes his way, "You don't even know." And although she hadn't meant to, she began to cry.

"What is it, Karen? I know how upset you must be about Ed, but is there something else bothering you?"

"I don't know how to feel," Karen answered, looking fixedly at her napkin. "I miss him so much. And yet... I thought I knew him better than anyone, Gene, but it turns out I didn't know him at all. Ed wasn't the man I thought he was."

"What makes you think that?" Gene asked gently.

"Just something I found out today," she answered, belatedly remembering that Gene was, after all, the president of the company. "I probably misunderstood it anyway."

"I know it's a cliché," Gene replied smoothly, "But try to remember all the good things you shared with him, and forget the rest."

"You're right, Gene. I will try. We had a lot of great times together, and I suppose I should focus on them. That's all I have anyway," Karen choked back a sob. "You're so kind to come and talk to me. I don't imagine you get a minute's peace at these things, what with everyone wanting some time with you."

"Comes with the job," Gene replied. "And I suppose I should head back into the fray. Will you be okay?"

"Y-yes. I was going to head straight up to my room, but now... well, I may even try to show some interest in these wonderful props. I hear there's a real live leopard around here somewhere."

"That's the spirit."

"I'll do my best, anyway. And Gene, thanks again."

"Any time."


Tim announced his presence to Laurie with a long whistle.

"This is some setup you've got here, Ms. Kilcannon, although I had the Devil's own time tracking you down." He didn't mention that he'd finally spied Juan and frantically asked the CSM where Laurie was likely to be.

Laurie was glad to see him, and said so.

"Where've you been, anyway? Doing those reports?"

"On the phone, mostly. I guess those reports will have to wait again. I've been checking in with headquarters, making sure Tim Jr. is focusing on his homework and not out with his girlfriend doing God knows what, the usual. But I wouldn't have missed this for the world, even without the investigation."

"And what's your professional opinion, Detective?"

"Impressive. The animals, the props, the fog machine, the food... you don't seem to have forgotten a thing, Laurie. I had no idea when you did your progress check this afternoon."

"Well, I may have arranged it, but there are a lot of people involved in making it happen," Laurie answered. "Hotel staffers, my freelance crew, the vendor and all of her people..."

"But you knew who to pick, didn't you?"

"I guess I did. I seem to be getting better at that. Knowing who to pick," Laurie said slowly, turning to face Tim full-on as she did so.

Tim swallowed and looked away, not daring to believe her subtle message.

"So how are the executives?" he asked, remembering why he was really here.

"They seemed fine when I saw them," Laurie answered, seeming a little disappointed, but relieved as well to talk about something other than the growing attraction between them. "You should see poor Wendell posing for pictures by the Land Rover. The reps won't leave him alone. God, I *hope* it's not him. He's just so great!"

"We'll see, won't we? How about Paulson? What's he up to?"

"Oh, he's here too, showing off for his freelancers as usual. Good thing he pays them."

"Probably is," Riordan agreed. "I'm going to poke around a little. I'll be nearby, but don't worry, I'll stay out of sight."

Laurie laughed out loud at that.

"Shouldn't be too hard tonight. Between the darkness and the mist, I'd say this environment was made for you! But Tim," she added seriously, wishing now that she'd never followed Wendell. "Do you have any more theories about who killed Ed Tradd?"

"I have a few ideas, and your little excursion earlier has made me think about other possibilities. I want to mull things over later this evening, then I'll run my ideas by you tomorrow. So long for now. I'll be around until the end of dinner."

And before Laurie could answer, he was gone.


For almost three hours, Vivian pointed reps toward bars and buffets, made sure empty chafing dishes were replenished, discussed the following day's agenda, and gave the more adventurous attendees directions to the clubs on Ocean Drive. Finally, finally, she had time to film.

Despite her own emotions, and the discomfort of the tape digging into her skin, she forced herself to be cold and professional. She refused to give in to her increasing distaste as she shot minute after minute of appalling footage. Gorgeous parrots with their wings clipped. A magnificent leopard who should have been streaking across the veldt somewhere, now docile. A bobcat on a leash, submitting to the delighted petting of smiling reps.

This was even worse than testing Zephyrex on rabbits, Vivian thought as she filmed, careful to face the animals head-on so the lens in her name tag would capture them. If people could just see how these proud, beautiful creatures were being exploited to provide the Connor people with "entertainment."

"What are you doing?" barked Dagmar. "Shouldn't you be checking on the buffet station back there?"

"Sorry, Ms. Gustafson. I must have gotten lost," she stuttered.

"It's that way," the F & B lead gestured. "Most people have finished dinner, but you should be making sure all the desserts are out. And every table in your section should have coffee cups by now."

"Yes. Thank you. I'll get right on it."

The Danish woman strode away.

Now if I can just get some footage that shows the Zephyrex banner *with* an animal, Vivian mused as her heart rate returned to normal, then I'll really have something worth showing…

"Laurie, come quick! Over!" Juan's voice shouted over her walkie-talkie.

"Where are you, Juan?" she asked urgently, so distressed by the alarm in his tone that she forgot to say "what's your 20?" – the usual code for "where are you?" In fact, she forgot all the standard walkie-talkie protocol she knew.

144

"In the bushes by the clearing! Near the plane! Over!"

"I'm on my way."

She ran.

A crowd of reps, district managers, VIPs, meeting staffers and banquet servers greeted her. Juan had enlisted Lew Paulson and some banquet staff to hold everyone back. Quickly, Laurie asked the Multimedia chief what was going on.

"It's Karen Shearing, Laurie," he said excitedly, "And I think she's dead!"

"Oh, my God. Where's Juan?"

"Laurie, thank God you're here," said the unusually flustered CSM. "We need to get the attendees back to the hotel and close down the event. I've called 911, and hotel security's already on their way."

"One thing at a time, Juan. What happened?"

"Karen Shearing's been killed," he said in a low voice.

Laurie's first thought was of a maddened leopard. *Why* hadn't she chosen Mardi Gras Night?

"Was it an animal?"

"No, Laurie," Juan answered more quietly, speaking just above a whisper now. "I think she was strangled."

Another murder.

Dear *God.*

"Juan, you're absolutely right about what needs to be done. I'll walkie Dagmar and she'll get the attendees inside and order the bars dismantled. Once the free booze is gone, the function's effectively over anyway. I know you've called 911, but Tim Riordan is here too. Or at least, he was earlier… "

The detective had just rushed to the scene.

"And I'm here now. I was about to go home when I heard all the raised voices. What's the fuss about?"

Juan told him, which was fortunate. Laurie couldn't have. As the meeting planner issued instructions to Dagmar, Tim gave orders of his own.

"Nothing's been touched this time? Let me see her then, and keep this area clear. I want to preserve the scene exactly as it is now for our forensics people. There's no doubt that *this* was a murder."

Karen wasn't beautiful anymore. Powerful fingers had made livid marks in her neck, and her face showed the slackness of the dead. Her tongue protruded slightly from her mouth. Her eyes, still staring, betrayed the horror she'd experienced as the air left her body.

Tim turned away.

Again, he asked Juan, "Please, do something about this crowd."

"I'll take care of it, Detective."

The people vanished as the enormous CMS fired off directions. Even Lew Paulson departed, although he was one of the last to leave.

Laurie and Tim waited for the ambulance from Fire Rescue and the forensics specialists in silence. Only a few hotel security guards remained, guarding the area against curious eyes.

Tim stared at the lifeless form of Karen.

"I guess I gave her bad advice after all," he whispered finally, turning to Laurie. Then he added incongruously, "Thank God you're safe."

# Chapter Eleven

Once the ambulance departed, the hotel staff drifted off, and the vendor led her trucks off the property, Laurie ordered Tim up to her suite.

"I know you have things to do and people to call, and so do I, but another half hour won't make a difference. You look awful."

"Thanks. I think."

"You know what I mean," Laurie said hurriedly as she called Dagmar on her walkie. "Laurie to Dagmar. Come in Dagmar."

"Dagmar here. Over."

"Everything okay on your end?" she asked the older woman, adding a perfunctory "over."

"Ja. The reps are upset, of course, and the VIPs are even worse. Most have gone upstairs to their rooms. I've alerted Room Service. Over."

"Good thinking, Dagmar. We'll need to talk about breakfast tomorrow, but if you don't mind, I'm going to be off walkie for a little bit. I'll call you later. Over."

"I'll be in my room. Over and out."

"Well, that takes care of the attendees for now," she said to Tim, forcing lightness into her tone. "So tell me, when was the last time you ate?"

"Must've been that box lunch."

"I'd guess Room Service is getting slammed right about now, judging from what Dagmar said, and even booze takes up waiters. Want to see what's in the minibar?"

"Sure," Tim answered dully.

It was amazing, Laurie thought, how worrying about someone else took her mind off things. One of her attendees – *another* of her attendees – had been murdered, the meeting was falling apart, the VIPs were beside themselves, and all she could think about was the distraught detective in front of her.

She tossed Tim some overpriced chocolates and a can of cashew nuts. He ignored them, and they fell to the floor.

"Laurie," he began.

"Tim, what *is* it? You're a police officer. You've seen people – die – before."

Karen was murdered, she admonished herself. Say the word.

"Yes, I have. I've seen people shot, knifed, beaten to death. I've seen overdoses. I've seen innocent children killed in gang wars. But they've never asked me, just hours beforehand, to look out for them."

"Tim, I told you I heard what you said to Karen, and I still think you were right. A person can't be ruled by fear. What should she have done? Gone home, stayed in her house, bricked up the door?"

"Laurie…"

"No, Tim, you couldn't have prevented it. It was terrible. It *is* terrible. But you couldn't have known."

"I should have… "

"Shhh," she said.

And then, driven by feelings she hadn't even realized she had for him until that moment, Laurie kissed him. Briefly, at first.

He was startled, but only for a moment. He embraced her finally as he'd been longing to do, gently held her face with one hand while the other undid her hair from its ponytail, and kissed her back anything but briefly.

Tradd... Karen... the unsolved mystery of their deaths... the meeting... none of it mattered to Laurie. Suddenly, all that mattered was Tim.

She relaxed into his comforting bulk, folded her arms around his thick, muscled back, lost herself in those lovely eyes...

But still, a nagging voice seemed to whisper to her, it's only been a few days.

She pulled away first.

"Tim," she murmured forlornly.

"I know," he responded, confident in the response from her body. "We both have things to do. We'll talk tomorrow. And Laurie... thank you."

He left too quickly.


Once Tim was gone, Laurie didn't know what to do with herself. She walked up and down her suite. She smoked a cigarette. She flipped the TV on. Spanish-language soap operas, an overwrought movie, local news featuring a car chase on the Julia Tuttle Causeway bridge. (Who was Julia Tuttle anyway? she wondered absently.) After a few distracted minutes, she turned it off and called Wendell, her earlier suspicions forgotten. Wendell was like a father to her.

"Sorry to bother you so late, Wendell. How're you doing?"

The older man responded in a shaken voice.

"I heard about what happened to Karen. She could've been my daughter, Laurie. I just can't believe someone would strangle Karen Shearing."

"I know, Wendell. This must be so hard for you. I hate to even mention it, but is someone going to talk to the reps at breakfast tomorrow? The thing is, they're pretty freaked as well. Two people dying at a meeting, and they all must know Karen was murdered by now…"

"You're right, Laurie. I guess I should talk to them. Gene's in a total state of shock, as you might guess."

"Yes, he must be. But you should try to get some sleep this evening, Wendell. I'll make sure there's a mic and podium at breakfast tomorrow."

"Thanks."

"And Wendell… maybe you should call Julie. I know it's late, but I think just hearing her voice might help you rest easier."

"Maybe I will," Wendell answered.

Once she'd spoken to Wendell and briefly discussed breakfast requirements with Dagmar, Laurie tried to sleep. Although it was long after midnight, she couldn't relax, and after futilely rearranging the enormous down-filled pillows and adjusting the angle of the small clock and portable fan she always traveled with, she gave up.

She turned on her lamp, fumbling for the legal pad and pen she kept near her phone, and tried to make a "to do" list for tomorrow.

For the first time ever, she simply stared at the page. She couldn't write a single word.

"…and there's the poor bobcat… can you believe they made him pose for pictures? 'Tame,' of course. Looks half asleep to me. Must be tranquilizers. Here comes the tree… see the snake behind glass? This is where things get dark and fuzzy. Sorry about that. I got interrupted by the head catering person at this point and forgot to turn the camera off... but this part is good coming up. Just look at that leopard. Tethered! And the Zephyrex banner right in the shot!"

"Vivian, this is great stuff," Jake admitted. "You've done AAPT a real service. Now all we have to do is make sure this footage gets into the right hands. Lydia?"

"I already have a reporter in mind. She works for a local station, but this might even get picked up by the networks. Nice job, Vivian," the slim woman added, almost as an afterthought.

"So back to the meeting for you, Vivian. You don't want to blow your cover, as they say," Jake put in with his winning smile.

They're dismissing me, Vivian realized. I ran the risk, I did the work, and here are the two of them acting like I don't even exist! Oh well, she thought, at least Jake finally knows my name...

"Yeah, I'll head back now," she muttered. "Some woman got killed at the dinner last night, so I don't want to do anything that looks odd."

"A woman murdered?" asked Lydia. "Well, that should help me with this reporter. Killing a person is still more sensational than abusing animals. You know what, Vivian?"

"Yes?" the plump girl replied on the point of leaving.

"You could help us even more by finding out if Connor has a public relations person at this meeting. Someone willing to talk to the press."

"Well, I'll try, Lydia, if you really think it'll help. I know there are management types at the meeting, but they seemed pretty close-lipped about the murder last night. One of the executives died of a heart attack before their first session, from what I hear, so I think they're pretty sensitive about talking to the media. Come to think of it, that's probably why your protest went nowhere, Jake. Everyone had other things on their minds."

"Hmm. I can see how they might be publicity-shy at the moment. Perhaps someone would agree to give an interview about the animals they used last night, though. If you don't know about the footage, it seems pretty innocent. 'What Big Companies Do at Meetings,' that sort of thing. That way, the reporter would have a contact."

"Oh, I see. Would the person who set up all the meeting arrangements be any help to you?"

Lydia's crystal-blue eyes lit up.

"Absolutely! If you could get us that name, it would be great."

"But I already know it from all the paperwork I got. Tell your reporter to ask for Laurie Kilcannon."


"Ana Sanchez here," said a clipped voice on the phone.

Lydia could picture the other woman, typing copy into a word processor one-handed, snatching spoonfuls of yogurt in between calls, trying not to muss the camera-ready waves the WFLA hairstylist had painstakingly created with mousse and blowdryer. She steeled herself to speak briefly.

"Ana, it's Lydia Emerson from AAPT. I have information about a murder at a national pharmaceutical conference that's in town. Video too. I thought you might be interested."

Ana rolled her eyes. She still had to record narration for a video package on a $2 million drug bust Miami-Dade cops had finally made and chase down a politician suspected of taking bribes, but still, murder sounded interesting…

"Forgive me for sounding cynical, but who got killed – a gerbil?"

Lydia was used to this reaction. It didn't bother her. Or at least she didn't show that it did.

"No, Ana, it was a young woman attending the conference. I don't have her name, but I *can* tell you who's organizing the meeting. Might be a place to start."

"Maybe," replied Ana. "But I still don't get why AAPT is involved."

Lydia told her about the failed protest demonstration and the amateur video Vivian had shot during the Safari Night dinner.

"The company is Connor Pharmaceuticals," persisted Lydia. "They're in town to introduce a drug called Zephyrex to their sales force. A drug that was tested on rabbits. Between that information, the girl getting killed, and the images of this 'Safari Night,' perhaps your angle could be how insensitive Connor is."

"Thank you, Lydia," Ana replied crisply. Like she didn't know how to frame a story! It wasn't enough that her bosses voiced their lack of confidence in her almost daily. Now this blonde gringa was telling her how to do her job.

Lydia sensed that she'd gone too far. All the good will she'd earned from Ana over the Premarin protest seemed about to evaporate.

"Of course, Ana. Whatever you think," she responded, doing her best to sound like it didn't matter.

Ana gave herself exactly ten seconds to brood before firing off a quick question.

"Where can I find you, Lydia?"


Ana climbed the stairs to the AAPT Southeast Region headquarters. She asked Lydia questions and reviewed the inexpertly shot videotape.

"You mentioned that you know the name of the person who set up the meeting arrangements?"

"Yes, it's Laurie Kilcannon."

"And you think she'll be willing to talk?"

"Well, there are no guarantees, but she might."

Ana sighed. This Laurie person could prove helpful or not, but the fact remained that a lot of legwork would be necessary before she could weave the footage and the facts into a coherent story.

"So do you think you can work the fact that Zephyrex was tested on rabbits into your report?" Lydia was asking.

"I'll try, Lydia, but as you said, there are no guarantees."


Defying convention, almost all of the attendees showed up for breakfast Thursday morning. Thankfully, most weren't hungry; despite the lower guaranteed numbers, there was plenty of food. Most attendees stayed in groups, feeling safer in the large, brightly lit room. It seemed impossible that danger could find them here, surrounded as they were by the familiar aroma of coffee and eggs, surrounded by each other.

Wendell McCarthy seemed to have become older overnight. Midway through breakfast, he approached the podium, his manner devoid of his usual energy.

"Ladies and gentlemen," he began as the crowd quickly grew silent. "I grieve with you at the tragic loss of our colleague Karen Shearing. Those of you who've listened to your voicemail this morning will have already heard from Gene Stockton about his great personal distress over her murder."

As Wendell hesitated over the last word, several people in the audience gasped.

"Gene's preparing to notify Karen's parents at this moment. It goes without saying that we have all been deeply upset by this recent turn of events. To have lost Edward Tradd to a heart attack just a few days ago only adds to our sadness about Karen."

At the back of the room with Dagmar, Laurie found it harder than ever to believe that Wendell had been involved in Tradd's murder. Wendell seemed genuinely shaken. No one was that good an actor, she reasoned.

He paused to sip from his water glass.

"I imagine many of you have questions about your own safety at this meeting, in light of what happened to Karen last night," Wendell said. "Rest assured that the hotel has increased security, and the police are heavily involved. The meeting will go forward as planned. Breakouts today, the banquet this evening, and tomorrow's closing general session. However… "

He waited until the murmuring quieted.

"However, anyone who wishes to leave immediately is free to do so. Our meeting planning staff will do everything possible to find flights for those who want to leave early."

Dagmar, listening unobtrusively from the back of the room, hastily turned to Laurie to make sure the younger woman was alerting Sue.

"I hope that the majority of you will choose to stay," Wendell said in closing. "The police will catch the madman who killed Karen. Let those of us who can, stand together in the face of fear. We're stronger together than we are alone. Thank you."

"Well, is there anyone here who doesn't know what happened last night?" a bleary-eyed Laurie asked her equally sleep-deprived staff.

They all knew.

"I'll save the explanations, then. But since the reps will ask, I want to make sure everyone has the same information. Karen Shearing was murdered toward the end of our Safari Night dinner. She was not mauled by one of the animals. She was strangled. The police are working diligently to find her killer, and the hotel has increased its security until they do." The police were also trying to solve Edward Tradd's murder, she added to herself, but although her leads might know or guess that both deaths were suspicious, the rank and file didn't.

"Dagmar and I just heard that attendees are going to be allowed to fly home today if they want, so we need to be prepared," she continued. "Sue, this will affect you most of all. I know you thought today would be fairly quiet, but I'll need you to be on the Special Services Desk to handle any requests we get. You'd better alert the ground operator too."

"No problem, Laurie."

"Dash, I'd like you to keep me informed about the Breakouts. If they're well-attended, that'll be an indication that most people plan to stay."

"Gotcha."

"Dagmar will keep an eye on the F & B situation. It's too late to change our guarantees, but I'm sure she'll have her hands full anyway with all the Breakout room lunches and coffee breaks and the big banquet this evening. As for the rest of you – for all of you – please direct any questions to the staffers at the SSD. Becky, I've changed the schedule so you'll have a full crew."

"Okey-doke."

"Any questions?"

There were none.

"Then get to work, everyone. Stay in groups of at least two, use common sense, and try not to worry. You've all got walkies. Check in with your department heads often. I think this will be a busy day," she sighed. "And as always, thank you."

The staff meeting over, the freelancers hurried to their assigned areas, some taking bagels from the coffee break station on their way, all making sure their walkies were fully charged.

When Juan called Laurie on her own walkie, her first thought was "oh Christ, what now?" But it just turned out that some reporter wanted to speak with her.

Well, Laurie thought, I won't tell them anything, so if they want to waste their time, why not? It should only take a few minutes. She told Juan she would see the reporter later that morning.

"What about the weather, Juan? Over."

"It looks like we might be getting rain. I'll keep you posted. Over."


Tim had only gotten two hours of sleep. After leaving the hotel, he'd spoken by phone with the Coroner and head of forensics and driven to his silent office to complete the new avalanche of forms necessitated by Karen's murder. When that was done, he'd ridden through empty streets to his apartment, drawn up a list of potential witnesses to the crime, grabbed some brief rest, and arrived early at the Hanover.

His eyes were still gritty. His mind whirled with unanswered questions. But his heart pounded in anticipation of seeing Laurie, and he felt like a teenager.

Now that the investigation was common knowledge, even if most people thought only Karen Shearing had been murdered, Tim could speak openly with Laurie. He found the meeting office quickly, and remembered what she'd said about Grand Central Station. He finally spied her huddled in a corner amid piles of lists, papers, and binders.

"Are these people all your staff?" he asked, trying to tell her with his eyes that although he needed to be professional, he hadn't forgotten about last night.

Laurie understood, and was grateful.

"Almost none," she answered. "You know Juan Herrara from the hotel, of course," she said as she indicated the tall man beside her, "But most of these folks are Connor reps or vendors for tonight's banquet."

She raised her voice a little.

"I'm glad to see the Miami Beach Police Department has sent you over. You're the detective I met when Mr. Tradd passed away, aren't you?"

"Yes, ma'am," he responded gravely. "May I speak with you somewhere quieter? We have no news as of yet, but I'd like to review last night's events with you if I may."

"Certainly, Detective. Just let me finish up here."

She turned to Juan.

"Dagmar's still supervising the end of the breakfast, so would you discuss those little umbrellas in the centerpieces with the florist and walkie Dagmar afterwards?"

"Absolutely."

She raised her voice again to address the milling reps in the office.

"And can I just ask any attendees with questions to visit our Special Services Desk on the main mezzanine? Meeting staff are there with plenty of copies of today's agenda for those of you who are unsure of which Breakout room to use, and they can also help out with flight arrangements for anyone who wants to go home early."

At that, a number of the more casually dressed people left, but the overly tanned vendors remained. Laurie led Tim to the café they'd visited just a few days before. The breakfast crowd had mostly come and gone, and once they'd been led to a fairly private booth and ordered coffee and Coke, both dropped their official manner.

"Tim, I barely slept after you left last night. I kept thinking about what happened. To Karen, between us... I'm trying to keep this meeting together, but I... "

"Take it easy now. One thing at a time. We'll talk about 'us' later. As for Karen, I've got to see everyone who might have noticed anything. Did I hear you say that attendees could leave if they wanted?"

"Yes, but it's only just been announced. And I don't think any of the VIPs will go home before the tribute to Tradd tonight. Wendell, for example... I don't think he's leaving early... one of my staff would have told me. And of course, the staff themselves won't be leaving."

"Okay. Hopefully I won't need to talk to the reps much. In fact, I thought I'd start with Lew Paulson."

"Lew!"

"Definitely. He was there, wasn't he? And you were right. He loves the sound of his own voice. I think he'll give me lots of useful information. Any idea where I can find him this morning?"

"Well, he's probably working on the tribute video backstage in the general session ballroom. You know, where Ed Tradd was killed," she said.

And where I met you, she thought.

"Okay, I'll look for him there. And I don't want to hold you up. I know how busy you must be at any meeting, especially this one, but there's something I want to ask you."

He glanced around quickly, then plunged.

"Laurie, did that kiss last night happen because you wanted to comfort me when I was feeling low?"

She tilted her head and looked at him.

"I wanted to comfort you, yes. But Detective, surely they taught you something about human nature in police school?"

"A bit," he answered, his slow smile matching hers now.

"Well, then... "

The server interrupted, bearing caffeine, and Laurie stole a glance at her watch.

"I hope you don't mind," she said to Tim as she hastily signed the check. "I really have to get back to the meeting office. I promised I'd talk to some reporter about everything I didn't see last night, and there are still a million details I need to iron out."

Tim's coffee got cooler and cooler as he tried to think about his upcoming conversation with Lew Paulson.

# Chapter Twelve

"Laurie," Juan said, "This is Ana Sanchez with WFLA." Laurie finished her conversation with Dash before turning toward Ana. Most attendees were in their Breakouts.

The walkie-laden, ponytail-wearing, unmade-up meeting planner faced the perfectly groomed and coiffed reporter. Only Ana's air of driven professionalism was similar.

"Good to meet you, Ms. Sanchez."

"Please. Ana," the correspondent responded with a warm smile.

"Okay, Ana. And I'm Laurie. But I have to tell you," she said, motioning toward Ana's silent cameraman, who bulged with threatening-looking equipment, "I didn't realize you were a television reporter. I thought you were with a newspaper."

Civilians, thought Ana. They're all alike. If you're print, they want to make sure you spell their names right, and if you're TV, they all want to be stars. Ana thought Laurie's earnest, clean look would emphasize the more sordid aspects of the story she'd decided to tell, but she didn't tell Laurie that.

"Oh, don't worry about Raul. He's pretty harmless. You know men and their toys!" she replied with a laugh. "Yes, I'm a television reporter, but I'm really just interested in hearing your impressions. When I learned that Karen Shearing had been murdered, I couldn't help but wonder how the person running this meeting was feeling. You must be so shocked! And you're so young!"

Make them feel important. Compliment them. Empathize. Ana knew just how to get a story.

Laurie's eyes narrowed.

"Yes, we've all been shocked. It's a terrible thing. But we have every confidence in the police, and we're sure they'll solve the case quickly."

Well that was a nothing response, Ana thought. Anyone could have said the same... the hotel guy, the police's Public Information Officer, the Connor VIPs who'd refused to be interviewed. Perhaps if she approached the murder sideways... well, AAPT would be happy, anyway...

"Wasn't Karen Shearing murdered at a safari-themed dinner you held here last night?"

"That's right."

"And isn't the purpose of this meeting for Connor Pharmaceuticals to introduce its new medicine called Zephyrex?"

"Yes, although I'm not sure how that pertains to the Ms. Shearing."

"The drug was tested on rabbits, I believe?"

"You've obviously done your homework, Ms. Sanchez. Perhaps you should speak with our Vice President for Public Affairs. I have his number right here," Laurie said, pointing to her binder.

"Perhaps I should," said Ana, pausing to write the number down. "And perhaps he'll be interested in the footage I have from your safari dinner as well."

*That* statement would get Laurie to open up, Ana guessed. For the first time, the younger woman seemed uncertain.

"You have film?" she asked, confused.

"Yes."

"From last night?"

"I do."

"But we didn't shoot any video last night," Laurie stammered. She remembered the photographer taking the posed shots by the jeep, but all of Lew's freelancers had been off duty. Whatever footage this reporter had, if there really was any in the first place, Laurie knew she shouldn't say anything else.

"I'm sorry I can't be more help, Ms. Sanchez, but this meeting is still underway and I have a lot to do. I'm sure you understand. If you need additional information, just call that number."

As the frustrated Ana departed with her cameraman, intent on filming the sign in front of the hotel, Laurie took a swig of her Coke and lit a cigarette. She went over every word of their conversation in her mind. Ana had surprised her with the revelation about the video footage. Who had shot it? But Laurie hadn't revealed anything important.

Had she?


Tim found Lew Paulson right where Laurie had predicted, in the backstage area of the general session room, splicing together photographs of Edward Tradd overnighted from the home office. Ed's wife Marcia had gone through all of her photo albums and picked out quite a few pictures. She'd asked only that they be returned, and timidly, for a copy of the tribute video. It would be too confusing for her young daughters now, but she knew they'd want to see it when they were older.

As a Multimedia staffer reviewed what seemed like a thousand tapes to find the perfect companion music for the video, Tim picked his way carefully through the labyrinth of cables and approached Lew.

"Mr. Paulson," he said after clearing his throat several times to get the department head's attention. "I wonder if I could speak to you for a few moments?"

"Sure thing, Officer. It really was awful, what happened last night. I guess that's why you're here? Looks like you have a case after all. You know I was one of the first people there, right?"

"Right on all counts, Mr. Paulson."

"Call me Lew!"

"Yes. Lew. Well, I was wondering if we could speak somewhere more private?" Tim said quietly, indicating the staffer choosing music.

"You're worried about Scott overhearing? Nah. Those headphones he has on block out everything but the tunes, Officer. Now as I was saying... " Lew continued.

"Why don't you start by telling me what brought you over to the clearing in the first place?" Tim interrupted smoothly.

"No problem. Let's see. My staffers and I had been there for a couple of hours. We didn't have much to do, for once. Usually we'd be up 'til all hours putting together footage from this meeting to show during the closing general session. We do a video of the reps arriving from the airport, giving the thumbs-up sign by the Zephyrex banner, missing golf shots, dozing in meeting rooms, that sort of thing. It's pretty funny, actually, and they always like it, but of course we're not doing that at this meeting, what with Ed Tradd and now Karen Shearing and all."

"Of course not," Tim replied, wondering if Lew was ever going to get to the point.

"And we knew these pictures wouldn't arrive until this morning, so we couldn't get started on the tribute package. Anyway, pretty much all of us went to the dinner last night. We stayed out of the way, but I've never known my guys to pass up free booze!"

"No, I guess they don't," Tim laughed encouragingly.

"Well, as I said, we'd been there for a few hours, and we were having a really good time. You know, exchanging stories and whatnot."

Tim could imagine the scene. From everything he'd observed, he guessed that Lew did most of the talking.

"So anyway, sometime after 10:00 p.m., I was starting to tell my staff about the time all the meeting slides got sent to the wrong airport – I got them recreated on site, of course – but they all seemed to have somewhere else to go. At that hour!"

Tim pictured Lew's long-suffering staffers planning in whispers to ditch their boss. Perhaps they just wanted to go to their rooms, perhaps out to a club. Lew must have been especially annoying if they preferred paying for their own drinks to listening to him at a function with open bars.

"It seemed like they all left at once," Lew was saying. "I went looking for them and wound up in the clearing. That's when I saw a pink flip-flop. It must have been Karen's. I called the hotel guy right away on my walkie."

"And Laurie? Wasn't she kind of running things?"

"Oh yeah. But I knew the hotel guy would walkie her once we knew what was going on. In the meantime, I thought he should take a look first."

Massive Juan or petite Laurie. Tim got the impression that Lew may have been afraid. Afraid of what would be found, or afraid of Laurie's brains, he couldn't tell.

"And then?" the detective prompted.

"Well, you saw most of it. Juan Herrara found the body, called Security, and asked me to gather volunteers to keep the area clear until they arrived," he said importantly.

"Did you hear anything?"

"Just a few of the birds squawking. It got pretty loud with all the people around, but there was nothing unusual. Like I always say... "

"Thank you, Lew. You've been a big help, and I appreciate your time. I don't want to keep you any longer from that tribute package. I'm sure you want to get it just right."

"Absolutely, Officer. Well, you know where I'll be."

"Yes indeed. And thanks again."

Tim stepped carefully out of the backstage area into the hotel corridor, allowing time for his eyes to adjust to the unaccustomed light. He still needed to interview Juan, the Safari Night vendor and her staff, the hotel's catering people who'd worked the function last night... yet he found himself walking toward the meeting office.

Laurie paced up and down, firing off instructions over her walkie-talkie and smoking cigarette after cigarette. The sight of Tim was a welcome one, not just because of last night, but also because he was the one person there who wanted to catch the murderer, or murderers, as much as she did.

"This place is driving me nuts!" she blurted to him in a rare show of frustration. "Meeting problems, murder victims, people asking questions every time I turn around... I don't know how much more I can take!"

"Well, then, why don't we go to a little restaurant I know?" he inquired, pushing the thought of all the interviews he still had to do to the back of his mind. "You could use a break, and I have a lot of ideas to run by you."

Abruptly, the frazzled planner stopped pacing, thunderstruck by his suggestion.

"You mean go off-property?"

"Why not?"

"But I can't. I mean, I don't. I mean, I need to be here in case…"

"Enough," he interrupted. "You'll only be gone for a few hours at most. Surely the meeting won't *completely* disintegrate between 11:00 a.m. and 12:30 p.m.?"

She pretended to glare at him, then quickly compressed her lips in a fake smile.

"Fine. I'll get Dagmar to take over for me. It's a little unusual, but then again, everything else about this meeting is, so okay."

"Now you're talking! Can we leave right now?"

"Just let me walkie a few people and I'll be right with you."

Fifteen minutes later, Laurie sank gratefully into the passenger seat of Tim's BMW, her green eyes widening as she took in the leather upholstery and wood detailing.

"You don't wear a uniform, so I wasn't expecting a police car, but this…"

"Another surprise, Ms. Kilcannon?"

She blushed.

"Well, since I live in a one-bedroom apartment and make a pretty good living even after alimony and child support, I figured I'd treat myself. I like to go fast, but I guess it wouldn't look too good if a member of the police department was caught speeding. You should see me on roller coasters, though!"

Laurie shuddered. "I can't stand them. All that jerking and spinning – ugh! And as for you, I would have thought you got enough adventure on the job."

"Yeah, you'd think that, wouldn't you?" he smiled.

The drive was brief, as he'd promised, but Laurie relaxed a bit as Tim played tour guide. She felt guilty at first, then curious about Tim, then worried about the murders, then finally free in a way she hadn't experienced since the day in her senior year of high school when she'd let a more daring friend talk her into blowing off classes and driving to the Jersey shore. Out of the corner of his eye, Tim watched the expressions cross her face.

"So how many times have you been to Miami Beach?"

"This is my first, believe it or not. Orlando plenty, but never here."

"Well, in that case, allow me to regale you with some local lore while we wait for these interminable traffic lights to change."

She sank even deeper into the passenger seat.

"Start with the lights, then. Why are they sideways? I noticed that on the way in. I've never seen it before."

"You *would* have to begin with a question I can't answer. There's probably a story behind it, but no one's ever told me what it is. Most likely, the traffic lights are just horizontal to make them more stable during hurricanes."

"Like Andrew?" she asked, having seen the dreadful footage on CNN.

"Yup, and that's a story I *can* tell you. I'm sure you've noticed that the majority of Miami Beach residents are Hispanic?"

"Of course. I always thought it was because of location, Miami Beach being so close to Cuba and all. What does Hurricane Andrew have to do with it?"

"Plenty. You're partially right about the location thing. After Castro rose to power in the late 50s, thousands of upper- and middle-class Cubans fled to the Miami area, and then of course there was the Mariel boatlift back in 1980, which brought a different class. Money was always a problem for the immigrants, though. After Andrew hit, a lot of real estate came on the market. White residents who didn't want to rebuild sold their houses at a loss instead. And guess who bought them?"

"The children of the first wave of Cuban immigrants?"

"Exactly. And even though this area is becoming a Mecca for people from all sorts of Latin countries, Cubans still dominate."

"Hurricane Andrew. Who would have thought? And here I was, assuming I was a minority just because Miami Beach is so tropical."

"You *are* a minority – so am I – but don't imagine that the Cubans haven't assimilated, because they have. I'm friends with a guy on the force, for example. His name is 'Jorge,' but he pronounces it 'George.'"

"You're a bit of a cultural historian, aren't you, Tim?"

Her beefy companion was surprised.

"Me? I never thought of myself that way... but maybe. How's this for cultural history?" he added as they drove past the gleaming hotel Laurie had noticed on her ride to the Hanover. "Do you know the story of the Spite Wall?"

"No, but it sounds fascinating," she said, turning to face him. "Tell me."

"Let's see, it must've been forty years ago at least. You know about the Rat Pack?"

"Frank Sinatra, Dean Martin, Peter Lawford, Sammy Davis, Jr., Joey Bishop? I've heard of them," she answered dryly.

"Well," continued an unabashed Tim, "They all used to hang out at the Fontainebleau Hotel. Drink at the pool bar, attract beautiful women, tell stories, that sort of thing. The hotel loved it, of course. Then another developer built the Eden Roc Hotel right next to the Fontainebleau, and the Rat Pack relocated. Suddenly the Eden Roc was enjoying all the free publicity the Fontainebleau used to get. So the owners of the Fontainebleau built an addition onto their hotel, one with no windows on the Eden Roc side. So Eden Roc guests, Rat Pack included, could no longer see the ocean from the pool bar, but instead were faced with this blank slab of concrete. It's always been known as the Spite Wall."

"Color me impressed, Detective. To think of all that planning and money going into a project with its origins in revenge."

Slowing down, he steered his dark blue sedan into the restaurant's parking lot.

"Javier's. Opens at eleven, but it doesn't get really crowded until after noon. Great Cuban food, if you like that, but I happen to know they serve terrific coffee too. And I think they have Coke as well."

"Sounds good, although I'm not too sure about the Cuban food. Maybe I'll just get something with 'pollo' in the name. That means 'chicken,' I think, although my Spanish is pretty poor," she said. "Actually, on this one meeting I did in Phoenix, all of the banquet cooks spoke Spanish, and our breakfast was something like ten minutes late. So into the kitchen I march, and needless to say, I can't pass for a Latina with this skin, and I break out some of the little high school Spanish I remember: 'Quiero los huevos ahora!' The words were probably wrong, but boy did we get our breakfast quickly after that!"

Tim led Laurie to a table in the back, past badly painted murals of Cuban landmarks, his hand grazing the small of her back unconsciously on occasion. Once they'd placed their order with a dark-haired, striking waitress whose name tag read "Carolina," Tim turned his attention, once again, to Laurie.

"So who's been asking you questions?" he asked, expecting to hear about nosy reps.

Suddenly, Laurie seemed to remember why they were there.

"A reporter," she answered soberly. "She was poking and prodding, trying to get me to ignore the camera guy she had with her, trying to get me to say something negative about Connor Pharma. She asked about Karen's murder, but I think she just wanted dirt. She even went so far as to tell me she had video footage from Safari Night! As if I'd buy that – it wasn't on the Working Agenda, for Pete's sake!"

"Hmm," said Tim, sipping thoughtfully at the excellent coffee Carolina had brought during this diatribe. "Did she mention what station she was with?"

"WFLA, I think, and her name was Ana Sanchez. But what does that matter? She's the least of our worries."

He noticed the "our."

"What I really want to know," she continued, "Is who's doing these awful things? Who killed Ed Tradd? Who killed Karen Shearing? I can't stand all this investigating business, wondering about Wendell, for instance. I hate suspecting the execs. I've known them for so long, and it feels terrible to be thinking of them this way. Do you have any ideas, Tim? I mean, you're the detective."

"Yes, I'm the detective. How about if I tell you my theory about each one? Remember, though, I don't know who the killer is. Not yet. You've helped me narrow the field, but I'm still not sure."

Laurie calmed down, grateful to pass the responsibility to him. She took a sip of her Coke and said, "That sounds ideal. Should I take notes on a napkin, or what?" She'd been so agitated when she left the hotel that she'd left her legal pad and walkie behind. She felt kind of naked without them.

Tim tried not to smile.

"Don't worry about notes. It's all in my head, believe it or not. Let's start with Edward Tradd, the first victim. We know he was blackmailing someone, but we don't know why. And according to almost everyone, he was ruthless, cunning, and unmerciful. Which leads me to our first suspect, our first still-living interview subject, actually. Wendell McCarthy."

"Okay, I'll admit that syringe packet looks pretty bad. I wish I'd never found it, actually, but it couldn't have been Wendell," Laurie insisted. "I thought you'd established that."

"But if we postulate that the same person who killed Tradd killed Shearing… "

Laurie winced at his casual use of the last names. Tim may have to refer to them that way, to distance himself, but she couldn't.

"…then McCarthy could easily be our murderer, and that would apply even if you hadn't found that packet. Whoever killed Shearing had to know about the blackmail note. If McCarthy is as approachable as he seems, what was to stop Shearing from confiding in him?"

"But then Wendell would have to be the person being blackmailed," Laurie insisted. "And about what? He told you about his daughter in the interview."

"Suppose he told me about his daughter to make it seem like he *hadn't* been blackmailed about her? But perhaps, in reality, Tradd knew something about – Julie, is it? – that McCarthy wanted to keep secret. Something he'd go to any lengths to keep secret. Don't forget, Julie worked in hospitals, and we know the poison used on Tradd was readily available to surgeons. Is McCarthy close enough to his daughter to ask her to steal for him? Maybe so. And then, when he found out that Shearing knew about the note… in any event, we don't know where he was when Shearing was strangled last night."

"But Karen was strangled in the bushes!" Laurie burst out. "Anyone could have done it. We don't fit our attendees with radio collars, you know!"

"Maybe you should," he muttered. "It would make my job easier, anyway. Okay, let's move on," he added in a more normal tone, "If you think McCarthy's not a good suspect. What about Mike DellaGuardia?"

"Mike? Are you kidding me?"

"Yes, I know, he's a good Catholic. And he's also, to quote Wendell McCarthy, 'big as a house.' I'd feel more sure of him if both victims were strangled, but perhaps he'd tumbled to the affair between Tradd and Shearing. Maybe the blackmail angle had nothing to do with it. After all, we know Tradd already tried to blackmail him once, with no success. He committed the first murder to save Tradd from himself, and committed the second one because he saw Shearing as a 'fallen woman.' He might not even remember what he did. That may be why he speaks with such conviction."

"And maybe you're just grasping at straws," Laurie responded.

"What if I told you that Mike DellaGuardia's sister heads up the pharmacy in a hospital? I've been looking into everyone, I told you. He could have gotten the Pavulon from her."

"That's just ridiculous."

"Alright then, try this: what about Jim Fisher?"

"What about him?" Laurie asked innocently, knowing there was a strong case against the man.

"Item: he was backstage when Tradd was killed, and even found the body. Item: his wife is not only a surgeon, from whom Fisher could have gotten the poison, but she'd also been hit on by Tradd, who'd gotten nowhere. Item: Tradd was Fisher's boss, and treated Fisher like dirt, which Fisher hated. Suppose Fisher was the blackmail victim. Tradd had discovered something unsavory about the sainted wife, say. Fisher decided to kill him at this meeting. Which he did, knowing nothing about the note."

"Then why didn't you question him further about finding Ed's body?"

"Because there wasn't any point. McCarthy mentioned talking to Fisher, but he may have gotten the time wrong. Besides, the administration of the poison is the main thing."

"Okay, but then why would Jim kill Karen?"

"Mistaken identity. Fisher goes off to do some thinking, get some quiet but still stay at the event, as you've told me all the VIPs are expected to do. So he slips away. He thinks someone has seen him kill Tradd. Remember the banquet person who was supposed to leave the backstage area after he set up the coffee break? It's dark, Fisher's scared and nervous. He hears footsteps and strangles the girl without meaning to, thinking she's someone else. As I recall, Shearing's outfit looked a lot like what the banquet servers were wearing, and you said yourself that Fisher's been jumpy ever since the first murder."

"We all are," Laurie put in dryly. Their food had arrived, the chicken swimming in peppers and tomatoes. Laurie took one look and reached for the bread.

Tim, on the other hand, tucked happily into his pressed Cuban sandwich, stuffing himself with pork, cheese, ham, and pickles.

"Okay, Detective," Laurie said between bites of bread, "So what's your case against Gene Stockton?"

He swallowed an enormous bite of sandwich.

"Stockton's a tough one, I'll admit. The 'why' I can make fit, if I go back to your inside information thing. Who'd be more likely to have special knowledge than the president of the company? And who else could talk to Shearing whenever he wanted? But I'm having trouble with the 'how.' Stockton seems unlikely to have access to a ready supply of Pavulon."

"Sounds like you're not going to get too far with that one. How about Lew Paulson?" she asked, searching her plate for what fragments of chicken she could find between the spicier ingredients.

"Ah, Lew Paulson," Tim replied. "He seems to be an officious know-it-all, yet he's admitted that his wife's an Emergency Room nurse. He could have gotten the Pavulon from her. I don't see the blackmail note as being his motive. More likely, Tradd targeted him for a slight or a series of slights and Paulson decided to take his revenge at a meeting. Remember, Lew said he was used to working in the dark. He'd probably think it was incredibly clever to murder Tradd backstage."

"And what about Karen?" Laurie asked dubiously. "I can't see her talking to Lew. What possible reason could he have for wanting her dead?"

"If he thought she suspected something, that might have been reason enough. He knew about her relationship with Tradd, remember."

Laurie brooded for awhile, then speared something that looked like a potato. It was actually quite good.

"So now that you've given me reasons that every single 'suspect' might have killed Ed and Karen, I'm more confused than ever! I thought you'd narrowed the field!"

"Sorry I can't offer you a pat solution, but this is a complicated case, and I've only been working it for three days."

Three days, she reminded herself. You've known this man for three days. In an instant, she became businesslike.

"Well, I'm sure you'll figure out the solution soon. And now I really think I should get back to my meeting."

He looked at her for a long moment.

"Laurie... "

"Take me back, Tim."

He settled the bill quickly, waving aside Laurie's insistent offer to pay her share, and the two rode back to the Hanover. In silence, this time.

The threatened rain had finally arrived.

"I should go back to headquarters now," Tim said as they pulled up to the elegant hotel entrance. "Make a few phone calls, fill out forms, do some thinking. I'll probably be back later. Where do you think you'll be?"

He asked it casually, but Laurie heard the meaning behind the words.

"In the meeting office for the next few hours," she said more softly. "Then I'll be checking on the big banquet setup later."

"Don't worry," Tim said. "I'll find you."

# Chapter Thirteen

"So in spite of all the great work that Lydia did getting her television contact to publicize Vivian's footage of Connor Pharma's Safari Night, it looks like the story won't focus on the plight of those exploited animals after all. A woman was murdered at Connor's 'party,' and the reporter wants to concentrate on that," Jake said bitterly.

Vivian had raced to AAPT headquarters after helping direct nervous groups of reps to a very subdued breakfast at the Hanover. She was due back to check on the afternoon coffee breaks at 2:00 p.m., and had decided to spend her few free hours among her fellow animal lovers at AAPT... although even Vivian had to admit that a murdered woman was probably more newsworthy than a tethered leopard. She hoped the killer would be found soon. The woman's family must be so upset.

"Once again," continued Jake, "The concerns of people are deemed more important than those of animals."

But a woman's been *killed*, Vivian thought. That's got to matter more. I care about the animals too, but still...

"The lives of wild animals are pure and true, and in the wild is where they should have been last night. Instead, those noble beasts were tied up, probably drugged, and used as – entertainment." He practically spat that last word.

Vivian felt like a traitor. Jake was right, he must be. Perhaps hearing that Connor guy speak at the breakfast had made her feel more for the dead girl.

"So let us redouble our efforts to protect these mute, but suffering, beings," Jake said in his rallying-the-troops voice.

"Let's resolve, here and now, to oppose their oppressors wherever we find them. If we are ignored, as we have been by Connor Pharma, we'll move on. If we find the plight of animals momentarily overshadowed by the petty troubles of human beings, we'll redirect our campaigns. The Fontainebleau's hosting an all-leather fashion show next month, and we'll be there. Demonstrating, protesting, raising awareness. Above all, and with every operation we undertake, we will continue to fight!"

The assembled AAPTers applauded as one, underscoring their commitment with whoops and whistles. Vivian clapped with the rest, but still she wondered.

She wondered about her priorities, and for the first time, she wondered about Jake.

Laurie arrived back in the meeting office to find a scene of controlled chaos. Freelancers wolfing down sandwiches from the restocked break station, vendors discussing tonight's banquet with Dagmar, Sue on the phone asking the ground operator about early flights and if the rain would cause airline delays. The familiarity of the scene calmed Laurie. She retrieved her walkie from its base, settled in at her table, and called Becky at the SSD number.

"Connor Pharmaceuticals Special Services Desk," answered an upbeat-sounding woman. "This is Becky speaking. How may I help you?"

"It's me, Becky. How's everything going?"

"Hi Laurie!" the SSD lead responded. "Things are great!" Becky would say that if her dog had just died, Laurie reflected, but even so... "We had a bit of a rush after the breakfast this morning, what with the reps who weren't sure where to go and the reps who had questions about today's flights. Sue was great with them, by the way. I'm sure she'll tell you, but I think only a handful decided to leave.

Anyway, it's pretty quiet at the moment, so I was just getting ready to call the Bell Captain about delivering the gifts tonight."

Laurie had chosen leather laptop cases with embossed Zephyrex logos as the meeting present that every attendee would receive. Experience had taught her not to give out golf shirts – too many problems with sizing – and at least the laptop cases would be useful in everyone's work life. She'd planned, as usual, to have bellmen deliver the cases to each bedroom while the meeting participants attended the banquet.

"I'd like to change the gift procedure this time, if it's not too late," she said.

"Of course not!" chirped Becky. "What would you like to do instead?"

"Well, I think our attendees may have had enough surprises for one meeting. Just in case anyone skips the dinner tonight, I don't want to spook them any further with the sudden entrance of a bellman, even if he *is* delivering a gift. Do you think we could set up a table outside the banquet room and distribute the cases there? Your people could check the name of everyone who takes a case against a list, and attendees who don't get one could pick it up at the SSD tomorrow."

"What a super idea! I'll walkie Juan right now to get it all set up!"

Laurie thanked her and hung up, rolling her eyes. The veterans on the meeting staff joked that Becky kept her husband chained up in a basement somewhere, and kicked him occasionally.


In another frenzied workplace several miles away, Ana Sanchez labored over her script for the report on Connor Pharma, set to air on the evening's local news. Her video editor had located a still photograph of Karen Shearing from one of Lew Paulson's suitably bribed freelancers. Interspersed with file footage of the Connor headquarters building, part of the homemade video AAPT had provided from last night's event, and Ana's in-person report from the front of the Miami Beach Hanover sign, the picture added a note of pathos to the story, even if that Laurie person hadn't cooperated.

It helped, Ana acknowledged to herself, that the victim had looked like a model.

A stunning sales representative, a nationally known pharmaceutical company, an exotic evening, a horrific crime... yes, there was a story. Without realizing it, Lydia Emerson had given Ana a newsworthy report, and if a few seconds of "Footage provided by AAPT" was all Lydia stood to gain from her tip, then too bad.

As Ana reached for her phone to call her stalwart editor with yet another change, a tall, rugged-looking man walked up to her.

Cop, Ana thought immediately. Even with the plainclothes ones, she could always tell.

"Can I help you?" she asked sweetly.

"I hope so," Tim Riordan replied, taking in Ana's wavy black hair, chiseled, sensual features, and sharp black eyes. She may not have been his type, but he knew a beautiful woman when he saw one.

"I'm looking for Ana Sanchez," he continued.

"Well, you've found her!" Ana answered. "And you are?"

"Detective Timothy Riordan, ma'am, from the Miami Beach P.D. I understand you're putting together a report on the murder of Karen Shearing?"

"That's right," Ana confirmed. "Are you investigating the case?"

Maybe she could persuade him to be interviewed on camera, Ana thought. Even though he wasn't Hispanic, he could add so much credibility to her report. And he may not be her type, but still, handsome was handsome. He'd look good on film.

"I'm looking into it," responded Tim. "And I understand you have some footage from last night?"

"That's right. My contact at the animal rights group AAPT gave it to me. I assume they have someone undercover at the Connor meeting, someone who took the video. It's clearly shot by an amateur, and I wouldn't have used it without this dreadful murder. Endless shots of animals in chains or something," she finished with a laugh.

Tim made a mental note to tell Laurie to keep an eye on her local freelancers before saying, "I'm sure it will be an excellent report, Ms. Sanchez, and I know you'll share any information you uncover with the MBPD. I'm afraid, however, that you won't be able to use the AAPT footage from last night. I've spoken to the station manager, and I'll need to take that tape."

Until that moment, Ana hadn't realized how important the AAPT footage was to her story. Even though she planned to use only a bit of it, the here-and-now aspect suddenly seemed irreplaceable.

"Perhaps you could wait until after I've aired my report, Detective," she said reasonably, although she was seething inside. Cops! Hispanic or gringo, they were all the same, thinking their badges gave them the right to do anything, take anything..."

"I'm afraid that won't be possible, Ms. Sanchez. I need to take the tape with me now, along with any copies that may have been made."

Ana thought quickly.

"Of course, Detective. I'll call down for it right now. Anything I can do to assist the police."

Tim waited for the tape, looking around at the warren of cubicles that made up the WFLA space and realizing how similar it was to the police station. Apprehending criminals, reporting on criminals... the two functions weren't all that different, when he thought about it.

"Thank you, Ms. Sanchez," he said as he left, tape in hand.

"No problem, Detective. I hope you find the murderer."

"So do I," answered Tim.

Ana could afford to be polite. The detective may have gotten the tape, but he'd said nothing about the report in progress. And Raul was fast.


Dash walkied Laurie that the Breakout meetings were proceeding with a minimum of hassles. Becky was handling the meeting gifts. In between phone calls, Sue coordinated under-the-door delivery of departure notices, those often-ignored sheets that told everyone to have their luggage packed and ready for pickup by a certain hour the following morning. At 2:00 p.m., it was far too early to check on the setup for tonight's banquet. For the time being, Laurie had nothing to do.

She didn't like it much.

I know, she thought to herself. I'll see how Gene's doing. A visit to the president of the company seemed not only appropriate, but under the circumstances, almost mandatory.

A quick phone call determined that Gene was in his suite, so Laurie entered the elevator and rode to the top floor. It was a different elevator from the one last night, she was a little shamefacedly relieved to notice.

When she stood outside the double doors on the 46<sup>th</sup> floor, she didn't forget to knock.

"Is that you, Laurie?" floated Gene's voice from somewhere inside. "Come in. The door's unlocked."

"Thanks for letting me come up, Gene," Laurie said after she'd navigated the suite's foyer, turning left to reach the opulent sitting area.

"Don't even mention it, Laurie. After all, you're keeping this meeting running, so how could I refuse? Can I offer you anything, by the way? Between your staff and the hotel, I'm well supplied!"

"Just a water, if it's no trouble," Laurie replied, noting with approval that the president's bar setups had been replenished.

"No trouble at all," Gene responded, fetching her a chilled bottle of Evian from a stocked refrigerator. "Now what can I do for you?"

"Actually, Gene, I just wanted to see how you're doing. Losing Edward Tradd, working on the talk you'll be giving about him tonight, then having Karen murdered on top of everything else. I can't even imagine how difficult it must be for you."

"You're kind to think of me, Laurie," responded the iron-haired executive, "The past couple of days have been hard on everyone, I guess. My heart just goes out to Marcia Tradd and her girls, and of course the Shearings are dreadfully upset as well."

"Yes, Karen's parents. I'd heard you were going to call them."

"That's what I did a few hours ago," said Gene, shaking his head, "It was awful."

"Oh, God, it must have been. Those poor people. To lose their daughter, such a beautiful young woman, in such an ugly way…"

Gene coughed suddenly. To cover tears, Laurie immediately thought.

"How're you holding up?" she asked. "Have you been able to talk to Cassandra today?"

"Yes, indeed," the company president answered, brightening as always when the conversation turned to his family. "She even put little Ben on the phone for a moment. He tried to eat it, of course, but it was still good to be reminded of what's most important to me. Cassandra and Ben certainly put everything in perspective. Even my job."

"Speaking of that – although I probably shouldn't – I was wondering if anything's been decided about the merger?" Laurie asked uncertainly. Like everyone else, she'd been preoccupied by the two deaths, but she still worried about her livelihood.

"Well," responded Gene, "Nothing's been finalized yet, but I'll just say that a consolidation wouldn't surprise me much."

Laurie knew what that meant. Time to blow the dust off her resumé and start looking around.

"Not that *you* need to worry, Laurie. If there's a merger, I'll make sure everyone knows what a stellar job your department does."

That was nice of Gene, Laurie thought. Too bad the execs always said that right before they fired you.

"Thanks. That's good to hear," she said mechanically. Quickly changing the subject again, she added, "How's the talk coming for tonight? I know Lew's hard at work putting together the tribute video for Ed Tradd."

"I know. I've been in communication with him about the timing. It's coming along, to answer your question, but the progress is slow."

Laurie nodded sympathetically.

"The stress must be overwhelming," she said. "Do you think you might have half an hour or so to relax before you have to go to the banquet? It may sound silly, but sometimes television helps me to decompress. Spanish-language soap operas are especially effective."

He laughed, as Laurie had hoped. Not wanting to stay too long, she rose.

"Perhaps I will turn on my TV if I can find the time," Gene said as he escorted her to the double doors. "It's strange. I've given so many speeches in my years here at Connor, but this time, I'll admit, I'm nervous."

Headquarters glared white in the afternoon sun. Tim didn't look forward to filling out the mountains of reports related to the latest murder at the Hanover. Even with a desktop fan pointed directly at his face, he knew he'd be sweltering in half an hour. He remembered that the maintenance crew, no doubt assuming everyone who lived here was used to the heat, had a decided laissez-faire attitude about air conditioner repairs.

What possessed me to move to Miami Beach in the first place, Tim halfway-wondered (recalling, of course, his determination to stay close to Tim Jr. even after his marriage to Dolores had failed). Somehow all the years of paying for track camp, saving for his son's college education, and rearranging his work schedule so he never missed a school function seemed like small sacrifices compared to this infernal, eternal heat.

Well, Tim Jr. will graduate high school in a few weeks, he reminded himself. Moving back north would be so welcome. There was that opening for a Chief of Police slot in Barcliff – he'd submitted a resumé for that one, should hear back any day about an interview. Barcliff may be boring, especially in winter, but at least it *had* a winter. Tim remembered growing up there... snow days only when the drifts were taller than he was, darkness at 4:30 p.m. in November, the utter contrast between tourist season and the rest of the year. The tourists were grateful if the temperature broke 80° there, even in August. Here, they were lucky if it went *down* to 80° – in February. No doubt about it, he thought as he sweated through his cotton polo shirt, he was ready for a change.

Was Laurie, though? He couldn't help but wonder how she felt. That kiss last night... but she'd seemed to think better of it this morning, hadn't she? Still, it couldn't hurt to look into job opportunities closer to Philadelphia than Barcliff...

Keep your mind on your work, Tim, he admonished himself as he reached for the tape he'd confiscated from Ana Sanchez.

"Mom! I didn't expect you to be here at this hour," said a rushed Vivian. She'd forgotten her Working Agenda, and raced home to get it before reporting back at the Hanover.

"Oh, I just came home for a late lunch," Earlene answered. "We had a few cancellations this morning, so they told me to take a few hours off. The salon'll be hopping later today, though. Prom season, you know. Lots of updos. So where are you off to? Still working that extra job Jeremy Smalls got you?"

"Yeah. I'll be late again tonight." She stuffed the agenda into a pleather purse on the new dining room table.

"How did last night go? Do you have time to tell me about it?"

Vivian looked quickly at her watch. She was cutting it pretty close, but at least there wouldn't be too many cars on Collins at this time of day. And she probably wouldn't even see her mother until tomorrow night.

"Sure, Mom," she replied, turning around one of the new chairs. "You would have really liked it. Well, most of it, anyway. They had a theme dinner for the sales reps, with props and sound effects and everything."

Vivian didn't tell her mother about the animals, though, knowing Earlene would ask far too many questions, questions Vivian didn't want to answer, especially given her real goal of exposing Connor's insensitivity.

"Wow!" enthused Earlene. "Sounds like it was quite a shindig! I'll bet it was great! Makes me wonder what part of it I wouldn't have liked."

Vivian told her mother about Karen Shearing. After all, the story would probably be on the news tonight, even if Vivian's surreptitiously filmed images of those poor animals weren't the focus of the report anymore.

Earlene was predictably horrified.

"Try not to worry, Mom. I'll have a walkie-talkie at all times, nothing happened at the breakfast this morning, and tonight's dinner is in a big ballroom. No dark bushes or anything."

"I can't believe they didn't stop the meeting right away and send everybody home!" exclaimed Earlene.

"Well, they didn't. I guess the police didn't think it was necessary. That rep probably got killed over a lover's quarrel or something. Nothing to do with the meeting itself."

"And tonight's your last assignment for them?"

"Yeah – I'm not working the breakfast tomorrow."

"And your friend Jeremy will be there?"

"Probably, I guess. How come?"

Earlene knew enough to keep her hopes of a relationship between the two to herself.

"I just like knowing you won't be completely among strangers, that's all. Be careful tonight, okay?"

Vivian laughed.

"Okay, Mom. But honestly, if you want to worry about something, just hope I don't get on the bad side of my boss, Ms. Gustafson. *She's* the scary one, believe me!"

Much earlier than he'd planned, Tim found himself driving to the Hanover. He had business to attend to, yes, but he also wanted to see Laurie again.

Laurie. Old-young Laurie of the almost-red hair. The tireless worker who kept her meeting going in the face of disaster. The vulnerable girl who'd told him of losing her parents. The passionate woman who'd kissed him back last night. The person he didn't want to lose.

Laurie, who'd leave tomorrow.

He had to tell her how he felt, preposterous though it was. He had to tell her that he'd been thinking of leaving Miami Beach even before they'd met, that what he needed most of all was to be where she was.

It had only been a few days, but he knew she was the one for him. Perhaps a force in the suburbs of Philadelphia *did* need a detective. He and Laurie could go to Barcliff in the summers. She'd like that, wouldn't she?

Tim had to know how she felt.

He pointed the car in the direction of the Hanover, and drove there determined to solve the case, and to talk to Laurie from his heart.

Becky looked up brightly from Connor's Special Services Desk, instantly noticing the Senior Vice President.

"Mr. McCarthy! What can I do for you?"

"Not a thing, Becky. I just wanted to experience your sparkling personality the way I did yesterday."

"Oh, go on!" Becky replied. "Let me guess, you've misplaced your name tag again and want me to make you another one!"

"Not this time," answered Wendell, "Although I wouldn't blame you for thinking it was a habit of mine."

"Well, then, perhaps I can give you another copy of the agenda, so you know where all the Breakouts are?" said the eager SSD lead.

"Nope," replied Wendell, just as another man joined them.

"Mr. McCarthy," interjected Tim, blessing the heaven-sent opportunity to question the VIP, and not quite ready to face Laurie, despite his earlier bravado. "May I have a word?"

"Of course," answered Wendell. "I'm always ready to help. And you've done me a great service, young man," he added as they left the SSD area. "I just escaped from a Breakout meeting and I was wondering what to do with myself. I'm sure you want to question me about last night. I know it's drizzling, but how about the poolside bar? It's covered."

Tim looked at his watch.

"Don't worry, Detective, they serve iced tea too. I know you're on duty."

Tim laughed. "Believe me, sir, if I weren't, I'm thinking those multiple bars last night would come in handy!"

"It was quite a spread," agreed Wendell. "But then, everything Laurie's department sets up is terrific. Last night, for example. Not just the food and the booze, but those props and animals too. She never forgets a thing, even down to having a photographer there – although eventually I started cursing her about that," he chuckled, noticing the look in Tim's eyes when the meeting planner's name came up. "No, it was a great event, right up until almost the end. And I imagine that's what you want to ask me about."

"It is, sir. Forgive me, but I need to inquire as to your whereabouts when the crime took place."

"'Inquire as to my whereabouts?'" Wendell guffawed. "Do they teach you that sort of language in detective school? Why don't you just ask me where I was?"

"Alright, then," a chagrined Tim replied. "Where were you?"

"Up in my room," the VIP answered with alacrity. "I'd pretty much had it with posing for pictures, so after I had some food, I disappeared."

Another alibi that couldn't be verified, thought Tim. Desperately, he asked the Vice President, "Did you order anything from Room Service, sir? A few beers, maybe?"

"Have you seen the Vice Presidents' rooms, Detective? And Gene's? Well, I guess I shouldn't really call them 'rooms,' but 'have you seen my suite?' sounds so lah-di-dah. Anyway, either Laurie's staff or the hotel people see to it that we never run out of our favorite beverage. And while mine may be beer, with my diabetes, my doctor told me I should only drink vodka or wine. What I wouldn't give for a Corona, though... " His glass of cabernet left red rings on the placemat. "I never need to call anyone when I want to wind down with a glass of wine. And after last night, believe me, I had several. Karen Shearing was around my daughter's age."

The daughter who'd been harassed by Edward Tradd, Tim thought.

"It must have been very distressing for you," he said dutifully, squeezing more lemon into his iced tea and wishing it was his day off.

"Yes," Wendell replied. "But I called my daughter, and felt a lot better after we'd spoken. You a family man, Detective?"

"Yes and no," answered Tim. "I have a son near college age, but his mother and I split up years ago. I'm from up north originally, but Tim Jr. lives with his mom, so when she followed a job down this way, I came along to stay close to him. Live on my own, of course. My ex is a very nice person, but boy was I wrong for her!"

"That's too bad. Best thing I ever did was to marry Jenny. This may come as a shock, but I'm not that easy to live with! Can't see why she stays with me, actually. Let me tell you, good women are priceless. When you find one, don't let her go," the older man concluded innocently.

Looking equally nonchalant, Tim agreed.

"That diabetes of yours must be a real annoyance," he said, thinking again of the investigation. "Don't you have to give yourself insulin for that? How do you manage with all the traveling you must do?"

"It's a hassle, alright," the older man sighed. "Wine instead of beer, keeping track of everything I eat, checking my blood sugar... well, I guess it could be worse. As for the travel, that's not really a problem. I just make sure I keep insulin in my carry-on bag, and I always carry disposable syringes on trips. I'm used to it now. Corona's not the only thing I miss, though. Sometimes I think I'd give my left arm for a chocolate cupcake. And as flattered as I am by your interest in my medical history," he added with a shrewd glance, "I can't help wondering why you ask."

"No reason," replied Tim, "Just curiosity, I guess."

So much for the syringe packet, he thought. Well, that fits in with my theory, and it would please Laurie at any rate.

# Chapter Fourteen

Vivian watched with Jeremy as the hotel staff began to prepare for Connor's final night dinner. She couldn't decide if Jeremy was a blessing, since he explained everything to her, or a burden, since he gazed at her adoringly every time she looked his way. Also, he never shut up.

"It's only 3:30," he was saying now, "So the banquet people and the vendors have plenty of time to get everything set up. You should see them race around when it's a tight turn! I've seen a hotel general manager pushing a vacuum when there've only been ninety minutes to change a meeting room to a dinner room. Anyway, I know you're familiar with catered functions, but the biggest party you've ever worked had how many guests? Three hundred?"

"Five hundred."

"Okay, then, this one is more than four times that big, and we don't do any of the serving. There are something like a hundred banquet people booked. Two tables of ten per server. I know we're used to having three or four tables apiece at Elegant Eats, but these pharma people are super-demanding, and Connor always makes sure there's one server for every twenty places."

He paused to take a breath, and Vivian seized her opportunity.

"So if there are so many servers, what do *we* do?"

"Plenty," answered Jeremy, "And we start long before the servers do. The Banquet Event Order is your bible again tonight. You've memorized it, right?"

"Almost," said Vivian, who hadn't looked at it yet. She held up her overstuffed binder. "And if I forget anything, it's all here."

"Great! First off, before the function starts, we want to make sure the vendors are bringing the right things. The tablecloths and chair covers should be dark blue, the napkins white, the chair bows silver, that sort of thing. Dagmar and Laurie will be checking on that too, of course, but it doesn't hurt for us to know what's going on. Now as for the centerpieces, you see this insert here?" He pointed to a piece of paper stapled to his BEO. "They've added two little umbrellas to each flower arrangement, because of the rain, I guess. Anyway, it's a recent change, so make sure to check the flowers at each table."

"Linens, chair covers, umbrellas in the centerpieces. Got it," echoed Vivian.

"The menu is easy, as it happens. Same thing for everyone, petite filet mignon and seared sea scallops for the main course."

Vivian shuddered to herself. Two kinds of flesh, as predicted.

"Long grain rice and seasonal veg on the side. Chef's choice, as usual. Plus a first course of spinach salad with walnuts, crumbled goat cheese, and warm bacon dressing," Jeremy continued.

Poor pigs, Vivian thought. And poor goats!

"Then for dessert, a chocolate mousse cup topped with the Connor Pharma logo in dark chocolate, along with raspberries for these freaks who don't *like* chocolate, and fresh whipped cream on the side."

"Do they make any extra desserts?" Vivian asked. That chocolate mousse sounded yummy.

"That's the best part. We get to test everything beforehand. Quality control!"

"Everything?"

"Well, we're supposed to, although there are always a few people in a crowd this size who are vegetarians or whatever. The chef usually makes a different salad and a pasta dish for them, but it's always a challenge to get people to taste those meals. I mean, who wants to pass up free filet?"

"I'll do it, Jeremy," Vivian rushed to say. "I mean, it's my first Connor meeting, and I want to make a good impression with Dagmar. I got the feeling she thought I was kind of useless last night."

"I'm sure you weren't," Jeremy said, "And even if Dagmar did think that, she's probably completely forgotten, what with everything else that happened. I can hardly believe they're even continuing with the meeting, but I guess they didn't want to change everyone's flights. Oh, that reminds me, we'll each have a section of tables to watch over, and we need to make sure the attendees get served quickly. They're going to show a tribute video about the guy who died of a heart attack on the first day, and the company president's going to make a speech or something. So we get to ride herd on the servers – be mini-Dagmars, really – to make sure they stay on schedule."

"Okay," Vivian said, "Banquet Event Orders, tasting, overseeing servers, schedule... I think I've got it now. So I guess I just need to review a little bit and get to work."

"Right," answered a suddenly much quieter Jeremy. "Um, Vivian, I was wondering..."

Oh God, she thought. Here it comes.

Still, you never knew.

"...When this meeting is over, would you like to, um, like, get together for coffee sometime? Or a movie, maybe?"

Vivian thought it over for a moment.

And as much to her surprise as his, she said yes.


After Laurie left Gene's suite, she decided to visit a few Breakout rooms on her way back to the meeting office. Briefly consulting her list, she turned left when she got off the elevator on the 22$^{nd}$ floor, and headed for the converted sleeping room being used by a Nebraska district.

The reps took the opportunity afforded by the coffee break to stretch their legs. They seized any excuse to get out of the cramped space, but the DM stayed behind. He added fresh handouts to every place and rummaged in his bag for small gifts to use as rewards in the Zephyrex role-playing exercises the reps would do when they returned.

As the break was refreshed, danish crumbs and stale bagel halves replaced by tortilla chips and chocolate-covered pretzels, Laurie slipped into the near-empty room with the banquet server.

"Hey, Laurie," greeted Jeff, the manager she'd spoken with the day before, "You weren't kidding about last night's dinner. It was wild alright."

"If you mean the animals and the props, then yes, the vendor did a great job. But I'm guessing you don't mean that."

"What *did* happen, Laurie? Do you have inside information? All I know is that my reps and I were told to leave pretty suddenly by your folks. Rumors got around like always, but we didn't hear the full story until Wendell McCarthy talked to us at breakfast."

"Did most of your district decide to stay?" Laurie asked, avoiding his question about inside information.

"Every one of them," responded Jeff proudly. "I guess those Nebraska winters make them pretty tough. Or maybe they're just curious. Who knows? Anyway, my reps wouldn't miss the big dinner tonight for three months of straight sunshine. It's odd, though, isn't it? First Mr. Tradd dying of a heart attack, and then Karen Shearing getting killed?"

"Yes, indeed, Jeff, very odd. Thank goodness Miami Beach has an excellent police force," she managed to add without expression.

From behind a closed door in the sleeping room, Laurie heard the sound of a toilet flushing, followed by water running. Jim Fisher stepped out of the bathroom.

"H-hello!" she said loudly to cover her surprise. "I'm doing spot checks on a few Breakout rooms. Making sure the banquet people are adding sodas to the coffee service, that sort of thing."

"Well, howdy!" responded an equally flustered Jim. "And I've been observing the sales aid review and brainstorming sessions. Seems like fate that we both chose the same Breakout room to check on!"

"Absolutely." And a perfect opportunity to question him, Laurie thought.

"Are you on your way down?" she asked. "It looks like the break is in good shape, so I'll probably get going. Once the reps get back, there'll be too many people in here anyway."

"Yeah, I've seen what I needed to," said the VIP. "Jeff, your people seem like they're doing a great job in spite of all the – distractions – at this meeting. I'm glad to see that you're all remembering why we're really here."

"Well, my reps have already started getting questions from their docs about Zephyrex, so it's good that now they'll be able to answer them," Jeff replied, concealing his pleasure that the VIP was finally leaving.

As the Breakout attendees began to squeeze back into the small room, Laurie and Jim crowded past them into the now-deserted hotel hallway.

Laurie made a point of using her walkie to let Dash know how the meeting was progressing.

"This thing is so convenient," she said to Jim. "It sure is nice to know that I can reach anyone on my staff instantaneously! And it's also good," she continued, "To see that the business of the launch is moving forward. One way or another, the reps do seem to be learning about the product."

"Yeah," Jim responded as they walked toward the elevator, "I'll admit I'm a little surprised by how hard they're all working. I guess once they'd decided to stay, they figured they should get down to business."

"Pretty amazing, considering what happened last night. Such a tragedy."

"Yes, it really was. Just awful."

Now how on earth was she supposed to approach her questions subtly?

"Were you around when it happened?" she blurted out. "I got there myself pretty quickly, but there was so much chaos that I can't even remember who was doing what."

"No, I was by one of the bars near the entrance. I think one of your staff told us what happened. It was someone with a walkie-talkie and a clipboard, anyway."

"Oh," said Laurie.

Think, she told herself.

"Did you know Karen Shearing at all?"

"'Fraid not. I wish I could be more helpful, but I didn't see a thing."

"And I guess, being so far away from where it happened, you wouldn't have heard anything either, would you?"

"Except for the sounds of people talking and beer bottles being opened, not a thing. Why do you want to know, anyway? You sound like a policewoman!"

"No reason," replied Laurie hastily.

Now what? If he hadn't even been near the clearing, what else could she ask him?

The elevator opened on the Hanover's busy lobby, sparing her the necessity of continuing the conversation.

Some detective I make, she thought bitterly.

What else can I do, though? I followed Wendell and discovered something that might be evidence. I asked Jim Fisher questions, however badly. And I *do* need to keep track of everything at the meeting...

Still, giving up didn't sit well with her, and she decided, after a quick glance at her watch, that she had time for one more effort.

Who hadn't she talked to directly yet? Who was strong enough to have strangled Karen Shearing with his bare hands? Who seemed to be (as the TV cop shows always said) the "unlikeliest suspect?"

Mike DellaGuardia.

Laurie dialed his suite, and amazingly found him there.

"Perfect timing, Laurie," he answered. "I was just taking a bit of a break before the big dinner tonight. What can I do for you?"

"Well," replied Laurie, using the cover story she'd dreamed up only moments ago, "I thought I could return those pictures of Ed that Marcia sent. If you have the time?" she added, partly hoping to be turned down.

"That's really kind of you! Lew Paulson promised he'd give them to me later, but this is a much better solution. I'd probably forget to get them, knowing me. Just let me grab a quick shower. Could you come up in about fifteen minutes?"

"Sure," Laurie said gratefully. Now she'd have time to retrieve the photos from Lew. "See you then."

Taking shortcuts through the back corridors, avoiding the main ballroom where she knew she'd be distracted (thank God for Juan and Dagmar, who'd have everything under control), she all but ran to the backstage area.

"Lew!" she called, just able to spot him in the dim surroundings. "Hold up!"

"What is it, Laurie?" the ponytailed Multimedia chief asked. "Don't mean to be rude or anything, but I'm kinda busy at the moment." He didn't notice her red face and flyaway hair.

"This won't take a minute. You know those pictures Marcia sent you? The ones you were going to give to Mike later? Well, he's asked me to bring them up to his suite now," she panted, figuring that a request from a VIP would carry more weight than any idea of hers. What's more, she was right. Lew practically leapt into action.

"No problem, Laurie. I have them all right here." He rummaged through a pile of tapes, plucked out a large, padded envelope, and handed it over.

"I guess DellaGuardia wanted to be sure he'd remember to get them. Good idea," he added sycophantically.

"That's right, Lew. Thanks."

She sprinted to the elevators.

Riding up, manila envelope in her sweating hands, Laurie did her best to think.

What should I look for once I'm in his suite? What questions should I ask? I know! I'll mention Karen's murder in passing, and watch his eyes and body language for signs of a guilty conscience when he responds. It wouldn't be a clue, of course, but it could be a start...

As it turned out, she didn't have to ask any questions after all.

Mike DellaGuardia answered the door of his suite with bandaged hands.

His arms had slipped when he was lifting weights an hour ago, he explained immediately and apologetically. The weights had bruised his palms in the process.

Hmm, Laurie thought. Or Karen Shearing had put up a fight.


Dagmar and Juan watched as the last few wooden round tables and standard-issue banquet seats were transformed with luxurious tablecloths and chair covers. Huge silver bows marked the back of each place, and the room smelled of freesia and delphinium as the florist added centerpieces to each table.

Dagmar nodded approvingly.

Once the linens and flowers were in place, banquet staff laid each setting with the special napkins, heavy flatware, excellent china, and soon-to-be-lit votive candles that told of the opulent banquet to come.

"Laurie, we were just about to walkie you," said Juan, indicating the impeccably turned out F & B lead. "What do you think?"

Laurie put aside her doubts about Mike for the moment. The Bougainvillea Ballroom was almost unrecognizable, and she said as much to Juan and Dagmar. As many times as she'd seen dinner setups before, the sight never failed to impress her. Granted, the hotel staff had access to the room all day. When turns were tight, she always made time to view the stop-motion photography of the transformation, enjoying the spectacle of what seemed like hundreds of hotel employees descending on a meeting room and changing it, as if by magic, into a setting worthy of a high-end restaurant.

But perhaps because the day's events had prevented her from checking on the ballroom until now, she was floored.

"It looks amazing!" Laurie added, "And I saw the cocktail area on my way in. Hard to believe it was just a pre-function foyer an hour ago. The perfect antidote to what was certainly a stressful day. And I see the floral vendor managed to find silver umbrellas for the centerpieces to match the chair bows. Terrific!"

"Glad you like it."

"Ja, they've done a good job so far," Dagmar responded, smothering a smile. She'd have thought Laurie's little-kid enthusiasm would have worn off by now.

"I should probably check on Lew," the planner put in. "I want to make sure he's ready for the tribute video."

"May I join you?" a new voice asked. Tim had arrived, dressed for the evening in black pants, cream-colored jacket, white shirt, and even a tie – black silk with a beige-and-white pattern that actually matched what he was wearing. Laurie found herself staring, then noticed gratefully that his black loafers were scuffed.

"There's something I need to discuss with you, Ms. Kilcannon," he added.

"I'm glad you're here, Detective. I need to talk with you too."

Breakouts were finally over. Exhausted reps returned to their rooms to change for dinner. DMs pulled flip chart paper with notes about Zephyrex down from the walls. Dash, getting reports from his weary staff, breathed a sigh of relief. Only tomorrow's general session to get through, then he and Marc could go home.

He doubted that Laurie would hold the usual post-meeting gathering in the lobby bar. Enjoyable as it was to order multiple rounds of drinks and gossip about the more annoying attendees, too much had happened on site this time.

The meeting planner moved quickly away from Dagmar and Juan, not wanting them to guess the attraction between her and Tim. They'd already stepped behind the huge screen left in place from Monday's general session when Tim said, "Laurie, I think I know who killed Karen Shearing."

"So do I," the planner replied soberly, "Hard as it is for me to believe it. I just visited Mike DellaGuardia in his suite, and both his hands were bandaged. I think he hurt them strangling Karen. He said it was from lifting weights, but I think it's like you said – he might not even remember what he did."

"That's a really interesting theory, Laurie. Mike does lift weights, though, as you'll remember from when I interviewed him yesterday. His explanation for the bandaged hands is probably genuine. Still, it feels like what you've discovered means something else... " He closed his eyes in concentration.

"Bandaged hands... banged-up hands... banged-up arms... thorny bushes... that's it, Laurie. That's our proof!"

"What are you talking about?" she asked. "You think Mike really did drop some barbells, but you're all excited about 'proof.' What's going on?"

"What's going on is that what you just told me helped me figure out how I can confront our murderer, and maybe even prompt a confession. Oh, by the way, it's not McCarthy. Turns out he's diabetic, has to give himself injections, that's why he carries syringes."

"Thank God for that, anyway. So you really do know who did it, don't you?"

"I think so."

"So tell me. Who – "

The balding Multimedia chief interrupted.

"Evening, Officer. We're all cued up and ready to go on the Tradd tribute, Laurie. The pictures and video are really heart-rending, and I've heard most of Gene's speech. There won't be a dry eye in the house. And the music! If I were you, I'd see to it that there's a box of tissues at each table."

"It sounds like you've got everything under control then, Lew. Just watch for Dagmar. She'll give you a signal when all the desserts are down and everyone has coffee."

"Sounds good."

"Now I need to show Detective Riordan those ballroom exits, so we'll get out of your hair," she added kindly. Lew still did seem busy, regardless of his claim to be ready.

"Okay, I'll leave you to it."

"I really just said that to get rid of him," she told Tim as they walked back into the brighter dinner area. "I'm dying to know who did it! We can't talk in here, though. Too many people. The Breakout rooms should be free by now," she said rapidly. "We'll use one of them."

She reached into her pocket for her lighter, then began searching frantically for something else.

"I can't believe it! I left my BEO in the meeting office! Damn it – I'll have to run back and get it. Don't go *anywhere*, okay?"

"I'll be right here," called Tim as Laurie raced away.

She almost knocked over the CEO as she left.

"Gene! I'm so sorry! Are you okay?"

"I'm fine, Laurie – just fine. I came down to chat with Lew about the timing for the video, since dinner doesn't start for another hour. You seem like you're in a terrible rush, though."

"I kind of am, Gene. I forgot the Banquet Event Order for tonight's function, and I need to go and get it."

"Well, don't let me keep you, then. I think I'll just stay here after I'm done talking with Lew. Will I be in anyone's way, do you think?"

"Of course not. If anything, they'll probably work more efficiently if they know you're here. I'll see you shortly. I just have to meet with Detective Riordan after I grab my BEO, and then I'll be driving the hotel staff crazy like always."

She deliberately didn't tell Gene that Tim thought he knew the identity of the killer. Better to wait for proof, she thought. Better to be sure.


Just a few minutes later, BEO stuffed into her pocket, a winded Laurie strode quickly down a deserted hotel corridor toward the dinner. The noise of her own breathing masked the sound of footsteps behind her.

Without warning, she was grabbed from behind and pulled into a pitch-black meeting room.

Gloved hands stretched a cord across her throat. Surgical gloves, she thought dimly. She could smell the latex.

She couldn't breathe.

As she struggled to draw air into her constricted lungs, Laurie didn't think of Karen Shearing's final moments, didn't think of her own parents' terror just before their plane dove into a mountain. She only knew that she needed to breathe – now! – and that someone was keeping her from performing that simple act.

Fight. She had to fight.

Her hands tried to pull the cord away from her neck, but she failed. The tension was too tight.

A person, she thought with waning consciousness, a person is holding this cord, trying to prevent me from breathing. People have eyes. Go for the eyes.

So with stubby-nailed fingers, she reached behind her in one last, frantic motion – and found the eyes. The cord slackened. Her attacker grunted briefly and fled.

As suddenly as it had started, the nightmare was over, and Laurie could breathe again. She heard footsteps running away.

She slumped against the wall, terrified and shaking, not even thinking to turn on the lights.

Someone just tried to kill me, she thought numbly. I almost died. She tried to think about the meeting, about the dinner and video that night, the closing general session and departures the following day, but her mind fixated on that single, horrifying thought.

Someone had tried to kill her.

Laurie didn't even notice it when she started to cry. She might have stayed huddled in that dark corner indefinitely, had it not been for Tim.

The detective ran into the room, threw the light switch, saw that Laurie was basically unharmed (corpses can't cry, he told himself), and gathered the shivering planner in his arms.

"Thank God you're okay. Thank God. When you didn't come back to the ballroom after a few minutes – I figured you'd run all the way to your office and back – I got so worried," he whispered to her, stroking her hair. "I went looking for you, then I saw someone run around a corner. People don't usually run in nice hotels. I checked every room off this hallway. Thank God you're okay," he repeated.

"Tim," she croaked, when she'd recovered enough to speak, "Take me to the ballroom. Somewhere with people."

He wanted to search for her assailant. Knew he *should* search for her assailant. But Laurie needed him.

Together, they stumbled into the candlelit cocktail area, complete with groups of early-arriving reps and smartly attired servers.

"Can I offer you a bruschetta?" one of the banquet staff asked brightly.

Fighting the impulse to laugh, Laurie responded faintly, "No, I think I'll pass. I need to find a bar."

"Of course," the well-trained server replied. "You'll find one over there. Nothing like a drink to whet the appetite!"

A drink, Laurie thought hysterically. Water! That's what I need to ease the soreness in my throat. Water, and lots of it!

"Laurie, are you really alright?" Tim asked anxiously, watching her down two glasses of iced water. He'd asked for a beer and a brandy, handing the latter to her.

"Drink this," he ordered. "It may or may not make you feel better, but it should help with the nerves."

"Thanks," she said gratefully, gulping down the unfamiliarly strong drink and feeling its effects almost immediately. After a few moments, she assured him, "I'm better now. Calmer, anyway. So you were going to tell me who you think killed Karen."

"Never mind about that now, Laurie. What *happened* to you in there?"

"I don't know. It was too dark to see anything. One minute I was coming back from my office with the BEO and the next minute I was being hauled into a dark room. Someone tried to kill me, I think, with a wire or something around my throat."

"Did you see *anything*?"

"No. I told you."

"How about sounds?"

"Nothing."

"Scents?"

"Not that I can recall. Wait a sec, though – I did smell men's cologne," she added. "Different from yours, I think."

"Well, I don't often wear any, but when I do, it's Versace. Call it Miami Beach solidarity, considering he lives down here. It's on my neck, if you want to make sure," he said mockingly.

"Anything for the cause, Detective," she replied, leaning in for a moment, then backing away, matching his tone exactly. "No, this was different. More musky, I think."

"So it was probably a male who attacked you," Tim said, trying to ignore Laurie's closeness. "If the same person who tried to strangle you also strangled Ms. Shearing, then that fits in with my evidence, such as it is."

"You have evidence?" she asked incredulously. "Did someone confess or leave fingerprints?"

"Not quite, but – "

"Laurie," Dagmar said. "If the cocktail reception is set to your liking, then we should check on the dinner arrangements."

"Yes, of course," replied the planner. Turning to Tim, she said quietly, "No one else knows what almost happened to me. I want to hear about your evidence, but right now I have to work."

"Will you be able to?"

"I think so. Just stay close."


It's about to begin, Vivian thought, and even though she knew the dinner would be served with clocklike precision whether she was there or not, she still felt nervous. She'd checked the umbrellas in every centerpiece twice.

The dreaded Dagmar approached with the Connor meeting planner and a guy who looked like the policeman from last night. Vivian stood up straighter.

"As you can see," Dagmar was saying, "Everything is ready for the dinner service, and Lew tells me he can begin the tribute as soon as every table has dessert and coffee."

Was Vivian imagining things, or did the planner look a little upset?

The Danish woman continued, "We've put a 'Reserved' sign on the table closest to the front, as requested. That's for the VIPs."

"Okay. The reps will seat themselves. They tend to sit by districts, so I doubt we'll have any problems. Now would you mind if we went over that BEO again?" Laurie asked as they moved on.

Vivian said a silent prayer of thanksgiving that her section didn't include the reserved table.


The ballroom was ready. All the vendors had come through, the power had stayed on despite heavy rain, and the Banquet Event Order was as thorough as Laurie remembered it.

All the servers had shown up.

Plates were warming in the enormous banquet kitchen. The food "prep" had been completed, filets ready to enter the huge ovens, scallops cleaned and resting in industrial-sized stainless steel bowls.

Bottles of Chardonnay chilled, bottles of Merlot breathed, urns full of coffee steamed.

A subdued hum of cocktail conversation reached Laurie in the back of the house. The reps began to unwind after their long day in the Breakout meetings, relaxed at the prospect of an excellent meal in the familiar ballroom.

Everything was ready, Laurie noted mechanically.

Then she looked for Tim again.

# Chapter Fifteen

"Plenty of tables over here," Vivian called. "No reserved places, just sit where you want." In the crush of the arriving attendees, many carrying their Zephyrex computer bags, she'd forgotten to be nervous.

"Wow, the room looks great."

"It sure does!"

"I wonder what they're going to feed us?"

"Do you know what's on the menu, ma'am?" asked a sharp-eyed rep, spotting Vivian's clipboard and walkie.

"The main course is filet mignon and sea scallops," she forced herself to answer with a smile (instead of saying "You'll be eating slaughtered cow meat and defenseless sea creatures" like she wanted). She must have used the correct tone, however, because several of the meeting attendees within earshot responded.

"Damn! They've spared no expense."

"Filet and scallops. Two of my favorite foods!"

A woman struggled to be heard among all the other reps. "What about me, miss?" she asked. "I don't eat meat or fish."

Vivian could have hugged her.

"Well, Ms. Perker," she responded after glancing at the rep's name badge, "That's easy. Just tell your server ahead of time. In fact, I'll make sure he knows. The chef has prepared a delicious alternate dish. You'll love it! Any other vegetarians at this table?" she inquired, trying not to sound too hopeful.

After determining that Ms. Perker was the only person in her section to need a special meal, Vivian pointed the lone vegetarian out to the server and returned to answering questions. Could they request an extra-rare filet, or did the hotel's liability laws require that all meat be charred beyond recognition? Were everyone's side dishes the same? What was for dessert? And the most frequent question of all, usually asked by the reps who juggled several bottles of beer: did the bar stay open during dinner?

Only two tables away, Vivian could see Jeremy responding to similar inquiries. When he caught sight of her, a radiant smile lit up his otherwise plain features as he gave her a thumbs-up sign.

Jeremy wasn't nearly as handsome as Jake. He didn't share her most basic philosophy, vegetarianism (the occasional cheeseburger didn't count, Vivian told herself). But at least Jeremy knew her name.

And he'd offered to protect her, however ineptly, last night.

And he'd asked her out.

Maybe it was just the candlelight, but Jeremy was looking better to Vivian all the time.

"Nice setup, Laurie," Wendell said as the planner made her customary check on the VIPs. "It's enough to take your breath away!"

"Absolutely!" agreed Mike, looking incongruous as ever in his business suit. "I almost passed out when I saw the change. And to think this space will be turned back into a huge meeting room tomorrow!"

Struggling to breathe. Almost fainting. Had Wendell and Mike used those phrases deliberately? Had one of them tried to murder her just an hour before? Tim had said Wendell was innocent, and implied the same thing about Mike, but still…

She'd turned into Tim, she noted ruefully, even as she searched the entranceway of the ballroom for his reassuring form. She suspected everyone now. It was odd. Just a few days ago, she'd protested when he cast doubts on everyone, but now that he seemed ready to exonerate all but one, Laurie saw them all as potential killers. Her recent experience in that darkened meeting room had upset her even more than she knew.

"Hopefully," put in Gene, "This excellent dinner will take everyone's minds off their worries."

"Yes indeed," Laurie said, glad to see that the company president seemed to have shaken off his earlier jitters, even though his bloodshot eyes showed just how little rest he'd gotten last night. "The hotel is doing a really good job."

As if on cue, a white-coated server arrived with a tray full of steaming entrées. Laurie glanced around the room, noting that most other places were empty and a few salad courses were still being cleared. As always, the executives got served first.

Without a word, the expert banquet server removed silvery covers and put a plate in front of each person, the steak cooked perfectly for everyone at the table. Laurie made a mental note to increase the banquet tip.

"I don't want to distract you from your dinners," she said easily, "So I'll just be on my way."

"How about you, Laurie?" asked the gangly Jim Fisher, seeming more at ease with her after their brief talk this afternoon. "When do you eat?"

"Oh, don't worry about me. I already ate," she lied. "Somebody has to test all this food, you know!" In truth, her "lunch" at Javier's was the last food she remembered consuming. Which reminded her...

"I'll see you guys later. 'Bye for now."

Pausing at only a few tables to make sure people were enjoying their main course, she made straight for Tim, even ignoring Dagmar. The now-lively ballroom, the hundreds of attendees slicing into excellent filets or spearing perfectly seared scallops, and most of all, the knowledge that the meeting would soon be over, served to ease her mind somewhat.

"Detective," she greeted him formally, noticing several of her staff standing nearby. "You wanted to see me, I believe?"

She thanked God Dash wasn't around. Or Sue, for that matter.

"Yes, there are a few points I'd like to clear up," he responded equally officially. "Could you leave the banquet for a bit? I'd prefer to talk somewhere quieter."

Almost every table now had main courses, so the attendees would be busy for a while. Laurie spied the imperturbable F & B lead saying something to Juan in a corner.

"Ms. Gustafson and the hotel staff seem to have everything well in hand," she replied, reaching for her walkie. "Let me just check with Mr. Herrara to see if any nearby conference rooms are available."

After a quick conversation with Juan, Laurie told Tim that the Hibiscus Boardroom was still open.

"No brioche, though," she added mischievously under her breath.

He chuckled briefly, glad to see her spirits returning after her frightening ordeal.

Seeing the gleaming table and plush leather chairs of the Hibiscus Boardroom again made Laurie realize how much had happened since Tim had used it for his interviews yesterday. Yesterday? Impossible.

As soon as the door closed behind them, Laurie turned to Tim and asked, "So who is it?"

"I'm not 100% sure," answered the detective, "And another few minutes won't hurt. In any case," he continued in a different tone, "I've been wanting to tell you something all afternoon, since before you were attacked."

He paused, feeling like a sailor searching for the right wave to carry him home, then said, "I care about you more than I've cared about any woman for a long time. I know it's too quick, and the circumstances are pretty much impossible, but I've got some vacation time coming up, and I'd like to spend it near you. We could go out to dinner, talk about something other than this case for once, just date like two normal people."

Then he kissed her, slowly, unhurriedly.

"That is, if you want to."

Laurie felt breathless, but in the good way this time. His words gave her permission, finally, to admit to herself that this might be more than a fleeting attraction.

Regaining control, she responded gravely, "I'd like that very much, Detective," and kissed him back to make sure he understood.

"Now who do you think it was?"

Tim laughed out loud as he forced himself to draw away from her.

"I did tell you to stay focused! Okay. The case. Well, when I got back to my office this afternoon, I did a lot of thinking (some of it even about the murders) and caught up on some work. One piece of unfinished business was to watch the AAPT tape that Ana Sanchez had gotten her hands on."

"That reporter. You visited her! And she really did have Safari Night footage! Where on earth did she get it?"

"I don't know," admitted Tim, "But you might want to check on the local people who worked the dinner last night. The tape came from the Southeast office of AAPT, headquartered in Miami. The important thing, though, is what was on it."

"And that was?"

"Animals, mostly. Whoever shot the video wanted to film that leopard. Remember, the one by the clearing?"

"Near where Karen was killed."

"Correct. What our uninformed cameraperson didn't realize, however, was that a crime was being committed just behind that animal. I checked the time stamp of the footage against the Medical Examiner's estimate of Karen's probable time of death, and the two matched. If the video captured someone coming out of those bushes, we might just have our killer."

"And did it?"

"It did."

"And the person?"

"You tell me. The footage is fairly dark, but I had one of our technical people clarify the video as much as possible and print a still image from it."

He withdrew the picture from his pocket. Laid it gently on the broad expanse of the conference table. Waited.

Laurie barely hesitated, shocked as she was.

"But that looks just like – "

"Exactly."

"It's impossible!"

"Perhaps. The explanation should be interesting, though."

"Let's get back to the banquet, okay? I need some time to make sense of this."

"I'd like nothing better. I want to keep an eye on him."


"So how are things going in your section?" Jeremy asked Vivian. "You look like you've been working meetings for years!"

"Thanks," she answered sincerely. "It's been odd, not serving, but you were right. We have plenty to do without that. Maybe now that desserts are going down, the requests will stop for a bit... although that group over there will probably want beer with their chocolate mousse!"

"There are some in every crowd," he said sympathetically. "So now that we have a little downtime," he added, "What would you like to do when we go out? Coffee or a movie?"

He wanted to get a firm commitment from her before she changed her mind.

Vivian eyed him thoughtfully once again. No Jake, certainly, but what the hell?

"How about a movie first and then coffee later so we can talk about the movie?"

"Perfect!" Jeremy enthused. "Just perfect! Are you free this Friday?"

Was she free, Vivian asked herself ruefully. She'd have to cancel those vital plans to eat Mallomars in front of the TV, but...

"Yes, I think so."

Jeremy looked like a kid on Christmas morning who'd been wishing for a shiny bike all year, and gotten it.

"Ladies and gentlemen," Gene began, the dimmed ballroom lights signaling the beginning of his speech.

"Ladies and gentlemen," he repeated as coffee cups were set down and conversation stilled.

"Before I progress to the more serious business at hand, I first want to thank the majority of you who stayed at this meeting and learned all you could about Zephyrex."

The crowd remained largely silent. Were they supposed to applaud themselves?

"And I'm sure we can all agree that the Hanover has done a magnificent job meeting all of our requirements in the face of these – unusual – circumstances."

This statement met with a more positive reception. No one had any quarrel with the hotel.

"Of course, I would be remiss if I failed to mention the near round-the-clock efforts of our meeting planning staff, ably led by Laurie Kilcannon."

A spotlight found Laurie hiding in a corner as the reps reacted with enthusiasm. Lew, she thought. I'm so going to get him for this.

"The main reason I want to speak to you tonight, however, is to honor the memory of Edward Tradd. In addition to the dreadful death of Karen Shearing last night, just as this meeting started, we lost one of our most tireless executives, tragically, to a heart attack."

And a heart attack is what it looked like, the killer reassured himself. The police might have their suspicions, but they could never guess the connection.

"Despite your shock, you stayed," Gene continued. "You learned about the drug Edward Tradd dedicated more than a year of his life to. In doing so, you celebrated his spirit in the best way possible."

The killer applauded dutifully. The threat Tradd posed was gone now.

"I first met Ed when he joined Connor Pharma ten years ago," Gene was saying.

Already a blackmailer? the killer wondered.

"Everyone could see he was ambitious, but he had real talent to back up his aspirations. From his days in the field, he was quickly promoted to a district manager position, then joined the home office staff as a Product Manager on one of our smaller products, the oral antibiotic Ceprel. In a field crowded with similar products, Ed's vision managed to turn the brand around, and suddenly this sleepy little antibiotic was earning double-digit market share. Upper management noticed, and placed him at the helm of Connor's newest product, Gromax."

Toying with the remnants of his chocolate mousse, Wendell sighed heavily.

"When early trial results for the drug that we now know as Zephyrex looked promising, there was really only one person to oversee its marketing. Edward Tradd. He wasted no time in creating the buzz that surrounds a blockbuster."

And when the opportunity for blackmail presented itself, the killer realized with grudging admiration, Ed Tradd wasted no time in exploiting it.

When had it all gone wrong? The killer had resolved to murder Edward Tradd months ago. Regrettable, but necessary. But the fear of exposure had led him to strangle Karen, and from there it didn't seem as big a step to killing Laurie too. Or trying to.

What had started as a foolproof plan to get rid of the one man who could really hurt him had become a string of murders and attempted murder. The killer couldn't help but wonder what he'd become along the way.

"Ed's wife Marcia generously made the effort, during what must be an incredibly difficult time for her, to send us the pictures you're about to see. Images not just of the businessman we all knew, but also of the husband and father she held so dear."

At this, the killer felt again the qualm that had been nagging at him all day. Those children, he thought…

"So let us raise our glasses in a final salute to Ed Tradd, and watch this tribute to his life and legacy."

The room grew even darker after the dutiful clinking sounded, images of Ed Tradd filling the screen in front of the diners.

Lilting piano and violin music accompanied the poignant images.

For once in his life, Lew Paulson had been right. There wasn't a dry eye in the house.

Laurie watched the video, moved in spite of herself.

Yet even as her eyes welled to see the happy blonde man on the screen, an arm around each daughter, her mind wrestled with the devastating impact of the picture Tim had shown her.

There must be a reason, probably quite a simple one, for the man in question to have been in those bushes around the time Karen was killed. Perhaps he heard something and went to investigate. Perhaps the times were wrong after all. Perhaps he'd lost something and went into the bushes to look for it.

The alternative was unthinkable.

She knew this man. She'd bantered with him. She *liked* him.

He couldn't be a killer.

Maybe he was.

Two innocent lives, and an attempt on hers?

Never.

Well, possibly.

Shaking her head in frustration, she approached Tim, mercifully just steps away.

Now that dinner was over, most attendees planned to extend the evening in the hotel bar. Normally, they'd be heading off to the nightclubs on Ocean Drive, but with danger still looming, the majority seemed to find the proximity of their sleeping rooms a strong plus.

As if by a signal, the crowd dispersed. In groups.

"So what's your next move?" asked Laurie quietly, disturbed by the prospect of the endless night that stretched ahead. Tim would have to leave eventually.

"I'll have to question him," Tim answered. "Confront him with the picture, if necessary. Tell him about the videotape. Would you like to come with me?"

She weighed her options: scurry back to the meeting office, do more work, then dart up to her own room, probably alone, or accompany Tim on his unpleasant but necessary errand. She opted for company and chose Tim.

After all, he was armed.

"Okay," he said, all business now. "Our best course would be to get to his room before he does. Can we do that, do you think?"

"Probably," she answered, trying to quell her nerves. "I think I heard him mention visiting the hotel bar with the rest of them. If we go now, we might get half an hour anyway."

Riding up in the elevator with a few reps who planned to go straight to their rooms, Laurie took care not to look at Tim. Their companions exited in pairs at several floors, but when the two were alone, she still didn't speak.

"Laurie," Tim asked gently, "Are you ready for this?"

"Nope," came her crisp reply as the elevator doors opened.


The hotel room looked as bland and well-lit as all hotel rooms did, but Laurie still felt like an intruder.

"Quickly," Tim said, donning a pair of thin gloves, "You check the bedroom while I take a look at the bathroom. Try not to touch anything."

Not wanting to get caught, she did as he asked. The first thing she noticed was a bottle of expensive cologne on the dresser. Instantly forgetting Tim's instructions, however, she opened it and slowly lifted the small container to her nostrils.

The scent was powerful, woodsy, unmistakable.

She replaced the bottle quickly, as if it burned her fingers.

"Tim," she croaked, then found her voice stronger on the second try. "Tim!"

For a big man, he moved fast.

"What have you found, Laurie?"

"This cologne. It reminded me so much of before, of what happened to me."

"Aromas can be quite evocative. I wouldn't call your memory evidence as such, but you may need to repeat it in any case. What I found in the bathroom, however..."

Her fear had subsided at the sound of his voice.

"What is it?" she asked, pointing to the hypodermic needle and a small vial of medicine Tim held in his gloved hands.

"This needle looks like one any medical supply house could provide. But the label of this vial says 'pancuronium,' the scientific name for Pavulon."

"But how did it get *here*?"

"An excellent question, Laurie," came a new, yet familiar voice. "Almost as good as the question of how *you* came to be here, rifling through my things. I wouldn't have expected that of you."

Laurie had always hated surprise parties.

This?

A hundred times worse.

In an instant, her heart rate seemed to double, her face turned bright red, and the back of her neck grew hot. She felt as guilty as she had at age five when her mother found her gorging on Valentine's Day chocolates in the forbidden lingerie drawer.

Tim, however, had been in these situations before. Situations much worse, if truth be told. At least this time, his enemy wasn't a hard-eyed drug lord.

"Laurie has keys to all the suites," Tim replied coolly, allowing the flustered planner to stay silent as she attempted to control her trembling. "Perhaps she just entered to check your bar setup."

"The bar's in the sitting room, not the bedroom, Detective. How do you explain that?"

"She was curious."

"And your own presence?"

"Perhaps I like Laurie. Follow her everywhere, just like a puppy."

The executive laughed at that.

"As likeable as Laurie undoubtedly is, I find that hard to believe. And what about the items you're holding? In very professional-looking gloves, I might add."

"The needle and medicine I found when I used the bathroom. As for the gloves, maybe I'm afraid of germs."

"Oh, let's cut this out," the other man said, tiring of their game. "You obviously suspect me of something. I'd like to know what."

"Alright, then, I have reason to believe you killed Karen Shearing by strangulation. I also think you murdered Edward Tradd by injecting him with Pavulon. And just a few hours ago, I suspect you tried to fatally harm Laurie as well."

"And what possible reason could I have had to perform all those outrageous crimes?" he asked.

"Edward Tradd was blackmailing you. I'm not sure of the reason yet, although I've been doing a little digging, and I have a few ideas. Karen Shearing found a draft of one of the blackmail notes hidden in between love letters she'd written to Tradd, letters she retrieved after his death. As for Laurie? Well, she knew too much. Too much about you, about Ed and Karen. She was asking questions, and you feared that sooner or later she'd realize what you'd done."

"And did you, Laurie? Do you believe all these awful things?"

"I don't know," she stammered. "I wasn't sure what to believe when I saw that picture."

"Picture?" the suddenly alert VIP said to Tim, "What picture is that?"

"A still image, time-stamped, placing you at the scene of the crime when Karen Shearing was murdered. An image from a videotape."

"That news report!" the executive gasped.

It was Tim's turn to be caught off guard. He thought he'd made it clear to Ana Sanchez that she wasn't to air that footage. Perhaps the reason she'd given him the tape so willingly was that she'd already extracted the shots she needed from it. Shots that the killer had obviously seen.

"Yes, that news report. I have the complete tape back at headquarters. If I'm right – and I believe I am – the killer would have been scratched by those bushes, hiding in the darkness last evening and strangling Karen Shearing. I can arrest you on suspicion based on this," Tim said, indicating the vial of Pavulon, "And then I can compel you to show them to me, but I prefer to ask civilly. Mr. Stockton, may I see your arms?"

# Chapter Sixteen

Tired but happy, Vivian eased her ancient Toyota out of the Hanover parking lot and into the still-busy traffic on Collins Avenue. She was glad to see that the majority of vehicles were cabs. Apparently, the tourists knew of South Beach's reputation.

As Vivian drove toward home, she saw other cars less frequently. The radio played softly, the windshield wipers swept her view clean over and over as she thought about the evening...

Animal flesh aside, it had all gone very well.

In fact, she'd never seen a more luxurious banquet, or one better staffed. The reps had noticed her walkie-talkie and assumed she knew all the answers. Thank heaven Jeremy had told her to memorize the menu and the next day's agenda.

Jeremy.

She'd dismissed him as short, pockmarked, and overly talkative, and it was true he was no Jake. Gorgeous Jake. Selfless Jake.

Sanctimonious Jake?

Hmm. That last speech of his *had* sounded kind of jerky. Jake hadn't even suggested a renewed protest against Connor, just a "let's go somewhere else" strategy that had sounded suspiciously like giving up.

Jeremy, on the other hand, seemed pretty nice, but how well did she really know him?

He liked her. He took his job seriously. He was chivalrous.

He liked her.

Strange how that one counted for so much. She wasn't exactly flooded with offers for Friday night. Perhaps she should look at Jeremy differently.

> *"Stocky and strong," she visualized herself telling her few friends. "Rugged," she heard herself describing him to Earlene. "Overly talkative" had become "open" and "not afraid to communicate."*

Vivian laughed. Here she was talking herself into a relationship with this guy, and they hadn't even had their first date! The projecting had started, though, and she knew she wouldn't get much sleep tonight.

As she turned onto Palm Drive, her eyes automatically sought the modest bungalow she shared with her mother.

It was after midnight, Vivian saw by the clock on the dashboard.

So why were all the lights still on?

At the word "arrest," Gene Stockton changed. Gone was the affable CEO Laurie knew, gone too the suspicious man angered by their intrusion.

"So you know?" he asked Tim resignedly.

"No, sir. I suspect. I have evidence," he said, indicating the needle and medicine, "that links you to the murder of Edward Tradd, and film back at the office that shows you leaving the scene of Karen Shearing's strangulation just after she was killed. They'll check your arms for scratches down at the station, since you prefer not to show me, and if they're there, they won't help your case. But who knows? A jury might view it all as circumstantial."

"Jury?"

"Certainly. There's enough here to take the case to trial." Even if there wasn't, Tim thought, that idea would probably get Stockton to open up.

"And my wife and son?" Gene asked, looking not at Tim but at the framed photograph by the bed.

"Would no doubt be as supportive and loving as they always have."

"Supportive of a husband and father charged with murder."

"I'm sure Connor Pharma has excellent lawyers. In fact, I need to tell you the following: 'You have the right to remain silent. Anything you say can and will be used against you in a court of law. You have the right to have an attorney present now and during any future questioning. If you cannot afford an attorney, one will be provided for you at government expense if you wish.'"

Gene laughed. A hollow, dead laugh.

"Yes, I can afford legal representation. I'm not worried about myself. But Cassie will always wonder, and Ben... he'll grow up under a cloud, won't he?"

"Not if you're exonerated, Gene," said Laurie softly.

"Oh, please," sighed Gene. "How could any lawyer, no matter how talented, explain away that Pavulon? I knew about it from pharmacy school, of course. Did you know vets use it to put animals to sleep?" he added conversationally. "Well, one of the charities I head up funded a new veterinary clinic a few months ago, and I got a behind-the-scenes tour right before it opened..."

"You should probably talk to a lawyer, Mr. Stockton. Before you say anything else."

"Yes," said Gene. "But I did kill them, you know."

Laurie gasped.

"Sorry to disillusion you, Laurie," Gene said with a ghost of a smile.

"But Gene, if it's true… well, *why*?"

"Yes, Mr. Stockton. Why?" Tim had read the killer his rights, advised him to get a lawyer. If Stockton wanted to talk, who was he to stop him?

"It must seem incomprehensible to you especially, Laurie. I have everything. A great position, more than enough money, a beautiful wife, an amazing son… "

Gene's voice broke a little as he thought of Ben.

"And Ed would have destroyed it all. He sent me a blackmail note. I knew it had to be him. He'd tried to do it with Mike DellaGuardia, only it didn't work. And what Ed found, he could have only seen in my private office. It would have hurt Cassie so much, and would have hurt Ben too, when he was old enough to understand."

Again, the thought of injuring his wife and son seemed to overwhelm him.

"Ed wanted me to step down, right after this meeting, in fact. That didn't bother me much. After that *BusinessWeek* article, I knew I could get hired again in a minute. But he'd always have that knowledge to hold over my head. I had to kill him. I had to," he whispered.

"So you planned to do it *here*?" Laurie wondered aloud, still reluctant to believe that the charming executive she knew was in fact a murderer.

"Yes. I thought I'd be able to catch Ed in a secluded spot somewhere… at your Safari Night, maybe… and no one would have suspected a thing. But I hadn't settled on a time and place. I kept the needle and some Pavulon with me always, just in case. When those protesters started up and all the people backstage were looking the other way, I thought it was perfect. A dark area, a bunch of witnesses to say how shocked I was. Then *you* showed up," he said, looking at Tim.

The detective only shrugged.

"I still thought I'd gotten away with it, though. After all, even if you suspected, what could you know for sure? I actually went so far as to follow a housekeeper and steal Tradd's briefcase out of his girlfriend's room. I figured she'd take it, wanting a memento of him."

"So that's where it went," said Tim. "Did you go through it?"

"Every inch," answered Gene, "And there was no blackmail note. I figured I was in the clear, until..."

"Karen Shearing," Laurie interjected quietly.

"Somehow she knew. Or I was pretty sure she did, anyway. Once she'd told me she'd 'found something' that disillusioned her about Ed, I got scared again. I knew *she* hadn't connected me to Tradd's scheme, but I didn't know who else she'd talk to. What conclusions would be drawn. So I... strangled her. And it was so simple," he said in an almost bewildered tone of voice.

Laurie remembered what Tim had said... it seemed like a year ago now... about murder being easier the second time around.

And the third.

Tim must have had the same thought.

"And Laurie? You tried to strangle her too, didn't you?"

Gene looked away.

"That was a mistake," he said, rubbing his eyes. "You really got me with that finger-jab, by the way," he told the planner.

"I thought Laurie knew too much already," Gene continued, addressing himself once again to Tim, "and if she'd watched the same news report I did, she had to put two and two together. When she said she was going to meet with you tonight, all I could think of was getting rid of her quickly, before she could talk about her suspicions. I really am sorry," he added, glancing at the open-mouthed planner as Laurie's hands unconsciously massaged her throat.

"I still can't believe you didn't come after me, Detective," Gene said. "I took such a foolish chance, with you so close. Why didn't you?"

"Perhaps that was my mistake," Tim answered softly. "The rule books would say so, anyway. But I wasn't lying to you before. I do like Laurie. More than like her."

And although his eyes never left Stockton's face, he reached for Laurie.

"What's going on, Mom? You're usually asleep by now. Are you okay?"

"I'm fine, Vivian, but there's something I need to tell you."

Earlene balanced on the edge of the new dinette set chair, still dressed in the Poly blend slacks and fern-patterned blouse she'd worn to work. She hadn't even removed her shoes. The red-tipped feet overflowed her white vinyl sandals.

Puzzled, Vivian took the other chair. Mom's Friday nights almost never varied. A Weight Watchers dinner, two dishes of Häagen-Dazs Chocolate Chocolate Chip, half a pack of Virginia Slims, whatever Lifetime was showing, and bed by 10:00 p.m. And she usually changed into shorts and a tank top.

"Do you ever remember me talking about your father?" Earlene asked.

"Only to say he left when I was a baby. Why?" Was that what this was all about? Had her father reappeared? Had

Earlene rekindled their relationship? It would explain a lot, Vivian thought.

> *Or perhaps, as Vivian had always secretly hoped, her father had come to regret leaving her as an infant. Perhaps he'd thought of her all these years, just as she'd thought of him. Perhaps he actually had been wasting away all this time in a – she knew it! – a foreign prison. He'd been a spy after all, just as she'd suspected, and his disappearance was necessary for him to complete his mission. No one had known about his secret romance with Earlene, no one had known about Vivian... and now that he was free again, the first thing he wanted to do was get to know his daughter...*

> *Well, I won't be upset with him, thought Vivian. I'll be calm and dignified and happy to have him back at last...*

"He was a real nice guy, your father, or at least he was nice when I knew him. Poor, of course, like pretty much every student, but a real gentleman just the same."

She exhaled noisily, smoke from her Virginia Slim clouding the air in the small space.

"When I told him I was expecting, I was sure he'd marry me and take care of us both. He said he would, anyway... after you were born. And he was great while I was pregnant. Went to birthing classes with me, drove to the grocery store at 2:00 in the morning when I had a craving for something or other. And he was pleased as could be when he saw you," she added in a kind voice.

"But then?" Vivian prompted, afraid to hear more, but needing to all the same.

"Well, I guess he got cold feet. A woman and a baby, a guy just getting out of school. He left one night after we were both asleep. I must've been extra tired, because I never heard a thing when he packed up. He just left behind a note. 'I'm sorry' and his name. I've kept it all these years."

That still fit in with her spy theory, Vivian told herself. The whole poverty-stricken student thing could just have been a cover story.

Emboldened and eager, she asked her mother, "And you only saw him again yesterday, right? Now that he's free to come back, he did?"

Earlene looked at Vivian like her daughter had suddenly sprouted an extra arm.

"What?" she sputtered. "What cockamamie story have you been telling yourself all these years?" Then, seeing her daughter's expression change back to its familiar bleakness, she continued more gently.

"No, I've never seen him since. But I do know what happened to him. He became a real bigshot, even got featured in one of the magazines that we keep in the reception area at the salon. Well, when I saw that, I wrote to him, reminding him about you. He sent all the back support money he owed, I'll give him that."

Vivian gripped the edge of their shiny new dinette table.

"Did he even want a picture of me?" she asked dully.

"Of course he did, honey!" Earlene said, "And he wanted to know how you were doing and everything!"

Vivian knew she was lying. So that's where the money for the new furniture and the planned trip to Disney World had come from.

"It's okay, Mom. I understand. But why are you telling me this now?"

Earlene dropped her pretence.

"Well, he *did* send all the back support. He must've cared about you some. And I'm telling you now because I got you a new car. And I didn't want you to think I'd robbed a bank or anything."

"So now that you know, Detective, what do you plan to do?"

The chiseled features seemed to have slackened. In the last few minutes, Gene Stockton had grown old.

"I'll have to arrest you and take you to the station. You'll be fingerprinted and have a mug shot taken, all the usual procedural things. You can call your lawyer first if you want."

"Thank you."

Tim had to force himself to think of Stockton as a killer. A man who'd murdered a colleague, who'd brutally strangled a young woman, who'd almost taken Laurie away from him. He found himself wishing Stockton weren't surrounded by ornate furnishings and the aura of power that still emanated from him. Tim was used to murderers who were vicious, unrepentant, not – well, *polite*.

But polite or not, Stockton was still a criminal. He'd felt cornered, and he'd killed rather than admit…

"Gene," Laurie asked, shaken. "What started all this? What did you want to hide that badly?"

Stockton sighed heavily.

"Well, you know everything else now. I guess there's no reason to keep my secret any longer. Years ago, when I was in pharmacy school quite near here, I had a relationship with a woman named Earlene. She got pregnant. When she had the child, a little girl, I ran. She must have thought I'd just disappeared. In any case, she never tried to find me. To be honest, I'd pretty much forgotten about her. Then last fall, the article in *BusinessWeek* appeared. Somehow she saw it, and wrote me a letter asking for the child support I hadn't paid her all those years. I was happy to do it, although I had the sense to send the money in cash so there'd be no proof. I don't think she had blackmail in mind, though. She just wanted what I hadn't sent her before. Tradd must have seen her letter lying on my desk. He threatened to make the matter public, and it would have just about killed Cassie."

Laurie tried to imagine the authoritative CEO she'd always known as a scruffy student, and she struggled to make sense of his story.

"But Cassie loves you," she said haltingly. "Why would it matter to her if you'd had a child years before?"

Gene shook his head.

"Laurie, Cassie's... she's delicate. She went through four miscarriages before giving birth to Ben, and she wasn't terribly stable even before that ordeal. If she'd discovered that I'd had a child, and *left* that child, what would she have done?"

The fear that had driven Gene finally came home to Laurie.

She couldn't empathize. She could barely even sympathize.

But at least now she understood.

"I know I have to go with you, Detective, but may I use the bathroom first?"

"Of course," Tim responded automatically.

Gene headed for the smaller room.

Once he had gone, Tim turned to his quiet, subdued companion.

"It's over now, Laurie. And, thank God, you're safe. Once Stockton's through in there, you know what I have to do. Maybe you should head back to your room. I'll be in touch tomorrow."

"Alright. I know there'll be a ton of ramifications from this. For one thing, what do we tell the reps? I mean, it's *Gene*. They'll be so shocked."

"Sounds like you are too," he said, joining her on the edge of Gene's bed.

"Of course I am. How could I not be? Here's this guy I thought I knew a little, this fantastic man who virtually everyone loves, and he's just admitted that he killed two people."

"And tried to kill you."

"That too. *And* he had an illegitimate child, *and* he abandoned her. It's just too much to take in. It's like finding out…"

"What?"

"Well, I was going to say that it's like finding out that a nun used to be a prostitute, but that's probably happened in real life…"

Tim smiled at that.

"It probably has. And this happened too. Everyone has secrets, Laurie, and fear can do strange things to a person. I think Stockton's a coward at heart. Afraid other people will discover his mistakes. What did you just call him? 'This fantastic man who everyone loves?'"

"But everyone does! Even that article…"

"That article only gave Stockton more proof that he was a great guy, and it set off the events that led to tonight. Terrible events. In fact, I'm probably the only one who's really benefited from that story. If Tradd hadn't been murdered, I never would have met you. But all things considered, I wish we'd seen each other in a club."

It was her turn to smile.

"Me too. However it happened, though, I'm glad we've found each other now."

Their fingers intertwined briefly before Tim became gruff once more.

"I hate to be the one to say it, but this looks to be a long night for both of us, and it's late already. What's taking Stockton so long, anyway?"

"I guess his stomach's a little upset, which is pretty understandable under the circumstances. But I don't think he'd take too kindly to me interrupting him. I'll leave that to you."

"As if I'd let you go near that door. In fact, weren't you just about to leave?"

Laurie was troubled, but her voice was firm.

"I've been thinking, Tim, and no. I want to see him before you take him away. I don't imagine he'll get much kindness over the next few hours, not until his lawyer arrives, anyway. And I'm not saying he deserves any. But he can't be all bad. He *can't* be. I'd like to be nice to him. Not for long, but still."

Tim sighed.

"Okay… but be careful."

She rubbed her neck again.

"You don't have to convince me of *that*."

After escorting Laurie to the sitting area, Tim knocked on the bathroom door.

"Mr. Stockton, we need to leave."

Gene didn't answer. Tim knocked again.

"You've had plenty of time in there, Mr. Stockton."

Gene said nothing. Tim tried the handle and found the door locked.

"I've seen the floor plans, and there are no exits from in there. If you don't come out immediately, I'm going to have to break down this door!"

Ten seconds passed without a word from the bathroom.

Tim charged.

The Hanover was no fleabag motel. That door was *strong*.

As Tim searched the bedroom for a tool to use as a battering ram, he heard Laurie come up behind him.

"What are you doing? And where's Gene?"

"He's barricaded himself in the bathroom. I'm looking for something to help me break down the door," he answered testily, red in the face from the effort. "Just stay back, would you?"

"He probably called his lawyer from in there." Laurie guessed. "Those bathrooms have two phones each. Gene told the lawyer what happened, and was advised not to move a muscle or say a word until he could get here."

"Resisting arrest in the process? I think you watch too many cop shows. I know – the wooden dolphin in the entryway. I'll try that," he responded, stalking into the foyer with Laurie right on his heels.

"But that's teak... " she started to say. At the sight of Tim's raised eyebrows, however, Laurie fell silent.

"Then it's heavy. Be right back with Stockton. Stay here, and practice 'being nice.' You'll probably need to."

"Fine!" she snapped.

"Good!" he snapped back, snatching the hard-carved fish, pedestal and all, from its place.

Armed with the weighty sculpture, he rushed the bathroom door. This time, it broke.

And Tim saw the body of Gene Stockton hanging from the shower head.

Then he saw the note.

> *Detective: Please ask the Coroner to list the cause of death as 'accident.' Thank you.*
>
> *Gene Stockton*

Suddenly, Laurie was beside him.

"What happened to… ? Oh my God."

What had happened was all too clear. As fast as she could, she turned away.

The detective, too, was shaken.

"I never should have let him go in there alone. I had no idea he'd do this, but still… I never should have…"

"Stop," said Laurie, looking only at Tim. She didn't want to see Gene's lifeless body. "No one could have foreseen this. Now can we please go into the next room?" She started to leave when Gene's brief note caught her eye. It took only a few seconds to read, and then she darted into the bedroom.

Tim followed.

"I still have a lot of work ahead of me tonight. It'll just be different from what I thought."

He sounded dejected.

"Tim, can't you – fix – the body first? Make it look like Gene had an accident like he asked in the note?"

"You mean lie? Tamper with evidence?"

"In this case, yes. Not for Gene's reputation, but for Cassie and Ben's mental health. Murder's hard enough to deal with, but suicide must be impossible. Gene's past helping now, but his wife and child aren't. And I'm sure you could convince the Coroner."

"I can try," he sighed. "She won't believe that the death was an accident, not with those ligature marks on the neck, but maybe I can pass it off as another strangulation."

"You think she'll go for it?" asked Laurie.

"I'm not sure, but I guess I can give it a shot. At least I know her number by heart now."

# Chapter Seventeen

The reps gathered one last time in the Bougainvillea Ballroom, set up again for a general session. This time, there was no walk-in music.

Solemnly, they took their seats, expecting a grim yet determined Gene Stockton to reflect on the extraordinary events at this meeting, and to give them their marching orders.

The subdued conversation ceased as Wendell McCarthy took the stage.

"The past few days have been difficult for us all," the elderly VIP began.

"First, we lost Edward Tradd. Then, senselessly, Karen Shearing was murdered. I regret to inform you that the same person who killed Ms. Shearing also took Gene Stockton's life last night."

Stunned silence greeted these words. It was as if the whole audience had been punched in the stomach at once.

Aside from Laurie and Tim, Wendell alone knew the full story. The planner, knowing she could rely on his discretion, had told him everything. He chose his words carefully.

"The police have informed us that this is a local matter, and that the local investigation will continue. They've promised to stay in touch with me, and I'll keep you apprised of developments. As for us, we're free to leave. And, of course, we mourn the loss of Gene Stockton as we mourn the losses of Edward Tradd and Karen Shearing."

Death after death. Name after name. The reps could barely take it all in.

In the front row, Mike DellaGuardia muttered a prayer as Jim Fisher shook his head. Backstage, Lew Paulson silently fiddled with dials, checking the volume on McCarthy's microphone.

"If a heart attack hadn't claimed Ed Tradd, if brutal violence hadn't taken Karen and Gene from us, this meeting would be ending differently. Ed would probably be up here encouraging you to perform ever greater feats in the field. Gene would be applauding him, and Karen would be preparing to put her lessons into practice."

All around the ballroom, reps nodded in agreement.

"Yes, terrible things have happened," Wendell continued, "But the essentials remain the same. You'll all return to your families. You'll all keep doing your jobs. I hope," he added, with a trace of a smile.

"Zephyrex is still a great medication. That hasn't changed either. Gene believed in it, Ed worked on it, Karen was busy learning how to promote it. This is the part of a launch meeting where executives usually come out to inspire you one more time to do your best when you get back to your territories. I won't do that today. You know what to do. On behalf of Connor Pharma, I thank you all for staying. Travel safely, go home, and hug whoever you hug."

Earlier that morning, an exhausted Laurie had told her staff much the same thing, asking them to keep the information quiet until after Wendell had addressed the reps.

"You've all performed admirably under what anyone would consider difficult circumstances. For that, I thank you, as well as for all the hard work you've put in over the last several days. That work hasn't been in vain. Despite

239

everything, this meeting has accomplished its goal. Zephyrex has been launched, the reps have learned how to sell it, and Connor Pharma will no doubt be stronger as a result. I hope to see you again on future meetings. And if not, I wish you all the best in whatever paths you decide to take."

Grimly, silently, the freelancers gathered their walkies from the chargers. In just a few hours, the Zephyrex launch would be over.

To a person, they just wanted to go home.

Laurie made one more visit to the backstage area to make sure Lew had everything he needed. She was so tired after her second near-sleepless night that she didn't even remember to hesitate. And there was no reason to. Not anymore.

"Packing up, Lew?"

"Yup," came his unusually taciturn reply.

"Safe flight."

"You too. See you back at the office."

As she left the ballroom, Wendell approached.

"When are you flying out, Laurie?" the older man asked.

"Not until tonight. I have a few things to do here still."

"Are you taking any time off, or will I see you Monday?"

"I was thinking of taking Monday off, but I'll be in anyway. I don't even want to think about my In-box. What I'd like to do is sleep for two days straight when I get home."

"I'm sure you could use the rest."

"Wendell," she blurted out, "I'm sure there will be a service of some sort for Gene. At the company, I mean. Could you give me a little warning? I think I'll have a 24-hour bug that day."

The VIP chuckled softly.

"Understood. I'll let you know. I wish I could get a 24-hour bug myself, but the Board will probably want me to speak."

"Well, you *are* good at it."

"Perhaps. But I'll need to be a good actor for this one too. Laurie, do you know why he did those awful things?"

"Who knows why anyone does anything?" she replied, ducking the issue. "All I call tell you is that Gene must have been deeply troubled."

"Clearly. And we never saw it coming."

"I don't think anyone can. By the way, what are you going to tell people who ask you for details of the 'ongoing investigation' into Karen and Gene's deaths?"

"Let's just say this: it's a good thing most people have short memories. Have a good trip home, Laurie."

"You too, Wendell."

Becky closed down the Special Services Desk, and wondered why anyone would set out to commit murder. It defied her understanding.

Dagmar folded her last few items, placed them in her carry-on bag, and prepared to exit the Miami Beach Hanover. She'd already decided not to go back to the meeting office, having said a calm goodbye to Laurie some hours before. Dagmar had her suspicions, but she knew how to keep things to herself. Perhaps she'd speak to Bjorn, her fellow ex-pat in New York City. At least he wasn't in the same industry.

Dash and Marc had said their goodbyes more recently. The oddly formal parting seemed to suit Marc. Usually, the meeting staff just drifted away from the lobby bar with a casual wave. Marc, stiff as an ironing board, shook Laurie's hand and thanked her for the work, as was customary. Dash, of course, threw his arms around the planner.

"Are you sure you're okay?" he asked, searching her face for clues. "You must be freaking *out* with all that's happened!"

"I'm okay, Dash, really. Or at any rate, I will be. Now go home, you two. And I hope you get a chance to catch up on sleep before your next assignment."

Dash eyed Marc appreciatively.

"I doubt it," he remarked, "But we'll try. So long for now, Lauriebell!"

Another bone-crushing hug, and they finally left, Marc berating Dash for being overfamiliar with his "boss," Dash ignoring his criticisms as usual. They waited for their airport van holding hands.


The morning passed. The reps boarded shuttles to the airport with luggage in tow, thanks to the diligence of the Transfers staff. When the last attendee left, Sue felt her knees buckle and allowed herself a moment of utter fatigue. At least she didn't have to get on a plane herself. She'd driven to this meeting, and a short ride would take her to the houseboat she shared with her husband.


Laurie busied herself with closing up the meeting office, signing papers as vendors arrived to take back printers, copiers, walkie-talkies. Sticky notes discarded, she gathered her far-flung possessions into an ever-smaller pile, drifting irresolutely from table to table like a late-summer bee. She thought about Gene.

And Karen.

Ed Tradd.

And Tim.

Juan stopped by to see how she was doing.

"You know, Juan, it's funny. Usually, I have such a sense of letdown when a meeting ends, but this time I'm just glad it's over. How were the Funeral Directors, by the way?"

"Not my group, but from what I hear, they were pretty sedate... for them. You'd be surprised how rowdy they can be."

"Maybe they sensed all the death at our meeting," Laurie answered tiredly.

"Maybe," Juan replied, abandoning his attempt to lighten her mood. "So what are your plans now?"

"Well, my flight doesn't leave until tonight, and I haven't even begun to pack. Any chance I could get a late checkout?"

"No problem at all. We don't have any big groups checking in until tomorrow, so take all the time you need. I'll make sure Housekeeping doesn't bother you."

"Thanks, Juan," she said. "I won't need to rush as much that way."

"Anything I can do," he responded. "I know this meeting's been hard for you."

He looked around the almost empty room.

"It looks like you're close to done in here, anyway. Should I have my guys come in an hour or so for the tables and stuff? They need to turn it over for a board meeting later today."

"An hour sounds fine. So if I don't see you again, thanks for everything. Oh, and by the way," she added, rummaging in her briefcase for the individually labeled gratuity envelopes, "I forgot to give these out last night. Would you make sure they get to the right people?"

"I'll take care of it. And just let me say that despite everything, it's been a pleasure working with you."

"You too, Juan."

They shook hands, and he left, contemplating his next group.


Laurie glanced at her watch, then scribbled out a quick list:

## Post-Meeting Tasks:

1. Write thank-you ltr. to Juan (copy his boss).
2. Write thank-you notes to leads.
3. Reconcile final hotel master account against estimated budget.
4. Track return shipments.
5. Send all vendor invoices to Finance with approval.
6. Get some sleep!

For the next twenty minutes or so, she threw out paper... the expected arrivals list, transfer manifests, spare agendas, and scores of reminders. All the information that had been so vital just days before. She was packing up her own dog-eared copy of the Working Agenda to ship home when Sue arrived.

"All the attendees are gone," related the older woman as she slumped into a chair. "And I just sent Wendell McCarthy off in the last limo we ordered, so that includes VIPs too."

"Thank God. Have the freelancers left as well?"

"Everyone but yours truly. I drove, so it doesn't matter when I leave. I just stopped in to say goodbye. How close are you to finishing up in here?"

"Almost done," Laurie responded. "I just have to drop a few boxes off at the Business Center to get shipped home, then

I'll be ready to go. No reason to stay, really. They've taken out the coffee break, so I can't even get a Coke."

"Well, then, how about I meet you in the lobby bar in half an hour? You can get a Coke if you want, but I'm definitely ordering a beer!"

"Done," Laurie replied. "I'm so sick of this room, I just can't tell you."

She didn't even return to her suite. Overfilled briefcase in hand, she went straight to the bar after shipping her boxes. Sue had already ordered. Beer for her, wine for Laurie. The planner just took a sip, having no energy to ask for a Coke.

The two toasted each other silently.

"Helluva meeting."

"I'll say. Let's hope I never plan one this – eventful – again."

"Yeah, I guess multiple murders pretty much trump lost luggage. You know, Laurie, I've been meaning to ask you… if Tradd was killed, and the same guy who strangled Karen got Gene too, then was it a Connor person after all? I checked my departure manifests and couldn't find anyone who wasn't headed home, but I can't think of any other explanation. I heard that Mr. McCarthy said it was a local crime, but somehow that doesn't ring true to me."

"Well, maybe it was, just like Wendell said."

Sue shook her head, still curious, but resigned.

"Okay, I probably shouldn't have asked. So you're sticking with the 'homicidal maniac' story?"

"In a way, I guess that's exactly what it was."

"Do you think the threat is gone?"

"Completely," Laurie said with finality.

"You know I live down here, right? Read the papers and all that. Will I see anything about this case?"

"Probably not."

"Cover-up?"

Laurie sipped her Chardonnay.

"Alright. I get it. Don't ask questions. But I will ask you this, and you'd better tell me! Where are you going after you leave this hotel?"

Confused now herself, Laurie asked, "What do you mean? I'm going home, of course."

"Really? I thought maybe you'd be staying in Miami Beach for awhile. With someone."

"Ah."

"Yes indeedy. Don't think I haven't noticed how you look at that detective. And he was glued to you like a first grader's art project last night."

Laurie grinned.

"Let's just put it this way: I'm going home, but I probably haven't seen the last of Tim Riordan."

"At last!"

"Now don't get your hopes up, Sue. I know you want to see me married off, but Tim and I haven't even been on a date yet. And we live hundreds of miles apart."

"Oh, those are just technicalities. If you're right for each other, you're right for each other. Love finds a way."

"Whatever you say," answered Laurie with a smile as the bartender handed over the bill.

"Anything else, ladies?"

"I think this'll do it for me. Sue?"

"Just the one, for now. I've got to drive later."

"Then let me see if the Master Account is still open," said Laurie, preparing to sign the check.

"Not a chance," answered Sue, reaching for her credit card. "This one's on me."


Back in her room, the light on Laurie's phone flashed. A message from Tim, she hoped. She was right. He left several numbers, and wanted to see her before she flew home.

After the long meeting, her belongings were spread everywhere. She found clothes in the closet, the drawers, on the backs of chairs, and not bothering to fold them, tossed them into her suitcase along with an ancient make-up bag stuffed with toiletries. Throwing a few essentials into her carry-on, she changed into her most comfortable jeans and called Tim back.

He answered on the first ring.

"Hi, it's me. I got your message. So did you want to see me for – how did you put it? – 'follow-up investigation'?" she teased.

"Okay, okay. So I wasn't very subtle. Actually, I'd like to take you out to dinner."

"And I'd love to go," she said in her normal voice. "But my flight leaves in a few hours, I won't land until late, then I've got to drive home and see if my cat's still alive, and I'm beat already. Whoever said traveling was glamorous wasn't a meeting planner, that's for sure!"

"And I guess flying home tomorrow is out of the question?"

Laurie considered briefly. That would mean she'd need to stay at the Hanover one more night, which she didn't want to do, or stay at Tim's place, which she wasn't ready to do.

"Not this time," she answered gently.

"Fair enough," said Tim. "Can I drive you to the airport, at any rate?"

Laurie could cancel the limo the hotel had ordered with one phone call. She really did want to see Tim tonight.

"Sold. And once I've checked my luggage, maybe we can grab a bite at the airport. Meet you in the lobby in an hour?"

"You got it. See you then."

Suddenly that jeans-and-sweatshirt ensemble didn't seem quite so attractive to Laurie. Digging through her suitcase, she found a pair of sleek trousers, a white silk blouse, and a pale pink cardigan.

She shook her hair out of its ponytail and stashed the elastic in her pocket. Dabbed on some perfume. Hunted for her good earrings.

Thankfully, Laurie thought, the Miami Beach Hanover kept an ironing board and iron in the closet.

An hour later, accompanied by luggage whose weight seemed to have doubled during the past week, Laurie boarded the Hanover elevator one last time.

As promised, Tim was waiting for her in the lobby, wearing a chauffer's cap and holding a sign with her name.

"Don't worry," he assured her. "I only borrowed the hat. Made the sign, though. And is this how you always look when you travel?"

"Nope. I usually wear jeans and a sweatshirt."

He grinned at her as he summoned a bellman to take her luggage to his car.

"It's about half an hour to the airport. Take a nap if you want."

She didn't need any more inducement. The darkness, the quiet – Tim had turned off the car radio – and the blessed feeling of safety lulled her into sleep almost immediately.

Once they'd arrived, a more awake Laurie faced a watchful Tim as they passed the time in an airport bar near her gate. Nachos congealed between them.

Both avoided discussing the meeting and their feelings, instead making inconsequential remarks to each other about the shops and kiosks, the people passing by... anything to stay away from the real subject.

Finally, Tim said, "I meant what I said before about spending my vacation near you. I was thinking of flying up in two weeks. Can I plan on it?"

"Please," she answered. "I'm glad you want to."

And if things go well with him, Laurie told herself, and if I still have a job, I'll ask to plan all the Florida meetings coming up...

*"Now beginning preboarding for flight 161 to Philadelphia,"* came an announcement. *"Passengers with small children or those needing extra time..."*

"That's me," Laurie said.

"Yeah."

"I'd better be going."

"I know."

She flashed ahead to her life at home. The condo she'd struggled to buy, the job she loved, the 'alone time' she cherished. Or used to.

This is crazy, Laurie thought. I've been on my own for years. I *like* living by myself. I *like* the peace of it, the control.

So why am I so sad?

She missed him already, and he wasn't even gone.

"Wait with me?"

"As long as I can."

All his plans lived in "someday." This was now, and Laurie was leaving.

Edward Tradd. Karen Shearing. Gene Stockton. It made no sense that he had found someone who made him feel so alive in the midst of so much death.

The gate agent made another announcement. Laurie always requested an exit row seat – for the leg room, and so she could leave the plane first in the event of an emergency, she said. He knew she'd make sure everyone else got out first, though...

"Laurie," he began.

"No, Tim. Don't say anything. The next two weeks will go by so fast, you'll be in Philly before you know it."

They were calling her section.

He pulled her into his arms, not kissing her, just holding her, breathing her, memorizing her.

"I won't say goodbye." He pulled away. "I can't."

"I can't either. Just know that however gruesome this meeting was, it led me to you, and for that, I'm grateful."

She reached up to touch his face. He caught her hand. Kissed it, looking at her all the while.

"I'll see you soon, Tim," she said huskily, and turned away.

He watched her walk, gait made awkward by the rhythmic thumping of the carry-on against her legs, down the jetway and onto the plane...

# Epilogue

Vivian Linsky gradually stopped going to AAPT meetings. She found a job as a veterinary technician, and was very good at it. She and Jeremy started to date. Vivian never learned the full story of her father, and eventually made peace with her fantasies of him. She became so enamored of the real world, in fact, that she invited Jeremy along on the Disney World trip. Earlene didn't mind at all about the extra room.

Zephyrex became a bigger hit than even Ed Tradd could have believed, and its success helped Connor Pharma avoid a buy-out. Connor's board persuaded Wendell McCarthy to delay his retirement for a bit longer and serve as interim CEO while they searched for a replacement for Gene Stockton.

Dash Tamaseko and Marc Masterson, inseparable as ever, continued to crisscross the country as freelancers for many large companies. Dagmar Gustafson eventually stopped doing meetings and opened an extremely well-run inn with her friend Bjorn on a small island near Greece.

Sue Palmer called a halt to her own freelancing days soon after the Zephyrex launch, becoming a full-fledged member of the houseboat-dwelling subculture she'd only sampled before. She sent Laurie nautical-themed Christmas cards each year, and the two women spoke often by phone.

Detective Tim Riordan resigned from the Miami Beach Police Department when his son started his freshman year Boston College.

Laurie Kilcannon continued to act as Connor Pharma's best meeting planner.

For a while...

$$2 \overline{)48.64}$$

$$\begin{array}{r} 24.32 \\ 2 + \phantom{0} \\ \hline 12.16 \end{array}$$

$$\begin{array}{r} 24.32 \\ 12.16 \\ \hline 36.48 \end{array}$$